I0831909

TYRONE M. EDDINS JR.

# *BAD INTENTIONS*

**A Novel**

Book One
of the
**CITY HIGH**
Series

Scripted Visions Publishing Group

For previews of upcoming books by Tyrone Eddins Jr. and for more information about the author and Scripted Visions Publishing Group, please visit: www.scriptedvisionspublishing.com

**SCRIPTED VISIONS PUBLISHING GROUP PRESENTS:**

# *BAD INTENTIONS*

Book One
of the
**CITY HIGH**
Series

A Novel
By

**TYRONE EDDINS JR.**

*SCRIPTED VISIONS PUBLISHING GROUP*
LAUREL, MD

BAD INTENTIONS

2019 Scripted Visions Publishing Group 2nd Edition (July 2019)



Originally published in paperback in the United States by Scripted Visions Publishing Group LLC, in 2012.

ISBN: 978-0-9850666-1-1 (print edition) & 978-0-9850666-2-8 (eBook)



Published in the United States by:

Scripted Visions Publishing Group, LLC Laurel, MD

www.scriptedvisionspublishing.com



Printed in the United States of America on acid-free paper.

Scripted Visions Publishing Group, LLC 2011

Cover Design: Kedi Darby (deluxe edition)

## *A note of thank-you from the author:*

Dear Reader,

Welcome to Scripted Visions Publishing Group. First and foremost, I want to thank you for purchasing ***BAD INTENTIONS.*** This novel is the first of what will be a long line of quality literary works from SVPG. It is the mission of Scripted Visions to provide a vehicle by which to allow new and talented authors to transport their unique styles and stories. This publishing house will serve as the bridge between the mainstream and the abstract, achieving a balance that results in the most enjoyable reading experience for you, the reader. Going forward, SVPG will continue to expand its horizons, providing you with a top-notch literary product that not only entertains, but also displays a true appreciation for the art of literature. I hope you enjoy ***BAD INTENTIONS*** as well as all future works from Scripted Visions Publishing Group. Again, thank you for your time and support.

*And now I present to you:* ***BAD INTENTIONS...***

***Tyrone M. Eddins Jr.***
***Author, BAD INTENTIONS***
***CEO & Founder, SCRIPTED VISIONS PUBLISHING GROUP***

*For Dad,*

*The best man I know...*
*For teaching me how to fly high, fight hard, and cast long...*
*For never letting me settle for less...*
*For always setting the standard...*
*For honor and tradition...*
*For teaching me how to "hook 'em to cook 'em"...*
*Words can't express my love and appreciation...*
*Here's to good food, good family, and good living...*

*"Boom, Boom the King"*

# *BAD INTENTIONS*

*"Nothing is more important than family, and everything I do, I do for my family."*

- **Ezra Harrell**

# *Prologue*

# *"NOTHING BEFORE FAMILY..."*

*Washington, D.C., more than a decade ago...*

Life is all about choices. The expression of one's God-given free will. An individual's prerogative to do what they want and live how they see fit. In life, a person makes choices that will serve as a kind of blueprint for how their existence will play out. Game changers. The kind of choices that will affect their life and the lives of everyone around them.

Sad thing is, sometimes, a person fails to think about the choices they've made until those very same choices come back to bite them in the ass. It's funny how that works. Hell, it's just plain funny how life in general works...

Speaking of choices, Maurice Broadnax had made plenty of choices over the years and just about all of them were bad. Most of his choices consisted of doing dirt and stepping on the neck of anyone who stood in his way. Like a broken GPS, his choices had led him all the way down the wrong path. Lost and fallen, he no longer had any choices left to make. Kind of like jumping off a cliff without a parachute or bungee cord.

Now, Maurice found himself at the end of his road and searching in the darkness for a way out. Hoping for a second chance to erase his long list of regrets instead of adding to it. But there was no way out and no chance of a do-over because it was much too late in the game for Maurice.

And someone had just made his final choice for him. Moe, as he was known in the streets, felt like he was dying as he lay the filthy basement floor of an abandoned apartment building.

With nothing left but his desperation, he clung to life like a fly clung to shit. Moe was trapped in a fight he had no chance of winning. Each strained gasp for air, each weakening heartbeat only delayed the inevitable as he felt the life evacuating his body. The Grim Reaper was closing in fast now, having seized the upper hand in this tussle thanks to the savage beating Moe had endured at the hands and feet of his assailants.

Moe attempted to speak but the blood pooling in his throat forced him to gag and cough. His breaths were nothing more than gurgled wheezing now. His hands shook as his muscles spasmed. Extreme pain seized his body and made him want to vomit. The crimson stains on the front of his shirt and pants forecasted tonight's outcome. Death had punched a one-way ticket on the expressway to hell for this man's soul.

*     *     *     *

The teenager standing a few feet away stared in open-mouthed silence, afraid to speak a word or even draw a breath. Horror and amazement washed over him and he wondered what message the beaten man had been trying to communicate as he'd struggled to speak.

His father called his name, but the boy didn't hear him. The shock of what he was witnessing transfixed him and blocked out all other sound. So much so that his father had to jar him out of his trance.

"Cuttino!" Ezra Harrell said again, raising his voice this time. "You hear me calling you?"

The teenager looked at his father and nodded but remained silent as he tried to swallow the lump in his throat. He hadn't known what he would see tonight, but he never would've imagined something like this. Never.

Even when he saw his father looking at him and motioning with his hand for him to come closer, he couldn't move. His feet were cinder blocks. The defeated look on the man's face and the fading light in his eyes, held Cuttino in a trance.

Half an hour ago, when their car had arrived at the broken-down building, the teenager had struggled to contain his excitement.

The shiny, chrome-plated Ruger .45 his father had given him felt heavy and real in his hands. His sweat-slicked palms had fought to maintain their grip, forcing him to switch the pistol between his hands and back again.

His father must have noticed his son's restlessness because he nudged him and said, "Relax son, you won't need that tonight. Put it away."

He smiled and winked at him, giving the boy's head a quick rub. "It isn't loaded anyway. I just wanted you to get a feel for it. You're here to watch and learn this time around, that's it."

Cuttino tried to hide his disappointment and looked up at his father who stood just a couple of inches taller than him. By his next birthday, he'd probably be tall enough to see clear over his daddy's head. Not that it would matter, because he'd always have to follow his father's law no matter how tall he grew. That would never change.

The .45 seemed to twitch in his hand, and Cuttino wanted to squeeze its trigger and blow something away. He wanted to empty the entire nine-round clip into anything, it didn't matter what, just to sample the pistol's raw power. Before tonight, he'd never held anything more hard-hitting than a tiny .22. But this

Ruger, shiny and magnificent, was a whole new animal to him.

Obedience overpowered curiosity, and Cuttino did as his father commanded. He slipped the pistol back into the waistband of his jeans and looked at the empty building in front of him. What a waste of time. If he wasn't going to get in any target practice, then why were they out here in the middle of the night?

Father and son stepped deeper into the darkness, moving towards the narrow opening of the building's basement. Meager lighting pulsed out of a fading yellow bulb dangling from the low water-stained ceiling.

The air in the room was stale and suffocating and it reeked of piss and sewage. The stench assaulted Cuttino's nose with all the force of an open-handed slap. He wanted to turn away and cover his nose, but if his father wouldn't, then he wouldn't either. He also didn't want to miss a second of what might happen in the next few minutes, whatever that might be.

On the other side of the light-starved basement, he saw his two uncles. His father's older brothers stood on either side of a beaten down man who was slumped on all fours. Through the thick, purple bruises and caked-on blood on the man's swollen face, Cuttino recognized him as one of his father's workers. *What could he have done to deserve this kind of ass-whippin'?*

This man was a member of their family, wasn't he? He couldn't remember the man's name right away, but he'd seen him many times around the family's house.

With a nod from his father, his uncles snatched the man up by his collar, forcing him up on his knees. His father motioned for him to stay behind as he stepped out of the shadows and into the flickering light. He watched his father lower into a crouch and edge closer to the man's face.

In a voice that sounded more like a growl, he heard his father say, "Hey Moe, can you hear me? Wake up, brotha. We got a few things we need to discuss here. You hear me? I said wake your ass up."

Cuttino saw the man stir as his father continued talking.

"You stole from me, Moe, didn't you? You greedy bastard, you. You stole from my family? What? You didn't think we would find out? Come on man, you can't be that damn dumb. Can't be. But then again, here we are, huh? Right here, right now."

The man's entire body shook with fear. He tried to shake his head in protest, but Cuttino's father stood and launched his right knee into the man's throat. The blow toppled the man backwards into a pile of trash and scrap metal. Clouds of dust plumed and the man's ragged coughs and wheezes echoed throughout the basement as he tried to catch his breath.

"That wasn't a question. I know exactly what you did. Ain't no mistaking it."

His father took a step back and brushed the dust from his black suit with both hands.

"Pick his ass up."

His uncles did as his father ordered, both of them holding the man up by his armpits. Moe slumped forward and looked close to passing out, his glassy eyes rolling as his head lolled from side to side.

"I trusted you and you go and shit on that trust. All over a few thousand dollars, right? Chump change," his father said as he lit a cigarette and took the first drag.

"Tell me something, Moe. Is that all your life is worth to you? A couple-few thousand dollars? That's a damn shame, man."

"Tino," Cuttino heard his father call to him, "give me that piece you're holding. Come on with it. Hurry up."

He edged forward and pulled the pistol from the small of his back. He massaged its black rubber grip one last time and handed it to his father. The pistol's chrome gleamed in the dim light as if the Ruger held a hungry anticipation of what was about to happen. *Time for some action*, it seemed to say.

His father took the weapon and jerked his head towards the building's entrance, signaling him to move away. He then took a magazine clip from the inside pocket of his suit jacket and loaded it into the .45.

"You're a piece of shit, Moe," his father said, flicking his lit cigarette towards the shadows. "And you know what we do with pieces of shit around here, right?"

Moe didn't bother to try and answer the question.

"Yeah, that's right. You know how we do. We flush shit."

Cocking a round into the pistol's chamber, his father raised the .45 and fired five shots point blank into Moe's chest. The Ruger bucked in his father's hand as it growled and spit fire in the direction of the condemned man.

The sudden and deafening boom ricocheted off the room's hollow walls, causing Cuttino to flinch. He'd watched wide-eyed as the man's chest exploded in a nasty collage of blood and torn flesh. The lethal impact of the gunshots had pushed the man's body into an awkward position, pinning his legs beneath him.

Now, Cuttino continued his watch, still mesmerized as Moe took the final breaths of his existence. He stepped close enough to see the man's eyes. Eyes that grew dark and took on a final kind of darkness that squashed all thoughts of seeing another sunrise.

He'd never seen a man die for real. Those movies he loved to watch didn't have anything on what he was witnessing tonight.

His father lowered the smoking pistol and spit on the dead body. "Done deal. Get rid of this garbage. Put him where no one will ever find his ass."

Then his father turned and walked in his direction. He used a handkerchief he'd pulled from his breast pocket to wipe away any blood that may have gotten on his suit.

"Let's go, Tino. Time to get on home," his father said, placing a strong hand on the boy's shoulder, guiding him out of the musty basement. They headed towards their waiting car and its driver.

"I want you to remember what you saw here tonight, son," his father said once the car pulled away from the building. "I don't like to use violence, but nothing ever comes before our family. Hear me? Nothing."

Cuttino didn't respond, just continued to stare straight ahead. He didn't know how he felt or how he was supposed to feel about what he'd just seen.

"Hey, boy, look at me," his father said. "You needed to see this tonight. You may not have liked it, may not have understood it, but I needed you to see this. This is one lesson you have to learn and never forget. If anyone, I mean anyone, ever tries to hurt us, we take care of it. No matter what, the family always comes first. Nothing before family."

Cuttino Marcellus Harrell couldn't have known he would see a man die that evening. Nothing in his short time on this earth had prepared him for tonight. He'd seen his father execute a man without hesitation or remorse. He hadn't wanted to look, but he'd been unable to turn away.

As their car transported them away from the darkened basement and away from Dead Moe, three words burned into Cuttino's brain:

*Nothing before family...*

# *Part I*

## *"JUST THE BEGINNING..."*

# *Chapter One*

***Washington, D.C., present day...***

Lucas Meadows tightened his gloved grip on the binoculars he held as he continued to watch from atop a five-story office building. It was time to get focused. "Game-time," as he liked to call it.

The hired assassin, known to his clientele as "The Clean," shifted his weight back and forth between his left and right leg. After standing in place for the last hour, a tingling numbness had begun to crawl up his legs.

He glanced at the sports watch on his left wrist. Its electronic numeric display read **5:14 AM** in large blue digits. This entire operation depended on his people's abilities to function with extreme attention to detail and precise execution.

*And they were running late.*

He was reaching for his cell phone when he noticed movement in the distance to his right. He adjusted his stance again and twisted on the ribbed plastic dial in the center of the binoculars. His field of view zoomed in, blurred, and then cleared, bringing a white work van into focus. It was coming towards him, chugging along on a one-way street a full eighteen minutes behind schedule.

*Strathman's and Sons Cleaning* was stenciled on the side of the beat-up vehicle in red lettering. The van appeared to be nothing more than a work vehicle traveling to its morning duties. But the five armed men inside the stolen van didn't belong to any part of the city's blue-collar workforce.

These men were "professional guns for hire" like The Clean. Well, not quite like him. To be honest, they weren't even close. He couldn't label them as professionals by his high standards, but this crew had come recommended by one of his local contacts. So, despite his doubts, he'd decided to give them a chance.

Per his instructions, the van circled the block once and then disappeared from his sight altogether. His cell phone pulsed with two quick vibrations, signaling an incoming text message. He took his cell from his pocket with his right hand and checked the display.

The message was from the men in the van and read:

**Good to go**

*Fucking amateurs...*

His thumbs pushed down hard on the phone's screen as he typed in a quick response:

**You're late. One more time and I void your contract. No deal. No payment.**

Everything needed to go according to the plan he'd designed, and these clowns were already making mistakes before the day's events began. He hadn't wanted to use this crew, but for a job with such intricate requirements, he'd had to sub-contract to locals.

He'd always worked alone, but this particular client had specified the how, when, and where of this job down to the letter. His newest employer was even paying extra to have those details followed without compromise or exception.

Seconds later, his cell vibrated again with a one-word reply:

**Understood**

He wanted to stay and make sure these amateurs completed their part of the job, but more important matters required his attention. This is what he'd paid good money for, to have someone else take care of the light work.

After sitting on a rooftop for the last couple of hours, he could continue with the rest of the day's business.

The Clean had no intention of putting anyone in the ground today, at least not with his hands, not just yet. Additional steps had to be taken before he could get dirty on this one. He couldn't rush into this job headstrong with his guns blazing. You didn't last long in this line of work without proper planning and details.

For now, he would watch, catch sight of his prey, and finish familiarizing himself with this city. He would let this crew of youngsters go to work first before he made his moves.

He'd visited Washington, D.C. once before as a tourist, but this was his first time working here. He would be sure to savor this trip.

The crew's lack of professionalism disturbed him, but he lowered his military spec binoculars and placed them in his duffel bag. Time to get moving. Hefting the bag, he pulled its shoulder strap over his head and let it rest across his muscular body. He clipped the phone to his belt and took one last look at the skyline before turning to exit the roof.

Dawn was beginning to rise over the city as the sun stretched its fingertips across D.C.'s pink and blue horizon. The August humidity was playing early bird and already beginning to muscle up. Lucas felt a sweaty dampness beneath the black V-neck t-shirt he wore. By noon, the infamous Chocolate City would be super-steamed and locked in the suffocating chokehold of the dog days of summer.

As the nighttime gave way to daybreak, the D.C. streets lived in a state of temporary peace and emptiness. Soon, the everyday grind would be renewed and picking up where it had left off the previous day.

To his left, he could see the sun-traced orange and silver outline of the city's architecture. The Washington Monument jutted straight up like a rocket, ready for blast off. He could also see the U.S. Capitol and the Washington Nationals' recently constructed baseball stadium, but none of these places interested him.

Straight ahead and about one mile out was the target area. The street corner he'd been watching sat at the elbow of two adjoining avenues, boxed in by a pair of graffiti-scaled warehouses. This part of the nation's capital existed beyond its political landscape and didn't receive any photoplay in the tourist brochures.

For the last several days, Lucas had spent hours observing this street corner. He studied the teenage crew in charge of orchestrating this area's heavy narcotics traffic and the soul-fried dope-fiends and crack-zombies they serviced.

After a week of watching this madness, he felt comfortable in his preparation to dispatch this crew of poison pushers. He didn't care why he'd been hired to rid the world of these cockroaches, but drug dealers represented the shit of the earth.

The black dealers were the worst of all because they sold to their people, his people. At least in his line of work, the taking of lives followed a respected code and professionalism, a damn sense of honor.

The Clean wasn't a gangster or some sort of street leech who fed off the weak. That's what these drug dealers did for a living. They didn't have any honor whatsoever. These monsters sold to whoever paid them.

Lucas considered himself as more of a cleaner than anything else, which is why he'd taken the moniker, "The Clean." When someone with the right kind of money needed a problem "cleaned," they called him. Didn't much matter where they needed him to go, he would travel where he had to for his retainer.

It was true that The Clean dealt in death, murder-for-hire, but he refused to kill the innocent or children. This was one of his few rules. He was a professional hunter, not some damn street-banger. What he did served the greater good in the grand scheme of life.

His first set of targets, these so-called Dope Boys, spent their time perched on this beaten-down corner. They arrived in the morning and departed late at the same time every day. The Clean had committed all of this to memory.

He'd also memorized the schedule of the periodic patrols conducted by the Metro Police Department's beat cops. He was ready now. He'd accounted for every angle and scripted every detail of how this job would go down.

Using a rusted metal fire escape attached to the side of the building, he exited the rooftop. He dropped the remaining few feet to the ground and walked towards the blue 2007 Chevy Impala parked in a nearby alley.

Pulling a set of keys from the side pocket of his brown and tan camouflaged cargo-pants, he unlocked the car's door. The details of this job continued to spin around his mind as he loaded his bag in the Impala's trunk. The teenage dealers he'd marked would be just the beginning of the blood he would shed in this city.

One month before, his employer had contacted him about this job via an encrypted email to his work account. Though the employer's identity remained a mystery, the large sum of money being offered spoke loud and clear. Someone with plenty of cash flow wanted to tear down a criminal empire within the Nation's Capital. Lucas had studied the job's specifics and gathered information from his network of contacts before accepting his client's terms.

The contract called for multiple hits that would take at least a few months to complete. This job was more long-term than he was used to, but it would prove to be his largest payday yet. The client had quadrupled his most expensive retainer rate due to the high profile and specific nature of each hit. $150,000 up front and then an additional $350,000 when he completed the contract.

*Five hundred thousand dollars.*

Premium money for a handful of clean hits. Sure, he'd felt the initial apprehension about the extended contract time and having to work with a crew. He was used to solo recon, and then in and out. Quick and precise hits. But this was the kind of payday he'd literally been gunning for his entire career as The Clean. No ransom, no drop-offs, and no worry of rotting away in someone's jungle or sandbox. He couldn't pass this up.

After receiving the first payment, he'd arranged for all of the accommodations needed during his stay in the Nation's Capital. Equipment, transportation, lodging and the subcontract crew; all paid for out of his pocket.

Then, he made the trip cross country to begin working. This was where The Clean came up to bat. Lucas Meadows handled everyday life and all business negotiations, while The Clean showed up for the hands dirty, animalistic work.

He always put forth extensive effort to ensure his clients never learned of his true identity. If a client ever somehow learned the truth, he'd be forced to terminate them without a second thought. And if a client were ever foolish enough to betray him, The Clean would hunt them down, obliterate them, and then disappear.

During a contract, The Clean took center stage, but in between jobs the vicious alter ego gave way to Lucas. His small home in Rosaritos, Mexico contained the bare minimum in furnishings and personal effects. A portion of his earnings went to living expenses and new weaponry and technology, but the majority he saved for retirement.

When he finally finished exorcising the demons of complete strangers, he would retire to the solitude of sandy beaches on foreign soil. After this job, The Clean's appetite for destruction would be momentarily sated and he would be closer to his ultimate goal. He would quit when the fire to end lives no longer burned in his heart, after he'd exorcised his personal demons.

Today, The Clean was once again a brilliant artist and Washington, D.C. would serve as his latest canvas. When he finished here, he would have a brand-new masterpiece to add to his already impressive résumé. And dust and memories would serve as the lone remnants of an underworld empire.

## *Chapter Two*

At 6:30 a.m., Mikey Stanley had no intention of getting out of bed. His mother, Bertrice Stanley, had other plans for him today.

"Michael Eugene Stanley!" Moms yelled for the fourth time in the last ten minutes.

Her voice rattled their second-floor apartment like the loud bass that boomed from the neighborhood cars as they drove by.

"Get your lazy behind outta that bed, and go clean up that mess in the kitchen!"

Mikey flinched at the sound of her yelling. *Now what was she fussin' about?* He tried to cling to the last bit of his sleep. Then he remembered the stacks of dirty dishes sitting in the kitchen sink.

Before she'd left yesterday, Moms had scribbled a note telling him to be sure to wash them when he got home. Of course, he hadn't done the dishes or any of his other chores. He'd had more important things to do with his time and forgot all about doing the dishes, sweeping the floors, or cleaning the bathroom.

Her voice came again, loud like a marching band drum and sounding like it was right on top on him. "Did you hear me, Mikey? I *said* get out of that bed!"

Moms had wedged her husky frame in the doorjamb of his small bedroom and wouldn't move until he got out of bed.

When he still didn't budge, she stepped across the room and yanked on the skinny string attached to his window blinds. The thin strips of aluminum shuddered and shrieked as they shot upwards, letting in the bright morning sun.

Mikey peeked from beneath his pale blue blanket and tried to blink away the sunlight tugging at his eyelids.

"Come on, Moms," he said, pulling the thin bedspread up over his eyes. "Go ahead with all that. It's like, five in the morning or something."

"No, it's after six, and I wouldn't care if it was half past the knot on the top of your head. I said get your narrow, wild-child behind up now!"

He snatched the blanket off his face, propped himself up on his elbows, and shot his mother a sideways look. He swung his skinny legs over the side of his bed until his feet touched the dusty, wood floor.

"You were supposed to clean up the kitchen before I got home last night, Mikey. You know I'm working doubles all week, and you are supposed to be helping me out here. *Get up!* And don't be rollin' your eyes at me either, boy!"

Yawning, he dragged himself out of the bed, the joints in his elbows and knees popping as he stood up. His eyes didn't want to open. After getting maybe four hours of sleep, he was exhausted.

*Damn, I'm working doubles too,* he thought, stomping towards the kitchen.

For the next few minutes, Moms rambled on and on about his responsibilities as man of the house.

"I'm sick and tired of this mess, Mikey," she yelled from her bedroom while she finished getting dressed for work. "I need your help around here; you know it's just us now."

He stood at the sink, now wearing black basketball shorts and his LeBron jersey, and pretended to wash the stacks of dirty dishes. "I know, Moms. I know, I know, I know."

He didn't feel bad at all about not doing the dishes. He didn't have time for any of that crap, but he did hate to hear Moms mad at him.

"Well, if you know, then why can't you do what I ask you to do, Mikey?"

"I meant to, Ma, I just forgot I guess."

"You forgot? You guess?" Moms said. "Whatever, Mikey. It's always the same mess with you, boy. You forgot, you guess, you don't know. Why can't you just do right?"

Moms shook her head. "Well, I know one thing—you better not forget about church this weekend. This is my first Sunday off in a while, and we're going to the ten o'clock service."

He sucked his teeth and threw the pink dishrag into the soapy water. The last thing he wanted to do was go to church.

"And what about your grades?" Moms continued. "I'm gettin' messages and emails from your teachers saying you aren't doing right in school. They said you are skipping class and not doing your homework. I don't have time to be going up to your school about you. You are fifteen and old enough to start being a man."

*Damn. Why did she have to bring up school and being a man?* He had things he wanted to do and none of this seemed fair to him. He hated church and school.

Was it his fault Dad left him and Moms alone with no money, nowhere to live? Hell no! It also wasn't his fault Moms had to work two jobs. He hadn't asked for any of this to happen. It just wasn't fair.

After she finished fussing at him, Moms started to leave for work at last. As she walked out of the front door, she turned to look back at him and her face softened just a bit.

"I know things are different, baby. I know it's harder now," she said, "but we'll be okay. This apartment and all, yeah, it's small and no, the neighborhood isn't that good. But us having to live here is just temporary until I can put our ends together."

"Yeah, you keep saying that," he said, avoiding eye contact with her, his words coming out harder than he'd meant them to. "But we still here, ain't we? Still in this dirty-ass apartment."

"You watch your mouth, Mikey," Moms said, her voice flashing with anger. She paused and closed her eyes as if to calm herself.

"I know we're still here, baby, and I know you don't like this place," she said in a whisper, her head down. "I miss our house too, but you know I couldn't afford to pay for it by myself even with these two jobs."

He still didn't look at Moms. Couldn't look. He'd hurt her with his last smart-assed comment and felt the knot of guilt wound tight in his stomach. He'd start crying if he looked at her now, and he just couldn't be doing that shit no more.

"Okay, Ma, I know," he said, his voice also lowering into a mumble. "I know it'll get better. And I-I'm sorry for what I just said. I didn't mean it."

"Hey baby, you know what?" she said, trying to smile. "It's Friday, and I don't have to work my part-time tonight, so I'll be home around seven for dinner. I'll cook your favorite spaghetti, okay?"

She turned to leave once more, but stopped herself again and said, "Please go to school today and stay away from them heathens you been hanging around, baby. And for Lord's sake, please stay your narrow behind off them blessed streets. There ain't no good for you out there, Michael Eugene."

*Michael Eugene.* Moms called him that when she meant to lay down the law on whatever point she was trying to make. She didn't smile much anymore. The look in her eyes and the constant frown of her lips reflected the sadness seeded deep in her breaking heart.

He watched his mother from their second-floor window after she left. She hustled to the bus stop as fast as her heavy legs would carry her.

He wished she didn't have to work so hard. He wished for a lot of things. Wished they didn't have to live in this shitty-ass neighborhood. Wished they had money. Real money. He would get all the cash they needed, and his dad could stay gone for all he cared. They didn't need his loser ass anyway.

When he got the money they needed, maybe Moms could take it easy some. Maybe they could move out of these raggedy-ass projects. Before his dad had bailed out two years ago, they had lived in a big house outside of the city. But when Michael Sr. decided he wanted a new life with a new woman, everything got all messed up.

He and Moms had to move from the Maryland suburbs to live with family in the city. When their welcome with relatives had worn out, Moms had gotten a second job and moved them again, this time into their tiny two-bedroom apartment in the Pruitt Palisades Projects on the Southeast side of the city.

Mikey hated living in this cramped apartment. He would often see roaches crawling around and even the occasional rat sticking his head out from a hole in the wall. It all felt so wrong to him. So unfair, every bit of it.

As usual, his mother's words stayed with him until just after she left and then he pushed them out of his mind. He also pushed far away any thoughts of finishing the dishes, stacking them in the lukewarm sink water instead. Then he left the kitchen, turned on the radio and flopped down on the faded green couch in the living room.

WPGC was rockin' one of his favorite new joints, which brought a smile to Mikey's face and a nod to his head. Five minutes later, he began to doze off without giving a second thought about school. Hell, he hadn't gone since he got his corner more than a month ago.

*No more hustlin' in the hallways and gym class,* he thought as he fell asleep once again. *Ain't shit them boring classes and clown-ass teachers can teach me about how to get out here and make this money.*

# *Chapter Three*

Two hours later, Mikey slugged his way off the couch and got ready for work. He showered and dressed in faded blue jean shorts, an oversized white t-shirt, and a pair of white Nike Air Force Ones.

After slurping down a bowl of Fruity O's, he grabbed a pack of strawberry Pop-Tarts and ran out of the door. Ten minutes and ten blocks later, he jogged up to his job right on time.

Mikey's "job" was located on a rundown corner in Southeast. He worked here for as many hours as it took to make his daily sales quota. In his line of work, there was no such thing as coming up short. His crew had pulled many all-nighters when business was slow just to sell their entire product load for the day.

They didn't work in one of the shabby storefronts occupying space along the narrow corridor. He and his friends worked on the street as a corner crew for the Harrells, D.C.'s criminal royal family. The Harrells had assigned Mikey and four other boys to operate here, pushing illegal highs such as crack, heroin, and marijuana.

This crew and other frontline scramblers just like them represented the low men on the totem pole. These boys earned their stripes by risking the most and getting paid the least while trying to climb the gangland food chain. Scramblers did the majority of the product handling and face-to-face dealing with the customers. They were also the most exposed to the police and rival crews.

Each youngster held aspirations of being promoted to better positions and making more money. But not all scramblers survived long enough to make it off the corners and onto higher ranking within their families. Many of these teenagers were lost to either the penal system or the violence of the streets or both.

"How we lookin'?" Mikey said as he approached one of the boys in his crew. Anthony "Ant" Cruz was thirteen, two years younger than him. His red t-shirt and black jean shorts drooped off his short wiry frame.

The two boys shook hands and gave each other a one-armed hug. Ant handed him a plastic bottle of grape flavored Gatorade along with a brown paper bag containing the morning's profits. Ant took a swig of his bottle and began to run down the day's first progress report.

"It's all good, Mike. Po-po came by and got they piece already so we cool for the rest of the week," he said, using his left hand to shield his eyes from the blazing sun overhead. "Said they be back next week as usual. Business starting to pick up, but it's hot as hell out here today."

The "piece" Ant referred to was the five hundred dollar bribe the MPD patrol unit collected every week. It was a tax. Part of the fee the Harrell family paid for being able to operate on this corner and many others.

The money bought the crew safe passage without any trouble from the law or rival crews. It was a small price to pay and one of the benefits of scrambling for the Harrells. Everyone knew the family's connections with the D.C. law system ran deep and wide.

"Yeah, it's hot as hell out here today," Mikey said. "Humid too, damn. Supposed to be in the nineties I heard, but we gotta make this money. Let's get this shit outta our hands quick, so we can shut it down before it gets real late tonight."

He went to check on the other boys before heading to his normal spot on the shaded stoop of a nearby building. From there he would oversee the in and out flow of the product and the exchange of money.

The Harrells had made him the boss over this street corner. Ant was his lieutenant, but it was Mikey who would pay the harshest price if anything ever went wrong on this corner. The Harrell family wouldn't tolerate their money or product going missing.

Each day he dealt with whomever the Family sent by to check on progress and drop off the resupply run. Ant picked up the first load and after it was sold, Mikey would call for delivery of the re-up of product.

After his crew sold the second batch, they would close up shop for the night. The same resupply truck would return, collect the day's earnings, pay him and his crew, and release them for the night. The next day, the boys would do it all over again. Just about every day went just like this. Same routine rain, sleet, or snow, like the damn post office.

The Harrell family recognized Sundays and a couple of holidays like Thanksgiving and Christmas as "no work" days. All other days were known as "grind days" for the Harrell corners in and around the city. Each location was open for business, everyone worked and the product got moved, even if it took all day and all night.

The boys in Mikey's crew all ranged in age from eleven to sixteen, teenagers posing as grown men in these streets. There were five including him. He was the second oldest, but he looked to be the youngest with his small, round baby face and large brown eyes.

He stood just five-foot-seven, but had grown up plenty in the short time after his father's abandonment. He'd seen and done things no teenager should ever have to see and do. He'd participated in various crimes, including armed robbery, burglary, and assault. He'd even spent a three-month stint at the Boys Village in Cheltenham, Maryland. After what he'd seen and done, Mikey didn't think there was much that could strike fear into his heart.

* * * *

Over the next five hours, a steady flow of junkies migrated to and from the corner like hungry fish to bait. Mikey watched each addict purchase his or her poison, all of them in search of a slow death.

The crew had sweated their way through their first load and was ready for a re-up. He pulled out his small, prepaid phone and sent a text message that read:

**#2**

The Family's resupply dispatcher would receive the text and match his phone number up with his assigned location. The order for the day's second load would be placed and delivered to his corner.

Every day that the Harrell corners conducted business, a designated operator coordinated all calls to the resupply crews. The four re-up rovers were luxury SUVs, each carrying armed three-man crews, which resupplied each of the Family's corners throughout the city. These rovers picked up from Harrell safe houses and made their way to each corner when contacted. In the event there was trouble, the resupply crews could also be called in as extra muscle wherever they were needed.

A minute or so after Mikey sent his text message, a return message chirped through to his cell phone:

**20 out**

This meant the resupply crew should reach his corner in the next twenty minutes.

Ten minutes later, the boys heard the noisy, metal grumbling of a vehicle approaching their corner.

"One up," Mikey called out from his spot on the stone stoop, signaling to his crew that the resupply vehicle approached.

He jumped over the edge of the stoop and knelt down near the side of the small porch. With two hands he pried away a board at the base of the stoop and reached inside with his right hand. He pulled out the brown paper bag Ant had handed him when he'd first arrived on the corner today. The bag had fattened to fifteen hundred dollars. *Not bad for the first half of the day.* If they could match this total before the night was over, then everything would be all good.

Mikey stood, brushed the dirt from his jean shorts, and walked towards the corner where the other boys waited. Here, he would hand over the crumpled paper bag and receive back a larger bag containing the second load for the day.

One cool thing about Harrell loads was that they came prepackaged: bottled-up, bagged-up, and ready to push out. This way there wasn't much downtime spent on packaging or too many hands on the product. This also helped the Family keep track of their money and keep their product exactly the way they had cooked it. Harder for anyone at the street level to get greedy and try to cut the dope again to stretch it out.

The Harrells didn't play any games. They ran their shit like a real live business, but here, getting fired came with a bullet instead of a pink slip.

One block up and from the left, a white van crept into view and stopped at the closest corner. The van turned right and edged towards the group of boys. Mikey assumed it was the re-up van at first, but as it approached, something didn't look right.

The Family had never used a beat-up van like this one. Something *was* wrong, but by the time he thought enough to say anything, all hell broke loose.

Without warning, the creeping van jumped to life and began freight training towards the boys.

"Who that, Mike?" he heard Ant say and could hear the fear in his friend's voice, but he didn't answer his question.

Mikey couldn't know who was in the van, but he didn't think they were Harrell people.

"S-Something ain't right. I don't know who that is," he said and reached for his cell phone. "Everybody back the hell up. Ant, go get our shit. Hurry up, man."

The other boys scattered while Ant ran for the pistols the boys kept stashed in a nearby trashcan. The van kept coming. Mikey tried to call for back up, but his fingers shook too much for him to dial the digits on the keypad.

Despite repeated warnings from the Family to remain sharp even during peacetime, he and his crew had lost their edge. It never occurred to him that someone could mess with their corner. Working for the Harrells, he thought he'd be safe. Now he knew he'd thought wrong.

Everything happened so damn fast. The speeding van bore down on the boys in just seconds and came screeching to a stop right in front them. The sliding passenger door flew open and out jumped four men dressed in black, sporting black ski masks and brandishing semi-automatic rifles.

Ant couldn't reach their weapons before the gunmen rounded the boys up and herded them like cattle into the van. Seconds later, the van rocketed away from the block leaving rubber on hot asphalt beneath clouds of dust and smoke.

In the rear cabin of the van, the kidnappers began beating the defenseless teenagers. Mikey saw two of his friends pinned against the rear of the van. He thought the backdoor might fly open and his friends would roll into the street. When the kidnappers finished, both of the boys laid on the van's floor unmoving, either unconscious or dead.

One of the men held Mikey on his knees with a gun to his head. He watched while the other men punched and kicked Ant and the last boy until they both slumped into a corner. The entire time, none of the gunmen said a word. They didn't ask about the crew's stash of money or drugs. This wasn't a robbery.

After watching each of his friends get beaten into the floor of the van, Mikey became the focus of the kidnappers' fury. He tried to fight back, but with four grown men jumping on him all at once, he didn't stand a chance. He ended up on the bed of the van in the fetal position, trying to shield his head from punches and kicks.

He fought to stay awake, but it wasn't long before the pain grabbed hold of him. His vision blurred and against his will, his eyes shut, making way for the darkness to swallow him whole.

# *Chapter Four*

A thick, muddy fog clouded Mikey Stanley's thoughts as he crawled his way back into consciousness. He forced his heavy eyelids open and a thunderclap of pain ricocheted through his entire body. He tried to contain the rising panic making his heart act as a battering ram against his ribcage. But for the first time since his father had left him, the teenager felt fear overwhelming him.

His head pounded as the raw, swollen tissue puckering his face sent jolts of pain to the backs of his eyes.

*How long had he been out of it?*

His eyes stung and felt full of grit. He tried to reach and rub away the irritation, but couldn't move his arms or his legs. Thick rope bound his limbs to the wooden chair he sat in, rubbing the skin around his wrists and ankles raw. The foul-tasting rag sealed in his mouth made him gag and dry heave. He strained against the ropes, but couldn't budge more than a couple of inches. After the initial wave of shock and confusion washed over him, he realized what was happening to him.

Through glassy, squinted eyes, he looked around and saw his four friends also gagged and bound to chairs. All of the chairs had been formed into a tight circle with the boys facing inward towards each other. The other boys' damaged faces looked as bad as his face felt.

He looked into the eyes of his friends and saw the frightened wildness of a trapped animal reflected in their stares. Mikey's body began to shake. His crew was looking to him for answers and help, and he had none of either to give them.

The dark and dusty room they were in stank of mold and stale piss. The space looked empty except for a few discarded McDonald's bags and several biggie size drink cups. Mikey began to remember what happened to him and his friends.

Business had been good and at almost 4:00 p.m., the crew had been ready to re-up when everything went wrong. He remembered seeing the white cargo van and for a half a second thought it might have been the resupply run. Then he remembered the masked men with the guns. He remembered the beating the men gave him and his friends.

Now he sat tied to a chair, gagged and bound, along with the rest of his crew. Bad thoughts of what might happen to them started swirling through his aching head.

*Who had been bold enough to snatch them off their corner in the middle of the day?*

He tried to calm himself long enough to think through the possibilities.

*Maybe a rival crew? No, couldn't be. This wasn't supposed to be happening. This was peacetime. Plus, they worked for the Harrells. None of this should be happening. None of it.*

He could see a couple of his friends struggling in their chairs. Like him, they couldn't move much because of their restraints. Each boy tried to speak, but their gags allowed nothing more than a few muffled grunts, cries, and muted yells for help.

When the door to the room creaked open, the group of boys became as silent and stiff as the dead. A streak of dim sunlight invaded the room but disappeared again with the closing of the heavy metal door. Through the shadows and poor lighting, Mikey could see two of their kidnappers walking towards him and his friends.

Both men were menacing-looking mountains cloaked in black and just like earlier, they wore ski masks over their faces. Each man carried something in their gloved hands, some sort of container or canister. *Gas cans*. Each man was carrying a large red gas can.

*What the hell is this?* Mikey thought. *What are they gonna do to us?*

*Wait, wait, wait. Okay, okay, it's all good,* he reasoned with himself, *they must not know who we work for. That's it, this is all wrong, some kind of mistake. Once they find out who we are, then they'll know they shouldn't have messed with us.*

As if the men could read his mind, one of them said, "This is them, huh?"

"Yeah, man, this is them," the other responded, "all of these lil' punks belong to the Harrell Family."

"Yeah, and they look plenty scared, too," the first man nodded and looked each of the boys up and down. "Well, let's get on with it. The man needs us somewhere else in a few."

Both men began circling the boys in opposite directions using slow, deliberate steps. They each twisted the small cap off their can's nozzle and poured gasoline over the boys' heads.

The flammable liquid burned the boys' swollen eyes and bruised skin as it ran down their faces. Their muffled screams began again as loud as their gags would allow. Each boy struggled in vain as their ropes wouldn't give enough for them to help themselves.

A horrifying truth set in on Mikey. He understood now that he was going to die in this dark hole of a room. There had been no mistake in their abduction, and there would be no salvation. His thoughts drifted to Moms.

He'd never see her again, would he? She'd be all alone with both him and his dad gone. Through the chorus of the boys' gagged screams, he thought he could hear her heart breaking.

His dad had run away two years ago, and he'd missed him every day since. But he'd also hated him each and every one of those days, too. Hated him for running away. He'd left his family to fend for themselves. No money, no car, no home. Hadn't so much as sent a Christmas or birthday card to his son. No calls. No visits. Nothing. He didn't even know where his father lived these days.

Mikey hated being named after that coward. He remembered the nights he'd spent crying himself to sleep. He remembered the days he spent asking Moms when Dad would be coming home. His hatred had burned deep in his heart. Hardened him. He'd lost interest in sports after his father left. Lost interest in everything.

He'd missed his dad so much he'd begun to run the streets to cope with his pain. Now, it looked as if all of his bottled up hurt and anger would come to an end once and for all.

*I just wanna go home,* he thought as his eyes rained tears that mixed with the stinging gasoline running through his braided hair and down his face.

For the first time since dropping out of the ninth grade, Mikey wished he'd stayed in school and listened to his mother. Her words from this morning rang in his ears again. *Please stay off them streets. There ain't nothing good out there for you, Michael Eugene.*

Why couldn't he have listened? He would've even gone to church. Done anything to avoid what was happening to him in this room. But it was too late, wasn't it? He wouldn't have the chance to do the right thing ever again.

One of the masked men set his can down and pulled out a long, skinny lighter from his back pocket. He lit it by clicking the black button on the handle twice, sparking a small flame from the tip. Then the other man pulled out his lighter and leaned in close so the boys could all hear him.

"Shut the fuck up!" He yelled above the boys muffled cries as he held the lighter over their heads until they were silent.

"This is just the beginning," he said through the small opening in his mask. "You hear me, you lil bitches?" he said and slapped one of the boys hard upside his head. "This is just the beginning."

Then he and the other masked man laughed like they'd just heard the funniest joke ever.

A queasiness rose from the pit of Mikey's stomach as the kidnappers' laughter bounced off the walls of the hollow room. Unable to muster another sound, he fell dead silent, as if to accept his inevitable fate.

The other boys started screaming again at the tops of their lungs. Their eyes streamed tears as their strangled cries shot toward the heavens. But it was all in vain because no one would ever hear or see these boys alive again.

The men touched their lighters' fiery tips to the gas on the floor, igniting a hungry flame that raced towards the boys. In seconds, the fire began consuming the legs of the wooden chairs and the teenage boys.

An incredible pain gripped Mikey's entire body. He felt the fire licking the flesh from his bones.

"MOMMA, PLEASE HELP ME!" He tried to scream and then the pain was too unbearable for words, too unbearable to think anymore.

He shook, kicked, and bucked in his chair. Again, he struggled; doing anything he could, but his effort was all for nothing. And then he couldn't move at all. He saw the blinding glow of yellow and orange all around him. The pain continued to rip through him as the fire burned the last of the life from his body.

Like a starving animal gorging itself on a long-awaited feast, the fire swallowed up Mikey and his friends. Their gagged screams and shrieks sounded off one last time in a sickening chorus. The last thing the boys would remember was the pain and the stench of their burning skin.

A short few minutes after the first flames were lit, it was all over. The internal fires of five teenagers had been extinguished forever. The boys' smoldering remains represented just an appetizer for the main course of carnage that would follow.

Like one of the masked arsonists had promised...*this was just the beginning...*

# *Chapter Five*

In a small tucked-away neighborhood in Southeast D.C., Death had come calling in the form of yet another gruesome homicide. The putrid stink of scorched flesh festered in the afternoon humidity and triggered the gag reflex of approaching rubberneckers.

The Metropolitan Police Department managed to cordon off the perimeter with yellow "crime scene" tape just as the rain and reporters began to arrive.

Newshounds from every local media outlet gathered to report on the bodies discovered in the basement of a burned down row house. Cameras flashed as the members of the media jockeyed for the best vantage point around the boundary.

Reporters spoke into their microphones and gave their individual accounts of the crime based on the limited information available. Law enforcement officials remained tight-lipped and deflected reporters' questions about the shocking discovery. One female journalist speculated that today's crime was the work of a serial killer on the hunt in D.C. She spoke of a modern-day monster that had cruelly burned five *human beings* beyond recognition.

Ramshackle apartment buildings and row houses sat jam-packed on both sides of the narrow streets running through this neighborhood. Like too many other parts of the city, the aged and dilapidated buildings suffered from years of neglect. Parked cars, news trucks, and emergency vehicles crowded the streets and slowed the traffic attempting to squeeze through.

Drug dealers and addicts often populated the dark, trash-strewn alleyways of this neighborhood. They used the shadowed corridors to conduct their illicit business. Fear had forced residents of this three-block district to ignore and hide from the crime problem. So, this neighborhood, like many others, remained infested and overrun, locked in a chokehold of narcotics trafficking and random violence.

In recent years, the violence had tapered off and though the trafficking continued to flourish, the rampaging bloodshed no longer accompanied it. Today's act of evil dealt this community a sorrowful blow and sparked new fears of old ghosts returning.

The MPD blocked off the vicinity from all approachable angles and diverted approaching traffic away from the scene. Despite the rolling clouds and downpour from the incoming storm, a large crowd continued to gather. People looked on in revulsion at the atrocity committed in their neighborhood as a growing tension circulated throughout the crowd.

Several stiff-legged officers manned the perimeter and tried to hold the crowd at bay.

One nervous officer squawked a shaky plea through his bullhorn, "E-Everyone needs to please remain calm and stay behind the perimeter. Please, move back and remain behind the yellow tape."

Patrolman Rodney Rogers was a newbie on the force, but he'd heard the stories of angry crowds escalating into riotous mobs. The bullhorn trembled in his hand. He prayed he could make it through this without becoming a part of one of those stories.

A metal gate at the entrance of the ruined house's front yard whined as the wind made it dance on its rusted hinges. Policemen, firemen, and other emergency personnel rushed in and out of the tiny square front yard. The row house itself had been hollowed out by an arsonist's handiwork, leaving nothing but a smoldering shell.

D.C.'s fire department had fought a two-hour battle before they were able to contain and extinguish the inferno within the two-story domicile. These row houses didn't utilize firewalls, and the homes on both sides of the house had suffered major damage from the fire. Both families on either side had escaped without injury, but would be forced to seek other shelter for the immediate future.

Throughout the crowd, sobs rang out towards the skies. The clouds seemed to roll in response to the people, heaving and releasing a heavier torrent of rain. Anxiety spread through the crowd like a virus as rumors about the identities of the dead bodies began to circulate. Cell phones were pulled out and fearful men and women tried to reach loved ones who hadn't been seen or heard from. Cries for justice rode the wind and drowned out the patrolmen's pleas for order as the scene deteriorated into chaos.

Men, women, and children of all ages absorbed the unbelievable sight. Parents covered their children's eyes. Like watching a fatal car wreck, no one could look straight on, yet all were too hypnotized to turn their attention away.

Moans and gasps sounded from the crowd when a charred arm slipped into view as med techs tried to situate the corpses. The wails and shouts of rage grew louder. The tortured living cried out in the name of the dead whose souls no longer belonged to this world.

Emergency crews and coroner techs would struggle trying to discern the gender of the victims by any visual means of inspection. A couple of the bodies were missing fingers and a hand or foot. Eyes were scorched out of their sockets, leaving blackened, sunken holes. The mouths of the dead remained open as if they screamed for mercy during their journey into the afterlife.

Four of the bodies lay in disturbing positions. Each corpse sported ash encrusted limbs pointed in different directions, appearing to flail as if they tried to outrun death himself. The last body lay in the fetal position as if it had given up and fallen with ease into the Grim Reaper's outstretched arms.

Lester Johnson, a tall, thin, middle-aged man dressed in a blue postal uniform, yelled out above the rest of the crowd.

"Hey! Hey, man! Hey, you police over there! Hey, I'm talkin' to you, Mr. Officer! You hear me?" he said, pointing in the direction of Patrolman Rogers.

"This shit is startin' up again! When are you cops gonna do something about these damn drugs around here? How many of *US* have to die before you crooked bastards do something? Protect and goddamn serve, right?"

The crowd howled in agreement, and a nervous shudder rippled through the patrolmen manning the perimeter. Each officer wanted to retreat towards the closest exit, but none of them moved for fear of further inciting the raucous crowd.

The crime scene tape stretched to its breaking point as the crowd swelled like a hot air balloon. Outraged men and women pushed against the barrier of policemen, pointing and screaming in the officer's faces.

The reporters continued to circle like vultures over roadkill, snapping pictures and hounding the policemen for comments. News of this magnitude would create a media frenzy and hell on earth for the city's authorities. Tomorrow, the headlines would read something like:

**Police Clueless as Five People Burned to Death in Apparent Gang Execution**

*   *   *   *

D.C. Mayor Ronaldus Dunbar and MPD Chief of Police Quinn Walters arrived in Southeast within a few minutes of each other. They conferred with the mayor's staff on the best approach before addressing the media. How would the mayor account for the five dead bodies?

Under different circumstances, he could soothe the public outcry and find a way to come out smelling like roses. An accidental house fire or even a random robbery was tenable, but today's crime had something much more sinister written all over it. There was no leeway for viable explanation of this mess.

The mayor had based his "Dunbar for D.C." reelection campaign platform on a successful war against drugs and gang violence. How would he answer the tough questions from the media and the families of the dead? Negative press could undermine his reelection efforts, unnerve his constituent base, and allow his adversary to try and steal the upcoming primary.

Mayor Dunbar knew the narcotics trafficking remained a serious issue, but the violence had dropped in dramatic fashion. With a younger, more vibrant opponent challenging him and promising wide-ranging improvements, he'd grown desperate. He felt his grip slipping on the office he'd held for the last three terms. In the decrease of violence, he'd seen an opportunity.

Channeling thoughts of self-preservation, he'd manufactured a false victory for his administration. Having to ignite a fresh war on drugs would be bad for him. It would do nothing but expose his campaign and depict him as a liar. The extra money for police meant budget cuts that would leave the school districts and city labor unions crying foul. His people would turn on him and he'd be out of office next year.

No, this was not the time for another expensive crime crackdown. He would deal with the lingering narcotics problem when it suited his long-term agenda *after* he won the election.

* * * *

Chief Walters stood at the mayor's side when he stepped to the portable podium and addressed the media. He watched his boss tap dance around the onslaught of questions the reporters hurled at him like rocks.

The crowd continued to grow larger and louder, drowning out the mayor's voice despite his use of a microphone. The synchronized chants of "STOP THE VIOLENCE!" and "NO MORE DRUGS!" could be heard from blocks away. When it was his turn, Chief Walters endured the same harsh treatment from the crowd and the media as he fielded questions.

"Chief Walters!" a petite brunette called out as she squeezed towards the front of the pack and extended her recorder in his direction. "Chief, are these killings drug related? Is today an indication that the violence is returning to our city's streets? How do you explain your department's lack of presence in an area known for its heavy narcotics activity?"

She'd bombarded him with her questions in an attempt to catch him off guard. Unlike his boss, the chief was able to maintain his composure and provide an even-keeled blanket statement as his answer.

"At this time, these deaths are being treated as an unfortunate, but isolated tragedy. Our department has yet to classify these deaths as homicides, but is also not ruling out the possibility of foul play. Furthermore, there has been no evidence linking this incident to any type of narcotics trafficking. As always, the Metropolitan Police Department maintains a strong presence throughout the city and especially in areas noted for high crime activity. After the victims have been identified, their names will be released after the appropriate time has been allotted for next of kin notification. No additional details are available at this time. Our department will release a statement as soon as more current information becomes available. Thank-you."

The questions continued, but he hurried from the podium, giving way to one of the mayor's senior staffers. The young man answered a few more questions, offering generic responses similar to the chief's, before ending the press conference.

After the brief but brutal press conference ended, Chief Walters examined the blackened row house. He massaged his temple with the fingers of his right hand, trying to ease the onset of a tension headache.

The chief still possessed an imposing presence at age fifty-six, still commanding the respect of those in his charge. His trim frame reflected diligent use of the precinct gym three times a week, but his body also told another story. The graying hair, worry lines entrenched deep in his dark skin, and his worn facial features spoke of accumulated frustration and exhaustion.

Elena Marie, his wife of twenty-one years, had been pushing him to retire from the force. She said it was just plain time for them to leave this city and begin their golden years in Savannah, Georgia.

He knew she was right. In the next year, their twin daughters would be gone away to college and Elena had already closed her real estate office. It was his turn, but he hadn't been able to leave the badge behind, not with things like this.

In his years serving the city he'd been born and raised in, Chief Walters had seen the best and worst of times. Without a doubt, the current state of his city placed near the top of his "bad" list.

Behind closed doors, the mayor demanded answers to the narcotics problem, but the chief and his undermanned force had none to give. Budget cuts were as big an enemy of the police as were the city's crime problems.

The MPD knew who many of the city's heavyweight narcotics traffickers were, but significant arrests came few and far between. When his officers did make an arrest, the district attorney couldn't obtain an indictment on any charge heavier than minor narcotics possession. Major drug trafficking charges just didn't seem to stick on most of these gangsters.

The chief had formed a drug and gang task force from his department's ranks, but it also had achieved very limited success. The task force had continued the trend of minimal headway towards toppling the bigger players in the city's crime syndicate.

In spite of the mayor's public boasts about winning the war on drugs, Chief Walters knew they had won nothing. He knew the drugs still flowed in his streets, and now it looked as if the violence was returning as well.

He didn't want to believe it, but the chief suspected some of his officers of running afoul of their sworn duties. In fact, he feared that widespread corruption had infected his force and even the other branches of the city's law system.

He'd launched an investigation into the possibility of corrupt cops and other crooked city officials assisting these criminals. It was no longer a question of if there was corruption, but rather how far up the ladder did it go.

The chief had been forced to take a more hidden and limited approach. Mayor Dunbar had approved his request to form an additional task force, but he wondered if it would matter at this point? Budgeting was tight and the mayor wouldn't allow a new public initiative that would contradict his campaign stance.

This new one-man task force would place an officer deep undercover into the city's underworld. His mission would be to disrupt the city's drug flow through the identification and apprehension of the city's largest narcotics distributers.

Chief Walters and his undercover would operate separate from the rest of the department and report to the mayor. Their goal would be to penetrate the city's organized crime ring at its highest level and bringing the entire thing toppling down. Now he only needed to sell his idea to the officer he had in mind for the job.

He'd chosen a young officer whose progress he'd followed since just after the officer's graduation from the academy. His name had first appeared on the chief's radar when he'd received two commendations for bravery in the line of duty. This young detective was a fast burner who'd aced the detective's test on his first try. His hard work had gotten him assigned to the narcotics division task force where he'd continued to shine.

The chief had finalized his choice after researching the young detective's rough upbringing and closeness to the city's drug-infested neighborhoods. He appeared to be a tough, street-smart kid itching to make a difference.

Chief Walters knew he had the right man.

He just hoped the youngster would be willing to become one of the animals they had been trying to catch. DC was a city of wolves and Chief Walters knew that becoming a wolf was the only way to survive out here.

With the current lack of funding and manpower, he knew it was a huge risk to put in an undercover now. Would his man be able to survive the heavy toll that came with this kind of life? Would he be able to steer clear of the corruption?

Chief Walters continued to watch as his detectives scrubbed the area for any clues that would yield a lead. His officers began their canvass of the neighborhood in search of witnesses. A search that would prove to be useless. No one would step forward. They were all too scared to say anything. Fear is a powerful and sometimes crippling thing. The group of protestors would return to their homes and refuse to get involved.

He couldn't blame the residents of this small community for their silence. His force had given them zero in the way of protection from these monsters. He often wondered how he even had a job anymore.

But the mayor couldn't fire him right now, could he? Not this close to the election; it would show instability and cause damage to his campaign. He had no doubt he would be forced into retirement if a new mayor took office, but none of that mattered to him. Saving his city was that all he cared about at this point.

The reporters and cameramen began to clear out after asking their questions, snapping hundreds of photographs and making their live reports. They all rushed to try and make the nightly televised news and the latest edition of the city's newspapers.

As the storm picked up strength, the crowd dispersed promising calls to the NAACP and the Reverends Sharpton and Jackson. The mayor also had seen enough and wasted no time retreating as soon as he thought the coast was clear.

*Jackass,* the chief thought as he watched the mayor and his staff leave in a chauffeured Lincoln Navigator. *He doesn't have a clue about what's going on out here in these streets and probably doesn't give a damn anyway.*

He walked towards his police cruiser, head hung, police cap pulled down low and his hands stuffed in pockets. He looked skyward and observed the shadowed clouds continuing their migration into the city's airspace.

*Yessir, we got a helluva storm coming this way,* he thought. *Plenty of rain and then some.*

Glancing at the house one final time, he shook his head in disgust. The engine of his blue Crown Victoria turned over, and as he backed the car out, Chief Walters had a disturbing thought:

*These murders are just the beginning. And when the beginning of the end comes, it's evidenced by the red flags we foolishly overlook. Then, before we know it, the end is slapping all of us upside the damn head...*

# *Part II*

# *"LIVE BY THE GUN..."*

*"The Harrell Way of Life"*

**Flying high, living right on life's edge, two small steps from darkness.**
**Real life, drowned deep in a cold-blooded rawness,**
**Scripted in jagged-edged mounds**
**Fueled by fear mixed with closed-fisted brutality...**
**Teeter-tottering on the thin line between life and death...**
**Not many peaceful sunrises on the wrong side...**

# *Chapter Six*

"Hey, listen up, everybody, look here," Ezra Harrell announced, standing up from his chair at the head of the long banquet table. "I'd like to propose a toast."

The black Armani two-button he'd bought especially for tonight's dinner suited him like a royal robe suited a king. He was a king, wasn't he? *The* king.

He lifted his crystal stemware high in the air, the sparkling champagne it held spilling over the rim.

"To my beautiful wife on her birthday," he said, tossing a wink at his queen sitting to his right in a camel-colored cashmere and satin gown.

Her caramel skin glowed and her cinnamon-hued braids framed her heart-shaped face just right. As usual, she was stunning.

Everyone seated around the rectangular table also stood, repeating his motion with their glasses as he continued.

"And to our family," he said and looked into each of the twenty-seven pairs of eyes staring back at him, locked onto his every word.

Each of those eyes belonged to the people closest to him. He looked from his wife, to his son, to his two older brothers. He looked at the rest of the table. The people sitting there, both blood and non-blood, had earned a place at his table through years of loyal service.

"And to the Harrell Empire. We built it by always operating as one and by always putting family first. Remember, nothing ever comes before our family. *Nothing before family.*"

"NOTHING BEFORE FAMILY," every person at the table repeated in unison and lifted their glasses up to their lips.

Ezra took a long swallow of the expensive, sweet tasting champagne before signaling to the maître d'. The middle-aged white man, with his thinning gray hair and starched demeanor, opened both glass doors of the private party room.

*"HAPPYYYYY BIRTHDAYYYYY TO YOU,"* everyone began singing on cue as two waiters carted in a huge, three-tier birthday cake extravaganza.

Fifty candy-striped candles stood in the thick white and pink butter-cream frosting. Ezra watched his wife's eyes grow big as the waiters parked the mountain of sweet sin near her seat. Her full, soft lips parted into a huge grin. The high wattage shine of her smile still warmed his soul after all this time.

He'd considered canceling tonight's celebration after the earlier events of this week, but he couldn't stand to spoil Liv's birthday. He wouldn't tell her about the family's recent problems until after her celebration concluded. He needed to sponge off his wife's happiness to help flush away his mounting stress.

The birthday meal hadn't disappointed in the least, and Ezra had no idea how he would manage dessert. The seafood buffet had consisted of broiled Maine lobster tails, seasoned snow crab leg clusters, and baked Atlantic croaker. He'd also enjoyed the thick monkfish steaks filled with cheese grits and the pan-seared black sea bass. He'd also been sure to sample the salmon stuffed with blue crab and the assortment of shrimp, clams, and oysters. The Moet, Cristal, Dom Perignon, and Cîroc flowed like tap water throughout the evening. He'd spared no expense for tonight's event.

The Seacatch Bar and Grill Restaurant in historic Georgetown was a longtime Harrell Family favorite. Its owners always catered to his requests, offering the restaurant's spacious Captain's Room whenever the Harrells hosted a private event.

After dessert, Ezra drifted away from everyone and onto the moonlit outdoor patio overlooking the half-filled C&O canal. He sipped from his glass of cognac and blew smoky circles from his cigar towards the half-moon in the cloudy, ebony sky.

*So, is this how things are going to play out for me and mine? Being dragged back to war after all of this time? So damned foolish of me to think we'd finally risen above the madness.*

The creaking of the patio door interrupted his thoughts, and the sound of heavy steps confirmed another man's presence on the patio. His street-borne reflexes kicked in and caused him to reach for the pistol strapped in his shoulder holster.

Most people didn't accessorize a $2,000 suit with a Sig Sauer P290, but Ezra Harrell wasn't "most people," was he? This was part of the life he'd chosen to lead so many years ago. It didn't much matter where he was or what he was doing. His life was always there, hanging heavy around his neck like a weight he was forced to carry.

The footsteps grew louder. He eased the pistol out of his jacket and clicked off the safety. Some things just never changed.

# Chapter Seven

"So what are we gonna do about this, lil brotha?" Montae Harrell said as he stepped out of the shadows.

He put a large hand on Ezra's right shoulder and squeezed. "How do we fix this mess?"

Relief washed over Ezra, and he was happy to reholster his pistol. He felt foolish as he remembered the many people watching his back at all times. *Old habits...*

"Don't know just yet, big brotha," he said turning to face his oldest brother. "I didn't see this one coming. Maybe I should have, but I didn't see it at all."

At six feet even, Ezra stood a full four inches over his brother. But what it lacked in vertical achievement, Montae's compact frame more than made up for in its muscular build.

"None of us did, not with the way things have been with the ceasefire in place. But that doesn't much matter at this point. Either way, we gotta do something, Ez," Montae said. "I mean we can't let this ride, right? Can't have people just invading our territory like that, right?"

"No, we can't just let it ride and we won't," Ezra replied, taking the last sip of his drink and flicking the remainder of his cigar towards the canal below.

"But we have to think big picture here. Going out and blowing up streets would do more harm than good for our operations."

"Streets are already blown up, Ez. Somebody snatched one of our corner crews and dumped them in one of our safe houses. They burned the damn bodies. Burned them to a crisp. Ain't tellin' you nuthin' you don't already know, man. The safe house was vacant and the crew's stash wasn't missing, so this wasn't a robbery. Looks to me like somebody sending us a message here. What you think?"

"Yeah, you're right. No doubt about that. Question is, who's sending us this message and why? We have agreements in place across the board and everybody's getting a good slice, so why rock the boat? It's bad for business all the way around and don't make no sense. Then, if we start shaking down the streets for answers, business could come to an all-out stop. I really don't want to risk further attention on this one."

"What attention, Ez? Police are on our side, in our pockets," Montae said. "We do what we want, and they turn the other cheek. Same as always."

"Yeah, they're in our pockets right at this moment but no amount of money in the world will matter if we start putting them in a position where they're forced to respond. We start giving the press reason enough to shout and the police won't have any other choice but to start cracking down on all of us. Then we'll really be left scrambling, won't we? We been there and done that. No need to revisit it this late in the game, man."

"Ez, I feel you, but..." Montae protested again, "all I'm saying is we need to hit back for what happened and then..."

"No, we can't do it that way. Who would we hit? We don't know anything yet. So, whatever we do, we'll do it on the low. This way, business keeps moving, money keeps flowing. Meanwhile, we get our answers and then we make our move. Cut the throats of whoever stepped in the wrong like that."

He could see from his brother's face that he disagreed, but he knew Montae wouldn't continue to argue the point.

"You got it, lil brother," Montae said. "Whatever you want to do. However you want to do it."

Ezra stood close to his brother and pointed out towards the skyline, waving his open hand across the city lights. "Look here. You see that out there, bro? See it? That's all ours right there, all of it. Trust me on this one, remember the big picture for us. We ain't street bangers no more, and a war won't do us any good. I know you want get-back and so do I, but throwing down out in the open won't help us. It'll hurt us now more than anything. Trust me."

Montae didn't look at him, but managed a nod of agreement. "Okay, Ez."

"Good deal," he said, clapping his brother on the back with his left hand. "Now, where's your other brother at?"

"Who knows? But if I know him, he's halfway to blitzed by now. Drunk and high," Montae said. "You know business ain't his thing at all. Drinks, smoke, and women? Hell, yeah. But business? No sir, no sir."

"Nope business ain't his thing, never has been and never will be," Ezra said and laughed, straightening his suit jacket. "But maybe we can learn from him a little? Ain't no doubt he knows how to relax. So, how about we go join him? I mean, it is a party after all."

Ezra turned and headed towards the patio entrance. "Come on, big brotha. No more stress tonight. Them streets will be there waiting on us, you best believe that."

# *Chapter Eight*

Olivia Harrell watched her husband reenter the restaurant from the outside patio with her oldest brother-in-law. She fingered her shoulder-length braids as she noted the worry lines etched across his face. Her husband was stressing about something, and his stress was always her stress. That was how their bond worked after so many years together.

When he noticed her deep brown eyes boring into him, Ezra pasted on his best smile, but she'd seen right through it. It was her job to know the innermost workings of her husband. Her ability to discern when something bothered him had long been second nature. He'd tried to hide it, but anxiety had weaved its way in and managed to distract him throughout the celebration. She'd picked up on it early in the evening. When they were alone, she'd ask him about whatever was bothering him.

Olivia turned to look at her son. At her request, he had remained sitting beside her when his father and uncle had first disappeared from the room. She knew he'd wanted to follow, but her mission was to delay his inevitable ascension into the ranks of the family business.

Her impatient child. He pushed his fork through his slice of the birthday cake, turning it into a pile of sugary mush and crumbs. He would never admit it, but she could tell he was angry with her. Well, he'd have to get over it because she didn't feel the least bit guilty for holding him back.

*You can't stop time, Liv, and he's not a baby anymore. He's a grown man now.*

No, she couldn't stop time, but she damn well could try to slow it down some. For the last few years, Ezra had promised her a new life away from Washington, D.C. and away from the family business. She hoped he would keep his promise before her son could take his place as the head of the family.

"Baby," she said, reaching out for her son's hand. "Go grab my coat please, and let's head on home. It's late and your momma's tired. I'll tell your father that we are leaving."

Cuttino looked up from his dessert. He shot her a look. She knew he wanted to stay, but when her eyes met his, the look vanished.

"Yes, ma'am," he said with a heavy sigh, and headed towards the coatroom to gather their belongings.

She smiled at her son as he walked away from the table. Her baby. So handsome. He looked like a taller, slimmer version of his daddy. But he was still her child, and nothing mattered to Olivia more than holding this family together the best way she could.

## *Chapter Nine*

Sundays were for church. Church, and then quality time with the family. No business was conducted on Sundays. No cell phones answered, no replies to texts or emails. Ezra knew his wife didn't ask for much, just Sundays for the family.

Liv never fooled with his business, never tried to control him, although she knew how he made every cent of their money. He didn't bother with keeping anything from her for too long. She knew him too well for that. But she never questioned his secret meetings and late nights. Never bitched and moaned about the simple things other women found a need to complain about just to hear themselves talk. Liv had what he called balance. She was secure in her place at his side and had helped him instead of trying to challenge and second-guess his decisions.

Early on, when he'd been young and dumb, he'd tried being a player. He'd seen how many of his peers had mistresses and even kids all over the place. Had thought maybe a different woman could give him something that Liv didn't. They couldn't. Thought maybe he was missing something by being loyal to just one woman. He wasn't.

He'd stepped out there, and Liv had gotten word of what he was doing. She hadn't freaked out on him, but she'd made it crystal clear that she wasn't weak. That she wasn't one of these other women out here that his brothers and partners liked to keep around. She'd threatened to leave and disappear forever; and had meant it, too, if he ever hurt her again. He never strayed again after that. Never even thought about it. He wasn't scared of Liv or of her leaving, but he wasn't a fool either. He respected her.

His wife was a rare breed, maybe even a once in a lifetime type woman. She was the perfect complement for a man like him. Never scared, always loyal, and loving. She'd put her life and future on the line all for him and the life he'd chosen for her. The least he could do was always honor that. What they had was deeper than love. There wasn't a word for it, but it just plain worked.

So, Sundays were non-negotiable, and he never, ever refused his wife on this subject.

*   *   *   *

Just before noon, on the Sunday after Liv's birthday party, the Harrells were participating in their normal Sunday routine.

Their pearl-white Lexus LX 570 glided to a stop in front of the Greater Southeast Baptist Church. Ezra, Olivia, and Cuttino stepped out and headed up the large stone steps leading to the house of worship. Several guards from a second SUV followed behind the Harrells. The men kept an inconspicuous but close eye on the family as they moved among the masses flocking towards the entrance.

Sunlight flooded through high glass ceilings and lit up the spacious, ornamented vestibule of GSBC. The church's sanctuary also boasted elaborate decorations as well as cathedral ceilings, multi-level theater seating, and two huge high definition screens. A two-level stage held the 120-person choir, five-piece band, and musical director on its top level. The Pastor and his nine-person staff sat on the stage's lower level.

Ezra wouldn't go as far as to say that he enjoyed this church, but he didn't dislike it either. The entire production bordered on the ridiculous, like some sort of Hollywood reality TV bit. As mega-churches went,

GSBC appeared to be legit, but Mom had taken him and his brothers to a much smaller church growing up.

The whole mega-church theme felt unnecessary and overdone, but Olivia had been raised in this church. The congregation had more than tripled in size over the years, but she'd remained a faithful member.

Pastor Malcolm Warner, GSBC's latest senior pastor, seemed sincere, so Ezra didn't mind the large amount of tithing Liv did each month. And he had to admit that he enjoyed the time alone with his wife and son away from their normal life.

He also savored the inner peace that church gave him, even one as overwhelming as GSBC. The music, the clapping, even the rhythm of the pastor's words while he delivered his sermon all seemed to settle Ezra. Most of all, he just enjoyed making his wife happy.

As much as he tried to resist the urge, Ezra sometimes allowed his thoughts to drift towards business. This Sunday, as he sat flanked by his wife, son, and personal driver, Ezra heard the pastor preaching about new beginnings. He spoke about the importance of family and taking action based on faith.

Ezra was sure those words weren't meant for a man like him, but he could relate them to his situation anyway. His family was important to him without a doubt and that was where he placed all of his faith. The more he thought about it all, the more he knew the truth: it was time for a new beginning.

After service ended, the Harrells went to the Beacon Bar and Grill on Rhode Island Avenue for brunch. The restaurant inside of the famous Beacon Hotel was known citywide for its Sunday Champagne Buffet Brunch.

Reservations were usually required almost a week in advance to get a table on Sunday afternoons. Of course, this requirement didn't apply to the Harrell Family. Their driver simply phoned a few minutes ahead and when they arrived, the Beacon's best and most private table always awaited them.

"Look at both of my men," Olivia said after Ezra had blessed their food.

As always, she beamed with pride at her husband and son. "You two always look so handsome in your Sunday best."

She loved saying that. It was her thing, like a ritual for her when they all were together on Sundays.

At Liv's request, father and son had dressed in the suits she'd had tailor-made for them this past Christmas. A taupe, double-breasted three button for him and an olive, single-breasted two button number for Cuttino. To Ezra, they resembled a "then and now" picture, one young and rising and the other older and on the decline.

He looked up from his crab omelet and glanced at his son. At twenty-six, his boy looked so much like he did at that age. Same strong chin, same cocoa skin. Same brown eyes and smile. His boy.

"Hey, so how's the new place coming, son?" he said, remembering that the family's realtor had just sold Cuttino's two-bedroom condo in Arlington and found him a townhouse near Rockville.

His son had wanted more space, but it was more than just gaining a basement, two extra bedrooms, and a garage. Ezra also thought he'd wanted to branch out a little further from home as well.

*Makes sense,* Ezra thought, *he's not a baby anymore.*

"It's good, Dad. Nice, real nice," Cuttino said through a spoonful of cheese eggs. "Ms. Baker did a good job finding it for me. Everything is just about set up. Can't wait for you and mom to see it."

"I thought Michelle was moving with you?" Olivia asked.

His wife couldn't help but pry into their son's love life. She loved Michelle, and she'd hoped to be planning a wedding and baby shower soon. Neither he nor Cuttino had the heart to tell her that the relationship had ended almost a month ago.

Ezra had played dumb for the past few weeks, while his son had skirted around the subject altogether. *Nowhere to run now.* He watched his son almost choke on his orange juice, and he wanted to laugh as the show began. Liv wouldn't let this matter die until she felt good and ready.

Cuttino cleared his throat. "Um, well Mom, me and Michelle didn't quite work out," he said, the excitement gone from his voice. "We, uh, we didn't see eye to eye on some things and well, you know how that is."

Ezra watched his son return his attention to his food, hoping his mother would somehow be satisfied with his answer.

*Nice try, but it's not gonna work. You know your mother. She's not letting this go, not this easy.*

"Didn't see eye to eye?" she asked. Ezra knew she was feigning ignorance at what their son had meant. "What things, Cuttino? You and Michelle dated for two and a half years and you break up just like that?"

Ezra saw his son look at him for help, but he wasn't biting. Not this time. He returned a look that said, *No sir, you are on your own.* Liv had never made a secret of her desire to see Cuttino married and making a few grandchildren for her to spoil.

"Mom, it's, it's just more complicated than that," Cuttino said, exhaling a heavy breath. "Chelle, well she wanted to get married, have kids and I, well I'm just not ready for all of that. Not yet."

"And why not, baby? What's wrong with that?" she said. "Your father and I were married at your age *and* we raised you. That's a good life, Cuttino."

"Livia, come on," Ezra said, placing his hand over his wife's. "Don't do that. Leave that boy alone. Times are different now. You know that. Kids these days and all that, you know. It's different from when we were coming up."

She pulled her hand from under his, never taking her eyes off their son. Ezra shook his head. He didn't feel like going through this today, not on a Sunday. Today was supposed to be a peaceful day for him, away from any foolishness. And this right here had the makings of some foolishness.

"So, boy, we 'bout ready to chase them fish?" he said, deciding to step in and change the subject. "I called Captain Dee and we're set for next Saturday. He said we'd have the whole boat to ourselves. Me, you, and a couple of our people. He also said them croakers are still hittin' hard. Be nice to get us a couple cooler-fulls and cook em' up right, huh?"

Cuttino looked at him and then at Liv. "Because Mom, I'm just not ready," he said, setting down his fork and ignoring Ezra's attempt to bail him out.

"Plus, I got the family business to worry about. I need to be focused on that, you know? Make sure I'm ready when Dad needs me. Kids and a wife right now wouldn't do anything but mess all that up. Chelle's not like you, Mom. She wouldn't have understood what's going on. How our family really works. I know she wouldn't. So... I just decided to break it off. It's better this way. Better for everybody."

Cuttino's words caught Ezra off guard. *Well, damn. Why did he have to go and say all of that?*

Olivia's eyes narrowed into dark slits, and she shot Ezra a dagger of a look. A pang of guilt shook him then. He didn't want his son making these kinds of decisions based on his aspirations to head up the family business.

He and Liv would be discussing this tonight. More than ever, he needed to make a decision about his family's future. He didn't want this life for his son or for the generations of the Harrells to follow.

# *Chapter Ten*

***Miami, Florida—one week later...***

A.J. Harrell had missed being down here, no doubt about it. This right here was the good life, how it was supposed to be. He took another sip of his Mojito and continued digesting the incredible view all around him.

The sparkling blue sky didn't have a cloud in sight and seemed to plunge right into the deep blue Atlantic Ocean. There were abundant amounts of white sand, mixed drinks, and beautiful women for as far as the eye could see. What more could one man ask for? D.C. was home, but there was nothing like South Beach in the summer.

The Miami sun baked everything in sight, leaving nothing to do but lie out, soak it in, and go with the flow. Watching gorgeous women walking around damn near butt naked was just what A.J. needed to relieve his stress. If he had to tell the truth, he could give a damn about the family business anyway. Life was too short to waste it working.

The fun side of life is what he loved, and these business trips were part of that fun. Except, the kind of business he conducted involved getting drunk and high and finding new ladies to get into his bed. Let his brothers worry about work; he would handle the sun, the alcohol, and the exotic women.

That was the thing about the women in South Beach, you could find anything down here—black, white, Dominican, and Cuban. Whatever you wanted. Race didn't matter; he loved them all. And they gravitated towards money like a submarine using sonar to find its target.

A slim Filipina waitress with eyes as blue as the ocean delivered a second carafe of mojitos to his table. She winked at him and licked her lips, ignoring the three long-legged women already keeping him company. Her full breasts damn near busted out of her skimpy top as she bent to place the tray on the table. A.J. nodded and returned the wink and the smile.

"Thanks, sweetheart," he said and slipped her a hundred-dollar bill. *This right here is why I love South Beach,* he thought, *now I got my choice of four tonight.*

The waitress's ocean eyes looked like contacts and her ample chest and perfect nose spoke of plastic surgery, but he didn't mind. He had every intention of doing a close-up inspection later that evening.

He watched her walk away; her petite hips and round ass performed a sexy switch beneath her short uniform skirt. A.J. smiled and made a mental note to find out what time her shift ended. *Gotta love South Beach.*

# *Chapter Eleven*

The oldest of the Harrell brothers watched the view of South Beach's main strip from his hotel room balcony. In the stifling Miami humidity, his black linen short-sleeved shirt and bone-white linen pants felt glued to his body.

At the peak of the afternoon on a Saturday, the famous strip buzzed with all kinds of activity. Well-tanned and coconut oil-soaked people, both native and tourist, young and old, crowded the narrow sidewalks and streets. They flowed in and out of the many restaurants, bars, and shops crowded along Ocean Drive.

*Ignorant asses,* Montae Harrell thought, *none of these fuckers have a clue about the real world.*

He couldn't wait to leave here and get back to D.C. With the exception of the business to be handled, Miami was a complete waste of time for him.

He would've preferred to stay in Miami's downtown business district, but A.J. always insisted on staying on the South Beach strip. This time they stayed at the Loews Miami Beach Hotel. It was too flashy for

Montae's taste, but right up A.J.'s alley. He couldn't get it through his knucklehead that these trips were about family business and not to be used for his pleasure.

But that was a battle Montae had given up on long ago. Instead of dragging A.J. along when it was time to get down to business, he always took care of it himself.

This trip marked their third time to Miami in the last year. Ezra had stopped making these trips years back, making it a permanent duty for him and A.J. Four times a year they caught a private flight south and met with the family's main supplier.

During these quarterly meetings, the two sides hashed out the details of their ongoing narcotics supply deal. Any adjustments, if needed, were made to account for the changing times. All issues were brought to the table and smoothed out. The meetings never ended until both sides walked away satisfied. It had been this way for years, since the very beginning.

"Face to face helps keep the relationship sweet," Ezra told him whenever he questioned the continued need for these trips. So, he kept on flying while his baby brother focused his attention on the political side of the family's business.

Ezra devoted too much time to getting in good with the politicians, wasted too much money building his unnecessary legal enterprises. He wanted to hide who the Harrells really were: cold-blooded, black-hearted gangsters. He'd forgotten what this life was all about. While he distanced himself from the family's roots, Montae embraced them more than ever.

During the first couple of meets in Miami, their business associates had questioned Ezra's absence. Montae had covered with talk of pressing frontline needs back home requiring his brother's personal attention. From then on, his handling of the negotiations became common and expected.

This trip had progressed like the others, two days of fun in the sun for A.J., while Montae took care of business. This trip couldn't end soon enough. Since the beginning, he'd handled the family's security and with the recent events in the city, he needed to get home. Things were starting to happen, and he didn't want to miss a minute of the action. In fact, he wanted to control as much of it as possible.

He checked the time on his black, leather-strapped Hamilton timepiece. It was almost one o'clock. The meet was set for five that evening. He sent two of his four guards to check out the area around the hotel and pick-up food for everyone. The last two remained behind with him. Three other guards watched over A.J. while he hit all of his favorite spots along the beach strip.

Montae continued to watch the beach bums walk, jog, and rollerblade their way up and down the strip. He observed the parade of Bentleys, Jags, Benzes, Maseratis, BMWs and other expensive luxury automobiles all creeping slow along both sides of the street. The scene reminded him of that Will Smith "Summertime" song.

With all of the money flowing throughout Miami, it was a damn shame the Harrells hadn't expanded their reach this far south.

*Soon, real, real soon,* he thought as a smile spread across his face, *it won't be long before the Harrells own Miami, too.*

# *Chapter Twelve*

Four hours later, a stretch Rolls Royce with dark tinted windows pulled across the street from the front of the Loews hotel. Montae saw the platinum automobile and knew it waited for him and his men.

He signaled to his guards that it was time. He had to steady his mind as they left the suite and headed towards the hotel lobby. Although this was standard procedure and his safety was guaranteed, he couldn't get used to riding with strangers to an unknown location.

As always, Javier Garrido waited to greet Montae and his men when they entered the air-conditioned cabin of the Rolls. The Garrido family boss had also given up attending these meetings some time ago.

In fact, Montae had seen the Garrido boss just once, back when The Harrells had first started dealing with the Garridos. This was when Ezra still cared about this business enough to handle these meetings himself. Since then, a representative from each family had shown up in their stead. Montae and Javier, one of the Garrido sons, had been dealing with each other for the past few years.

"Montae, my good friend, my partner in crime," Javier said, extending his slim, manicured hand. "It is good to see you again. You are looking fit as always."

"How you doing, Javier?" Montae said, his large hand grasping Javier's in a firm shake. "How's business down here in the fun and sun?"

"Mmmm, all is well my friend, all is well," Javier laughed and nodded his head. "People are always looking to get high, and so we are always in style. How are your brothers and the rest of the family? I trust they are well also?"

Montae also nodded and settled into the limo's soft leather seats. "Everything's good, man. Everything's everything."

The Rolls Royce glided away from the curb and eased into traffic heading away from the beach strip.

Javier was a tall, pretty-boy Latino in his late twenties with slicked black hair and a bleached white smile. Montae didn't trust the Garrido errand boy's fast talk and wanna-be Hollywood style.

Whenever the Harrell brothers came to town, Javier promised beautiful girls, booze, and whatever else they wanted to indulge themselves in. Of course A.J. ate it up every time, but Montae kept his distance. He made sure not to offend his hosts, but he refused to let his guard down even for a minute. He did all of his indulging off duty and in the safety of his territory.

A few miles from the Port of Miami in the city's industrial district, the Rolls pulled into an office building garage. The twenty-story structure's glass exterior sparkled beneath the midday sun and blue sky. After the limo parked in the garage, two armed guards opened the doors for Javier, Montae, and their men.

"So, my friend, as I was saying on the ride over," Javier said as the group walked towards an elevator at one end of the garage, "Our family has heard of the recent troubles in your city."

"And like I said, it ain't nothing we can't handle," Montae said without looking at Javier. "Just someone tryin' to kick up a little dust. Happens every once in a while. We just gotta remind folks who still runs D.C. Don't worry about it, everything's still all good."

He didn't feel the slightest sway as the elevator began the ascent from the bowels of the building up into its heart.

"And we are sure this is very true, and of course it is none of our business," Javier continued as the elevator doors opened and a female's electronic voice signaled their arrival at the requested destination. "Your brother, Ezra, has always run his business with an admirable and uncompromising efficiency. But, in the interest of protecting our significant investment in your family, we would like to offer, eh, what you might call 'a helping hand' if needed."

"What kind of *helping hand,* Javier? Like I already said, everything is under control."

"Of course it is, and we don't doubt that one bit," Javier said. "But as you will see, it is always good to have friends like the Garridos helping you out."

Javier opened an office door inward, revealing a large room containing a long rectangular table. A heavy security tint darkened the room's bay windows, and hanging fluorescent lights provided the room's lighting. On the table in large, neat stacks of packaged blocks lay the normal shipment of uncut heroin, cocaine, and marijuana. Montae couldn't help but think of the stacks of cash that would be made from this shipment alone.

"Okay, that's our normal thing in there, so what?" he said. "I don't have time for games, man. So, what are we talking about here?"

"Please, be patient my friend. How long have we been dealing with one another? A long time, no? Yes, that is our normal arrangement you see in there," Javier said with a broad smile as he pulled the office door shut.

"But come, let us sit and talk over dinner about how my family can help yours in addition to what you have seen in that office. We shall have lobster and steak, or 'Surf and Turf' as I believe it is called? We will eat, drink, and discuss some wonderful new ideas. Come, I think you will be very, very interested in what I have to say, my friend."

# *Chapter Thirteen*

***Washington, D.C.…***

*Family. Nothing is more important than family, and everything I do, I do for my family.* Ezra Harrell remembered those words as he stared at the overcast sky stretched out above him. He'd lived his entire existence by those words.

Cumulus clouds streamed in from the edge of the horizon, disrupting the clarity and tranquility of the summer's day. A new storm was gathering its strength and preparing to flex all of its muscles for the D.C. metro area.

The clouds resembled a caravan of camels, tethered together, their humps full of water, marching through the desert. These dark shapes floated through the sky, heavyset and miserable, primed to shower the city with their tears.

The DC metro area had been experiencing one of the longest and driest heat waves in recent history. Last night's thunderstorms had made for the perfect recipe to break the oppressive drought that had been suffocating the city.

"A little rain won't hurt business any," he said to himself. "Addicts are like the postal service, they need to get high through rain, sleet, or snow."

Without a doubt, he knew his customers would be out and about in spite of the weather. They always were, and his employees would be there to serve them up.

Ezra Darnell Harrell, current king of the D.C. narcotics and crime syndicate, was the All-American Hoodlum reborn. He was cut from the cloth of the old-time criminals who were hard and hungry, but unconsumed by greed.

With all the efficiency of a CEO over a multi-billion dollar corporation, he ran his large family and this city's entire underground. He'd succeeded where many others before him had failed by establishing longevity in a lifestyle where such a thing no longer existed. Not since the glory days of the Italian mob and Harlem's Golden Age had a criminal organization flaunted this kind of supremacy.

Known as tough but fair, he commanded the respect of his family while striking fear into anyone who stood against him. He rewarded performance with money and promotion. This was how he'd maintained the allegiance of his workers for so many years. He also never tolerated anything less than perfection and an unconditional devotion to The Harrell Family. Misplaced loyalties and betrayal of the family were met with an unyielding hostility. In his eyes, second place was last place.

He made sure everyone from the Family's top tier to its bottom rung workers had a seat at his table. But he never let anyone forget that he and he alone provided all of the meals at that table. Ezra was the unquestioned head of The Harrell Family and would be until he said otherwise.

Armed with a winning smile, a convincing voice, and a confident, reassuring manner, he had a way of winning people over to his side. The power of persuasion...this had been his best weapon coming up, better than ten guns and fifty fists. He'd learned to believe in finesse first and violence as a last resort, and that belief had served him well. As a major player in the booming drug game of the '80s, he'd built this city's narcotics flow from the ground up.

He watched the clouds for a while longer through the moonroof of his Cadillac CTS-V before deciding to get out and walk. He admired the sedan's streamlined angles and sexy shape as he exited the driver's side. Her thunder gray exterior was polished and flawless from a recent wash and wax. He hadn't driven her in almost two months, and she'd seemed to purr for him when he'd started her this morning.

His brothers both drove the ultra-luxury vehicles like Maybach, Rolls, Bentley, and Mercedes' higher-end models, but Cadillac had always been Ezra's favorite. Cadillac was classic luxury and American-made, but low-key enough to keep him from standing out.

Recent times hadn't yielded much time for him to stop and smell the roses. In fact, he rarely got to drive himself around much these days, let alone walk anywhere for leisure. There was always a meeting, a move to make, and some business to check on. For his protection, his family insisted on driving him everywhere he needed to go and he complied, knowing they were right.

Occasionally, like today, he overruled everyone, jumped behind the wheel of his car, and took off. Of course, he never really went anywhere alone. The black Suburban parked several feet away held his driver and several armed guards who wouldn't let him out of their sight. He turned and looked at the SUV driving close behind him. Similar to this country's guarded government officials, he had a personal protective detail.

His loyal soldiers would follow him to hell and back easy, but why? For what reason? Was it the money?

Sure, he paid them well, always had. He made sure all of his people lived well; that was how he maintained their loyalty. But he could never quite grasp the psychology behind the devotion he garnered from his people. He didn't understand it and didn't think he ever would. He'd never had that type of allegiance for anyone that wasn't his blood.

But they were always there, watching over him like he was a VIP or some great man or something. But he wasn't, not even close. Hell, he was just a damn criminal, plain and simple, nothing more. And there was no greatness to be had in that at all.

* * * *

On this sizzling hot afternoon, Ezra had driven to East Potomac Park, not far from the Southwest Waterfront and The Wharf. Hains Point sat on the banks of the Potomac River and had always been one of his favorite meditation spots.

Today, his thoughts were heavy and troubled. After all of these years of hustling, he was tired. Tired of the risks and constant danger to his life and the lives of his family. Tired of the greed and corruption. Tired of making a profit off the suffering of others. Because that's what this was, wasn't it? There was the truth of it all, no matter how he tried to dress it up. He had always been a predator hunting and preying on the weak. Now, he didn't know where he was leading his family anymore.

This way of life had begun as a game of survival, a way out of poverty and into the good life. But somewhere along the way, everything became blurred. Greed had clouded the search for that better life. Money and power were addictive drugs that everyone wanted a hit of, and life in D.C. had spun beyond even his control.

His mind drifted towards thoughts of retirement. This wasn't his life anymore. *But how do you retire from being a professional criminal? No such thing as 401(k) plans and social security for a drug CEO.*

He'd stashed away enough money so his family could live at least two lifetimes in high style, so money wasn't an issue. His legitimate businesses and investments would also help take care of their needs. Still, he faced the same question: *how do you walk away from this kind of life?*

A drug kingpin's announcement of retirement was the same as an admission of weakness and an open invitation for a hostile takeover. The bottom-line? There was probably no leaving this way of life alive. His associates would assume the worst. That he'd gone soft on them. Or he'd at long last gotten caught by the law and turned against them to save himself.

Fearing for their freedom, they would feel forced to take him and his family out. No compromising, no discussion. There would be no retirement party with cake, presents, and long-winded speeches. No, there would be just the bloodbath as the rest of the underground destroyed the Harrells and then turned on itself.

He prided himself on being a realist and knew his time was coming to an end as the King of D.C.'s underground. Kings can only rule for so long before they are forced to vacate their throne. *Father Time is fickle like that; he harbors no love for anyone.*

Ezra didn't want to be forced. He'd never been to jail because the police could never accumulate enough evidence to make anything stick. His payroll ran long with judges, lawyers, and police, both local and federal, but how long before his luck ran out? He didn't want to find out.

For the last twenty years, he had controlled the city's underground, pushing the drug trade into a whole new world of organized business. Intelligence, patience, high-priced legal protection, and the proper use of force had allowed the Harrells to thrive in this do-or-die lifestyle. But he'd had enough, and this day had been a long time coming.

The drug game wasn't how it used to be when he first started his hustle. Rival crews were springing up all over the place like wildfires during a drought. These young thundercats had itchy trigger fingers and roamed the city's blocks in packs like wild, rabid dogs. They were full of spit and fire, but lacked the honor and respect that used to govern the streets. This new kind of criminal rebuked the lessons handed down from the elders who first established this game.

These kids ran amok throughout the city, targeting anything and anyone, all in search of that next adrenaline rush. These wanna-be gangsters were more interested in making a name for themselves than making money. There was no thought given to the past or the future, just this moment, the right here and now.

The art of hustling had been lost on this new and ignorant generation. Some had plenty of heart, no question. But most had no brains to complete the package.

These young guns were also getting a lot bolder these days. The recent attack at his safe house left him with five dead bodies. Someone was sending a harsh message, and Ezra knew he needed to find whomever was responsible and burn them to the ground. He would end them in the same manner. Not because he wanted to, but because he had to. Retaliation slowed business and drew unwanted attention. He was losing his taste for this life, but he needed to remind everyone that this was still his city.

When the bodies started piling up, the police would stop turning the other cheek. At that point, it wouldn't matter how much money the Harrells threw at them. Times were changing, and the cost of stomping out his enemies crew by crew would be expensive to his business.

He thought of his wife and his son, whom he loved more than anything. His boy was a man, no doubt, but not quite ready to head the family. He didn't want this life for his son. He wanted him to succeed in a legitimate life without worries of police or rival gangs or any of that other shit. He would move his family away from D.C. and then hand his legitimate businesses over to his son.

Damn the odds, he *would* do the traditional retirement thing like normal people his age. There were plenty of ripe markets everywhere, and he could start over anywhere, doing anything he wanted. There was life outside of D.C. He longed for a change of scenery away from death and destruction, where no one knew him or his family. He would have to find a way to deal with his partners. Either they would trust him and allow him to exit in peace, or he would force his way out.

His two older brothers also wouldn't take well to this change. He knew this. They had been in the life with him from the beginning and neither showed any signs of slowing down. Montae lived to be a criminal; for him, there would never be too much power or money. While A.J. didn't share his brother's lust for power, he loved the luxury that came with this life. Even at his age, he remained fascinated with living in the style of a sports or music star.

No question, they would disagree with his plans for retirement, but they didn't see the world as he did. They didn't see the madness waiting for them, didn't see the storm on the horizon.

When everything fell apart, the authorities would be forced to close the net around the crime in this city. One way or another, things always fell apart.

After all these years, there would be federal intervention—FBI, ATF, DEA, one of them, all of them. He no longer felt untouchable. It wouldn't be long before something or someone caught up to him. And jail was not an option. He preferred to die in his old age surrounded by his family if he had any say at all in the matter. Ezra Harrell was nobody's fool and knew now was the time to get out while his head remained above water.

## *Chapter Fourteen*

At six p.m. that evening, rush hour traffic congested the city's major arteries. Fender benders, rubbernecking, and sheer volume combined to create a bottleneck effect across D.C., Maryland, and Virginia. Washington, D.C. was notorious for its gridlock, and the slightest addition of bad weather made traffic stall to a stop-and-go. Cars, SUVs, and busses inched along the crowded streets as miserable commuters slogged their way through the storm to their various destinations.

The rain had picked up and was relentless in its lashing of the metro area now. The wind howled, and like an audience anticipating a rock band's grand finale, encouraged the rising storm, pushing it to a climax. Nonetheless, for the head of the Harrell Family, the workday continued. There was business to be conducted tonight that couldn't be delayed because of a little rain, a little thunder and lightning.

Ten stories up, Ezra peered out of a window in the office building he'd purchased and renovated just over a year ago. This latest acquisition in Rosslyn, Virginia was the new home of Harrell Enterprises, the legitimate side of his empire. His growing real estate and construction companies were headquartered here now. This new building afforded him a view of the city he never could've dreamed of having as a child.

The ice in his glass clinked as he downed the last of the Crown Royal he'd been nursing for the past half hour. The dark amber whiskey went down smooth and warmed his belly. He wanted to pour a refill just to take the edge off, but thought better of it. He also decided against smoking the joint he'd rolled a few minutes earlier. As hectic as life could be, Ezra savored his few vices, but nothing ever came before business. He hadn't gotten to where he was by being a slave to his bad habits.

*Better to be all the way clear tonight,* he reasoned as he closed the glass door of his liquor cabinet and placed the glass in the small sink nearby.

Montae had called earlier to say that he and A.J. would be home in time for the second half of tonight's schedule. Tonight would be a long one, and Ezra wished he could skip it, but he knew that was impossible.

He continued to watch the rat race below, shaking his head at the robots below shuffling along from their nine to fives. These people were clueless to anything outside of their monogrammed briefcases and triple shot espressos. They had no idea of the real world lurking just beyond the tips of their noses. They knew nothing about the dark side other than what they heard the reporters babble about on the news.

He knew he didn't fit into their world, but he'd spent many hours becoming educated on the squares, as he called them. He'd read many books on them, trying to understand their world and how he could carve out a spot in it.

*They just don't know, do they? These people have no idea that I walk among them as if I'm one of them. But I'm not "one of them," am I? Never have been and never will be. I sell poison to them and their children. They don't know me, but they fear me and everyone just like me. To them, I'm the devil.*

*But I'm just a businessman. No different from the legalized criminals stealing our wealth, money, and souls with their high interest rate loans, high credit score requirements, and their corrupt government policies. No worse than some of the thugs in Congress, the corrupt and racist lawmakers and politicians.*

*Only difference is they just haven't legalized what I do... not yet.*

He'd come a long way, there was no denying that fact. But he would never forget where he came from. He'd never forget how basic things used to be for his family, trying to survive each day to the next. So how had it all become so damned complicated?

What seemed like an eternity ago could be remembered like it all happened yesterday. Everything remained so fresh in his mind, every detail from the very beginning.

# *Chapter Fifteen*

Fifty-three years ago, Lamina "Mimi" Harrell gave birth to the youngest of her three children. Ezra's earliest memories of his mother included watching her struggle to put food on the table and clothes on her children's backs. Worst of all, he remembered how constant disappointment chipped away at his mother's youthful good looks. Her coal-colored locks turning to gray, the worry lines creasing her mocha complexion, and her vibrant smile turning into a facial flat-line.

Young and mostly alone, Mimi always kept her sons close to her chest. Like any good mother would, she sacrificed whatever she had to and raised her sons the best way she could. She worked long hours at multiple jobs to try and provide for her babies.

The boys' fathers both suffered from the same disease: "deadbeat daddy syndrome." Montae's father, LeOtis Hill, was an alcoholic whose favorite pastime was getting drunk, high, and beating on his son's mother. He never held a steady job and walked out on her and their son for good not long after Montae's second birthday.

Two years later, Mimi married James Bridges, dropped her maiden name of Harrell and assumed Bridges for both her and Montae. James was a hustler and nightclub owner who treated her and her son like a queen and a prince in the beginning. He moved them out of their tiny efficiency in Southeast and into his huge house in Northwest D.C. It wasn't long before she bore him two sons of his own, Arthur James and Ezra.

Life was good for the Bridges family. That was before everything changed—before James changed from a loving husband and father into a distant, neglectful, mean-spirited man. Boredom with married life, coupled with his bitterness over failed business dealings, reduced her husband to a man she no longer recognized. It wasn't long before late nights at the office turned into him not coming home until the next day or day after. Mimi tolerated it all and did whatever she could to hold her family together.

Years spent living the hard way had taught her to trust her instincts. After five decent years, she could feel something bad creeping up on the horizon and heading towards her family. She was right. One sweltering day after the Fourth of July weekend, she returned home with the boys to find their home locked and boarded-up. Outside on the porch sat large cardboard boxes containing her and the boys' belongings. James was nowhere to be found. He'd vanished without so much as a Dear John letter. They would never hear from him again. Ezra was just a year old then and couldn't remember that terrible day.

Mimi sent the boys to live with her oldest sister in North Carolina while she found a new place to live. When the boys returned home just before the start of school, she'd settled in the Pruitt Palisades Housing Projects in Southeast. The dream of a better life for her children had taken a serious blow, but she refused to fold. She willed herself to push James out of her mind.

She dropped Bridges as her last name and reassumed her maiden name of Harrell. She also changed the last names of her three sons to Harrell, severing all ties to their no-good fathers. LeOtis Hill and James Bridges, they had both left Mimi and her kids alone to fend for themselves. Two different men, but in the end, the same sad result.

# *Chapter Sixteen*

The Pruitt Palisades Housing Projects made for one of life's harshest classrooms, but the Harrell brothers were willing students. Tired of cockroaches and government handouts, the Harrell brothers set out to find the good life the best way they knew how.

Back then, Pruitt Palisades had been run by Big Benny Jenkins, a small-time dealer with small-time ambitions. Big Benny had been known as "Big" for his waist size, but not much else. He didn't have the heart or hunger to do any real damage in the drug game. His territory didn't extend beyond the Palisades and a couple of neighboring tenements, and his grip on those was shaky at best.

Big Benny had grown up with Ezra's estranged father and was happy to look out for an old running partner. He hadn't hesitated to put the Harrell brothers on as scramblers for his corners. Ezra never bothered to ask him about the whereabouts of his father, wanting to let the past remain in the past.

He'd overheard Benny mentioning his father once, telling a friend that he had the son of Killer James

Bridges working for him. The same Killer James that had earned his name for his prowess with the female persuasion. The same Killer James that had walked out on his family and then disappeared on the run from gambling and business debts. The very same Killer James that had been put in the ground four years earlier by an angry husband. The man had caught James all up in his wife and had put three bullets all up in James's ass.

Ezra had heard folks speak of a Killer James before, but hadn't known until then that they were talking about his father. He never told Big Benny he'd overheard that conversation. He also never told his mother or his brothers what he'd found out about their father. He promised himself to never live like his father had lived or die like that bastard had died.

The Harrell brothers started like many dealers did, as corner boys, near the bottom of the food chain. They were runners for Big Benny's corners in the projects, but Ezra held onto bigger aspirations than nickel and diming. He wouldn't keep sweating it out on the corners while Big Benny sat back, got fat, and collected money he hadn't earned.

For the next few years, the brothers worked the corners with minimal trouble but also without making any real money. It was near his fourteenth birthday when Ezra got the present he'd wanted since the beginning: a real opportunity.

A crew of stickup boys had started targeting the Palisades. In a month's time, they'd hit many of Big Benny's corners, dropping bodies, and making a serious dent in his profits.

Ezra knew of Big Benny's distaste for violence, but he also knew this problem had to be handled. If it wasn't, other crews would begin hitting the Palisades, and Big Benny would find himself squeezed out altogether. The Harrells would be left out in the cold, looking for a new dealer to scramble for; Ezra wouldn't let this happen.

"Why don't you let me and my brothers handle this for you, boss?" he'd asked Benny when he approached him about the problem. "We know where they lay heads at. It wouldn't be nothin' to take care of this for you. No problem."

Big Benny had just stared at him at first, obviously surprised and maybe even impressed at Ezra's nerve.

"We'll keep it real hands off for you, so you don't have to worry about police coming your way. When we're done with these dudes, everybody will know not to mess with you. Consider it a favor, even. No charge."

Of course the fat man had agreed. He'd even offered to finance the operation, which Ezra declined. He'd told the fat man to simply relax and keep business running as usual. He would let him know when the problem had been made to disappear.

The nervous sweat on Benny's wrinkled brow seemed to evaporate when he'd heard Ezra's proposal. He'd licked his greasy chops at the happy thought of having someone else do his dirty work, and for free at that.

The Harrell brothers took their time putting a plan together. They watched and put their ears to the street to find out any information they could on the stick-up crew. It took two weeks after the last robbery before Ezra felt they were ready to take care of business. He wanted the crew to let their guard down. Wanted them comfortable in feeling like they had gotten away with the robberies. After studying the stick-up crew and getting their pattern down cold, Ezra and his brothers made their move.

The crew operated from a one-bedroom apartment in a rundown building on the northeast side of the city. The Harrell brothers had gotten an ID on them from a few addicts who had witnessed their last robbery. They trailed the crew enough times to know when they would all be together in the ramshackle building.

Ezra may have been the youngest of the Harrell brothers, but he was also the smartest. His plan required patience. His brothers both itched to dive in guns first, but he accounted for each and every detail. This move needed to be "airtight with no mistakes," he reminded them.

"This is where we get at them once and for all and put an end to this shit before they come for our corners," he told his brothers.

The Harrells memorized the layout of the building, each floor, the entrances and exits, and the patterns of nearby police patrols. At nightfall on their chosen day, the brothers approached the building, each dressed in a black hoodie, black jeans, and black work boots. Ezra came in through the building's front entrance, stepping through the cracked glass door. A.J. snuck through a rear entrance and climbed the stairs through the musty and cobwebbed darkness. Montae entered the building last, climbing the fire escape and crossing over to a fifth-floor balcony.

The stick-up crew didn't know what hit them when Ezra kicked in the front door, brandishing two 9mm pistols. Four of the five-man crew sat at a wooden table in the cramped kitchen, along with three females standing near the sink.

As Ezra and A.J. charged into the apartment, two of the crew tried to escape to the rear of the apartment. There they found Montae waiting for them. He pointed one pistol in their direction and the other at the head of the crew's fifth member.

The Harrell brothers forced the five men and three women into the main living room. They duct taped the hands, feet, and mouths of each man and laid them side by side on the floor. The three women were forced to watch from a nearby couch as Ezra stooped and looked into the eyes of each man. They were all at least in their mid to late twenties. Ezra told them who he and his brothers were by name.

Then, he pulled his pistol and put a single bullet into the forehead of each man at point blank range. Montae followed up with gunshots to the body of each fallen man while A.J. kept his pistol trained on the women.

The Harrells left the three women alive to spread the word of the violence they had witnessed that night. The brothers exited the apartment building, leaving behind five dead bodies and three horrified witnesses. The women would probably be forever scarred and would never utter a word about the identity of the killers.

For the Harrells, this night would serve as their catapult to stardom. In just a few days, word of the hit burned throughout the underground and earned the boys instant respect in the streets. Young Ezra Harrell had organized the perfect hit. With a single act of bloody payback, he gave birth to his reputation as a man to be both feared and respected.

# *Chapter Seventeen*

The ruthlessness with which the Harrells had eliminated the stick-up crew impressed Big Benny enough for him to promote Ezra. He made the teenager his right-hand man and a crew lieutenant. This move put him in charge of the Harrells' corners as well as several other crews and corners around the neighborhood. A.J. and Montae were both older, but they had always deferred to him as the head of the family. Now, his new street ranking made it official.

It wasn't long before the Harrells assumed control of the entire Palisades drug flow while Benny collected his share as their supplier. Everything just fell into place after that.

Heroin and marijuana were the flavors of the month, and the brothers served up the menu buffet style. They became larger than Big Benny's size 48 waist around The Palisades. Then in the mid-1980s, the drug game witnessed the arrival of an all-new high to compete with marijuana and heroin.

Cocaine had always been thought of as a rich man's drug habit because of its high cost. Many of the inner-city dealers avoided it until crack cocaine sprang up in Miami, Los Angeles, and New York. Its nickname, crack, was inspired by the sound the drug made while being cooked and smoked. This new poison rolled throughout the ghettos in cities nationwide in a way never thought possible.

This highly addictive, freebased form of cocaine was cooked to form a rock that addicts smoked in a small glass pipe. Its suffocating grip left no one untouched. Young pregnant mothers on welfare, sports stars, and prominent city officials. There was no discrimination.

This newest wave of money-making potential further intensified the forming of numerous rival gangs looking to corner the market. Like other major cities, D.C. became segregated into a dangerous maze of gangland territories divided among its many blocks and avenues. The war for control of the metro area drug trade spawned destruction and death that spread like the plague.

No one was safe from the unpredictable violence that could erupt without warning. Bullets knew no names, and the homicide rate in the city skyrocketed close to five hundred bodies per year in 1990. Washington, D.C. became known as the nation's murder capital.

It seemed like those who weren't selling the drugs, and fighting for the territory to sell them on, were using them. Crackheads had become a permanent neighborhood fixture, like the corner stores the kids grew up stealing from, except the crackheads did the stealing.

The sight of a person when the crack monster had them in its clutches was a scary and pitiful thing. A crackhead would bust you over your head in broad daylight just like they would climb through your bedroom window at night. Once addicted to crack, a person would sell their baby's diapers and even their body in pursuit of that next high.

What did this mean to Ezra and his brothers? It meant, "play or be played," "kill or be killed." Unwilling to risk being squeezed out of a game he'd worked so hard to establish himself in, Ezra expanded his operation. The Harrell brothers formed a new crew unmatched by any other at that time, and they were just getting started.

# *Chapter Eighteen*

The Harrells had started as corner scramblers, but like a child outgrows their shoes, the brothers outgrew Big Benny's limited supply. Ezra began making plans to guide his family past Big Benny's middleman reach.

He ceased to buy from Benny, moved past Benny's supplier, and bought from the major narcotics traffickers themselves. These were the heavy hitters who manufactured and shipped the drugs into the country. This would increase Harrell's risk, but it would also increase their profit and dominance over the D.C. narcotics trade.

When his product demand outweighed Benny's supply, Ezra sought out a more potent connection in the form of a Colombian dealer. The Garrido Cartel operated through Venezuela and Mexico and up into the states via Florida, Texas, and California. Using these routes, the Garridos could funnel in enough premium-grade narcotics to get the entire Eastern seaboard high off their product.

The successful establishment of a partnership with the Colombians allowed the Harrell's operation to double, then triple in size and strength. The brothers squeezed out middlemen like Benny and other mid- and low-level suppliers. They restructured their business and revamped the narcotics game in the nation's capital.

The new-look Harrell Family hit the streets with the force of a runaway freight train, crushing anyone who stood in their path. The Family swallowed up the competition by offering the highest quality product and carrying the most muscle. They gobbled up control of the city's drug trade through the use of money, intimidation, and acts of violence.

Dealers on nearby blocks lacking the Family's numbers and organization didn't stand a chance. They either began to buy their product from the Harrells or they relinquished their corners altogether without much static.

The Harrells' takeover devoured corners throughout the city, but not everyone bowed down to the Family without a fight. Those that had to learn the hard way were dealt a lethal judgment at the business end of a smoking pistol.

The resulting turf war caused major damage to the narcotics business as the violence slowed the movement of the product. The damage to the public was even worse, and the number of innocent citizens caught in the crossfire continued to rise. The Metropolitan Police Department became targets themselves as they tried to intervene in the madness.

In an effort to counteract the violence, police attention, and profit loss, Ezra thought of a different approach to the drug trade. He called for a meeting with the city's other major dealers to try and put an end to the war. What he proposed had never been done in D.C. with any long-lasting success. He offered the dealers an end to the violence through the forming of a cooperative alliance. Under this new arrangement, the major dealers were given access to a top-notch narcotics connection with Ezra serving as the controlling middleman. Ezra also provided access to his extensive contacts in the legal system. By this right, he assumed control as the co-op's chairman.

After an expected period of negotiation, each of the major players agreed. They were all happy to end the fighting while gaining substantial legal protection and returning to the business of making money. With an end to the war, business eased its way back towards normal. Everyone appeared to be satisfied with getting a healthy slice of the pie.

This newfound peace even allowed Ezra to start a couple of legitimate businesses to serve as laundering fronts for his dirty money. But he never allowed himself to feel too comfortable, always remembering the violent and unpredictable world he dwelled in.

Through it all he remained untouchable. The closest law enforcement could get were petty charges on a few of his employees, but nothing that could be tied to him. He continued to grow in power and so did his influence over important officials like policemen, lawyers, and judges. With layers upon layers of protection, he managed to buffer himself against both the law and the streets. He built the Family's operation to the point where he never handled the product himself or made appearances on his corners.

While hundreds of his workers operated a citywide assembly line, manufacturing and distributing his family's product, he watched and counted his dollars. He'd risen far above his humble beginnings as a street corner scrambler and midlevel dealer. Ezra Harrell had become a CEO at the uppermost tier of a narcotics conglomerate.

# *Chapter Nineteen*

Ezra continued to stare out of the large office window, thoughts of the past lingering in his mind. The raindrops cascading down the windowpane reminded him of happier times.

Reminded him of his mother. He often thought of her whenever he managed to free his thoughts from his daily grind. He remembered how his mom used to fix chocolate and peanut butter cookies for the boys whenever the rain kept them indoors. Remembered how his mother always had a smile for him, even during the worst of times. A smile that always made everything alright. He wished her smile could fix everything now.

Montae and A.J. didn't mention Mom much anymore, and he wondered if they still remembered her. Or had shame buried their memories? A familiar pain plucked Ezra's heart whenever he thought of his mother looking down on him and the man he'd become. Ezra remembered his mother's late-night tears when she thought the boys were asleep. He remembered her pain, caused first by the boys' fathers and then by the boys themselves. He remembered all of it.

*I'm so sorry, Momma. I know this isn't the life you wanted for your boys.*

The ringing of his cell phone snatched Ezra away from his memories, back to the present and his view of the rain-washed skyline.

"Yeah," he said as he raised the phone to his ear. "How we looking?"

"Mr. Ezra, your limo is waiting downstairs."

"Thanks, Donnie. Is my wife with you already?"

"Yes sir, she is. Picked her up on the way."

"Sounds good, Don. I'll be down in a few." He ended the call and placed the phone in the inside pocket of his tuxedo jacket.

Donnie Gainsford was a sixty-five-year-old widower who Ezra had known since his childhood. For the past twenty years, Donnie had served as his personal driver and bodyguard. But the soft-spoken giant of a man was much more than just an employee. He was family. Ezra often confided his thoughts to Donnie and regarded the big man as one of his few close friends.

Giving himself a final once-over in the mirror, Ezra plucked a few errant threads from the front of his black tuxedo. His shoes shone like black glass, and his cufflinks sparkled like miniature stars. Everything was in order, just as it should be for the king of D.C.'s Underground. It was time to put away the past and come back to the right here and right now. It was time to make some money.

He didn't care for these black-tie events, but he'd deemed tonight necessary for the sake of business. Some of his important business associates would be in attendance, and therefore so would he. With the plans he was making, he would need to close the loop on some of the deals he'd been working on. When things got going, he would need each of his friends in high places.

The limo waiting for him was a custom-designed stretch black Lincoln Navigator, one more thing he no longer wanted. But in this line of work, image was everything and the proper maintenance of one's image was essential for success. People wouldn't do business with someone that didn't look and sound like money.

"Hey baby-love," he said as he stepped into the limo and planted a kiss on his wife's lips. "How are you? You look gorgeous."

The closest members of his family were the privileged few that knew this softer side of him. Most only ever saw his hard side. And for those who crossed him: all they usually saw was cold steel and hot lead.

"Hey yourself, handsome," Liv said and flashed him her sexiest of smiles. She was gorgeous in a white chiffon evening gown. "Are you ready for tonight?"

"Yes ma'am, I'm ready to get this thing over with," he said and winked at her. "With you here by my side, this will be easy."

He smiled at the woman he'd loved for what seemed like forever. They had been together for thirty-one years, the last twenty-eight as man and wife.

From the beginning, she'd accepted him and the life he'd chosen to lead. She'd stood beside him through the worst of times, and he knew he owed her much more than this type of life.

As Donnie pulled the limo away from the curb, Ezra thought again of years gone by. Then, he forced himself to push those thoughts out of his head. He couldn't change the past, but the future and present were well within his control. That was all he could worry about. The rest no longer mattered.

# *Chapter Twenty*

Downtown D.C.'s Friday nightlife moved along in full swing, undeterred by the intermittent storm. Like the rain at its peak, people flowed into the city seeking the bars, clubs, and lounges situated throughout downtown.

For Ezra and Olivia, tonight's destination was a fundraiser ball being hosted by the mayor of D.C. himself. The good mayor found himself engaged in a heated battle for his job. His poll numbers had slipped, and he needed serious help to complete his reelection bid in the upcoming fall election. Tonight's fundraiser proved he would spare no expense to gather campaign support.

The Walter E. Washington Convention Center lit up the night sky with a brilliant radiance that could be seen from blocks away. Much of Washington's high society looked to be present and accounted for, all of the big pockets the Mayor would squeeze for donations.

As the Navigator approached the convention center, Ezra thought he recognized a few of the city's heavy hitters making their way inside. The owners and CEOs of D.C.'s professional sports franchises and prosperous law and land development firms looked to be in attendance. He even saw D.C.'s district attorney making his way towards the convention center entrance.

He smiled to himself: *this would be a very good night.*

Limousines and other expensive luxury cars lined up for valet parking in two lines, both stretching at least a block long. The dazzling lights and growing crowd full of the beautiful and wealthy gave the entire setting a Hollywood red carpet feel.

Inside, the bright lights and gaudy decorations hanging from almost every inch of the ceiling made the entire ballroom shine. Platinum and candy apple red streamers crisscrossed one another, and a large silver and glass globe hung from the middle of the ceiling.

As Ezra and Liv entered the room, he was reminded of the '70s TV show, *Soul Train*. He half expected Don Cornelius and his afro to strut out in a powder blue suit and introduce "The Mighty, Mighty O'Jays!"

Each of the three hundred or so tables had a miniature bronze figurine likeness of the Mayor in the middle of it. The man had no shame.

The night felt like it would never end, but when it did, Ezra had to admit that it was a success. Under the guise of conducting legal business, he'd lined the pockets of some of Washington's important power players. He continued to lay the groundwork for what he planned to be his "exit stage right" from this lifestyle. He'd even managed a few minutes with Mayor Dunbar before the night ended, making a sizeable campaign contribution in the process.

Olivia had also done her part. She either stood by his side or mingled with the wives of his associates, keeping them busy while he worked their husbands.

*The perfect partner,* Ezra thought to himself as he watched his angel work. *Perfect.*

After four and a half hours, the Harrells headed home at close to midnight, both exhausted, but satisfied with the evening. Donnie drove the limo towards their home in the city.

Ezra promised Liv he wouldn't stay out too much later, but there was other business to tend to that couldn't wait. He didn't bother to change clothes. Instead, he kissed his wife goodbye, snatched off his tuxedo's bowtie, and headed back out. He was running late and his brothers were waiting for him. There was *always* business to handle.

# *Chapter Twenty-One*

Seventeen-year MPD veteran Art Grimes had plaques and citations hanging all over his office, lauding him as a bona fide crime fighter. He had also been the focus of many news stories about his heroic police work throughout his career. The mayor and other top officials had shaken his hand and patted him on the back more times than he could remember. They thought of him as a living legend.

Hell, he even looked the part of a supercop. His athletic frame reflected hours spent sweating in the gym, and he kept it draped in tailored suits and Italian leather. He kept his blonde hair close cut and barbershop neat and his clean-shaven face had a trustworthy look to it. The thin wire frames he wore added to his professional appearance, and his bleached white smile finished the entire package. Without question, he was a poster boy for the MPD.

Art Grimes was also a dirty cop. In fact, on a police force knee-deep in the filth of corruption, he had to be in the deepest. He was thirty-eight and had been on the force a long time. Too long. He'd grown tired of risking his life for $60,000 a year and a pension he may not live to enjoy. He was a "taker" now. He took whatever he wanted; however, whenever, and wherever he could.

Of course, his wife hadn't known about his extracurricular activities. He'd managed to keep his second job a secret up until the day she walked out on him. Patricia left him a few years ago for a freakin' dentist not long after his youngest son's fourth birthday. *She'd actually left him?* What an ass-backwards joke that was.

She hired a lawyer with his money and dragged him into divorce court. Not only did she get full custody of his sons but also a ludicrous alimony and child support payment. She would even get a chunk of his pension whenever he retired from the force. Month after month, the majority of his MPD earnings went into her account, leaving him just enough to break even.

So, when the Harrell Family first approached him, he dove into their world headfirst without giving it a second thought. Without their dirty money, he'd have nothing. Working for the Harrells had at least given him a taste of the life he deserved for all his work. Taking drug money was a dangerous situation to be entangled in, but with it, he'd been able to do more than just survive.

He hadn't wanted to get this deeply involved with the Harrells, but with child support and alimony, he had no other options. The system failed him and he decided to get his by any and all means, both legal and illegal. This was his survival money. He called it his "head above water" fund. Anyone that thought he was wrong could take their morals and go fuck themselves.

Besides being a money-grubbing whore, Patricia also refused to abide by the limited visitation rights the judge had granted him. He saw his sons when and how she dictated, which wasn't too often. Hell, she hadn't even been a good lay the last few years of their marriage. The sight of her now with all the weight she'd put on made him gag and happy to be rid of her. His mistresses, or "his girls" as he liked to call them, were a much better fit for him in all ways.

The problem was that he loved his two boys more than anything and couldn't stand being apart from them. Ricky and Josh were the bright spot in an otherwise shitty existence. So, for their sake, he tolerated Trish, made his support payments on time, and tried to see them as often as possible. Otherwise, he had a good mind to make Patricia disappear forever.

Throughout his career, Grimes had always pinched off his share here and there anyway. If he busted a perp carrying a stack of cash, he never failed to take a piece for him and his boys. Working for the Harrells was like a long overdue jackpot for him. Natural progression, he'd called it; an under-the-table pay raise that he more than deserved. He even brought along two of his senior detectives that he'd worked with since his academy days.

He trusted Vincent Morris and Robbie Hankerson with his life. Both men had families and had also grown tired of the reward never justifying their risk. Together, the three men kept major heat off the Harrell Family over the years. They provided every service the Harrells required, from intel on MPD operations to security service to the elimination of marked targets. In fact, Grimes considered him and his men the chief reason for the Harrell's long-standing success.

*Without my help, they wouldn't be able to run this city like they do, not a chance in hell,* he always reminded himself. *They need me to keep doing their dirty work.*

Grimes had enjoyed a long and prosperous, but uneasy relationship with the Harrells. Of course, he didn't trust Ezra Harrell and his family. Hell, why should he? After all, they were a bunch of dope dealers and sociopathic gangsters. To be honest, he despised them to the core and envied the life they lived. He'd busted his ass his entire life, but didn't have the mansions or the expensive clothes and cars. He resided in a cramped two-bedroom condo with an expensive mortgage and a greedy ex-wife to show for all his effort.

He'd like nothing more than to bust the Harrells, but he needed the stacks of cash they threw his way each month. All that extra cash was like an additional lifeline for him. So sure, he needed the Harrells… for now. Soon enough "Supercop Art Grimes" would take down the entire Harrell operation and be the hero all over again. That was his endgame.

There wouldn't be any trials for these assholes, just bullets and shallow graves. The Harrell Family had too much dirt on too many important people for them to go down any other way. After he put Ezra Harrell and his brothers down, he would be well on his way to making captain and then chief. *Chief Grimes.* Yeah, he liked the sound of that. *Hell yeah, shit yeah.*

But before any of this could happen, there was business to be handled. Business that if not handled with decisive action could spoil all of his future plans. The recent weeks' events had put him on edge. How much longer could he stay in this criminal arrangement before the entire thing exploded in his face? Corpses were starting to pop up throughout the city, and no one had a clue who was dropping these bodies. One thing was for sure: a gang war would be bad for all business, including his.

Things were going downhill fast, and to make it worse, Ezra Harrell had requested a face-to-face meeting tonight. This type of meeting never happened.

When it came to receiving instructions and payment, he always dealt with one of Ezra Harrell's flunkies. Maybe even one of his brothers if it was something really heavy. Montae or that jerkoff A.J. might visit him, but he never, ever saw the head of the Harrell Family face to face. No one outside of The Family did anymore, from what he heard.

This was how thc headman had managed to stay out of jail. He couldn't be linked to anything outside of his legit businesses. *So, why take the risk tonight?* Grimes had to wonder. Whatever the reason, it couldn't mean anything good for him.

He pulled a gold money clip from around a thick wad of cash and left six crisp twenties on his table. He loved eating at upscale places like the Ruth's Chris Steakhouse on Connecticut Avenue. This was his style, and he deserved it. The steaks, salmon, and Jameson were all top-notch. It was one of the few luxuries he afforded himself these days. He knew he'd earned it, but more than ever, discretion was paramount, so he kept his indulgences to a minimum.

Leaving the restaurant, he observed the fractured night sky filled with thick gray clouds and a sliver of moon. The rain had fallen at a steady clip throughout the day and looked as if it would continue into the night. He shoved his hands into the pockets of his beige trench and headed for his unmarked cruiser parked in a nearby garage. He needed to pick up his pace. There were rounds to finish up and then the meeting with the Harrells in a couple of hours.

And that's when Art Grimes would have his fortune read by the man himself.

## *Chapter Twenty-Two*

Ezra had four men stand post at his home while he and Donnie headed to his office in Rosslyn. Montae and A.J. had called earlier and would be waiting for him when he arrived.

"You're late, lil' brotha," Montae said when Ezra stepped out of the elevator and into the entranceway of his private office.

He was sitting on the edge of Ezra's desk fingering one of the many marble figurines decorating its surface.

Ezra nodded at his oldest brother, removed his black hat and black raincoat, and hung both on a nearby coatrack.

"You know it's funny you would say that, big brotha, since I didn't see either one of you jumping at the chance to show face at the mayor's fundraiser tonight," Ezra said as he reached into the cherrywood cabinet next to his desk and poured himself the drink he skipped earlier. "And hey, watch the desk, man. Don't go scratchin' my shit all up. I paid a nice chunk of change for that."

"Be cool, Ez. Ain't nobody scratchin' up your pretty-ass desk," Montae said. "You know attending those fancy black-tie parties is your thing, not ours."

"Yeah man, that's why you did the night school thing, right?" A.J. said and stepped forward from his spot in the rear of the office. "Went and got yourself all educated, so you could take care of *that* side of the family business, right?"

Ezra wanted to ask A.J. just what the hell part of the business *he* took care of these days, but didn't bother. *It is what it is...*

A.J. had lost his taste for the business years ago. Ezra knew this was the truth. In fact, he doubted his brother ever had a real taste for it in the first place. His brother was a follower and didn't know anything beyond going along with what Ezra said was best for the family.

"That's what I thought, so I guess this means I'm not late after all, huh?" Ezra said. "Since I'm the one who always does face time for this family, I had to go and rub elbows with this city's uppity folks tonight.

"Look at that, Montae. Our little brother out there with the rich folks. Would love to see that one of these days," A.J. said with a laugh. "But I am digging the tux, Ez. You do shine up real nice like, bro. No doubt. So, how'd it go?"

"It went like it always did. Boring, lots of business talk. The mayor, the DA, all of those clowns were there tonight. Dunbar talked his usual bull about continuing the war on crime in his town, as if he was even considering doing something crazy like that. But I guess it sounds good to the people, right? At this point, he's saying whatever he can to get reelected. The young brother from the Fifth District? Owens, I think his name is? Yeah, he's creeping up on Dunbar something serious from what I understand."

"Yeah, I heard about him. Real sharp brother from what I hear, and he's starting to pull votes, too," Montae said. "You think he's got a chance? Dunbar is in, what, his third term? This city has been with him for a lot of years now."

"Yup, he's in his third. But he might not get to number four. Not sure how this election will go. Couldn't call it if I had to. Poll numbers ain't looking too hot for our man. This race is so tight right now, we are hitting the home stretch and still don't know a damn thing. Dunbar won the last few easily, but this one looks like it's going down to the wire."

"Wouldn't be good for business to get a new administration next year," Montae said. "A new mayor means new people, new changes, and all new money we have to put out. We don't need that shit."

"No, we don't need that," Ezra agreed. "But we can't afford to take any chances just in case our boy Dunbar isn't on top of his game come November. I'm putting big dollars behind his reelection campaign, but not too much so as to stand out. We need to stay ahead of this thing and make sure everything is airtight on our end in the event we do have to deal with a new administration."

"We'll stay on top of everything, Ez, no worries. We'll make sure we keep our end together."

"Yeah, I know we will. We've been doing this a long time. Can do it in our sleep. I ain't much worried about that. Anyway, so what about Miami? How did that go?"

Ezra saw A.J. smile at the mention of Miami, which meant he had an all-new batch of freaks to tell them about. He was sure his brother had lured more than a few females to his South Beach hotel room. But none of this interested Ezra in the least. He didn't care to hear about his brother's latest sexual conquests. All he cared about was the business side of the trip.

"Everything went good, Ez, as usual. Same terms in place, no changes," Montae said. "Everyone's happy."

"Cool. Glad to hear that. When and where for the deliveries?"

Montae's face curled into an expression like he smelled something sour, an expression that said he didn't like Ezra's line of questioning.

"Since when does all that matter? You know I got it handled."

"I know you do, big brotha. You always do, no doubt." Ezra said without looking up from his drink. "So, like I asked you: when and where?"

Montae sucked his teeth and said, "Four loads like always, all mixed up. Two up from Miami on rails, one down from Canada rollin' on eighteen wheels and one coming through Jersey Shore soaking wet. Our people will meet the last one up at the docks and bring it home. Staggered arrivals, one each week starting next Tuesday. Everything done in a month."

"Alright," Ezra nodded, "you put eyes on the product?"

"Man, of course I did. I always do, don't I? It's top shelf as usual. Like I said, the deal is same as always, and we mix up the deliveries each time to keep it fresh. You know this already, so what's the problem, Ez? Since when do you care about the details anymore?"

"No problem at all. Calm down. I asked a question, you answered. Done deal," Ezra said and took a sip of his drink. "But the details always matter to me, even when I don't ask. You know this."

"Yeah okay, but what the hell, man? Since when do you even ask anymore, Ezra? You got trust issues all of a sudden?"

"Well, I ask whenever I want to ask. I am still running this show, right?"

"Yeah but, Ez," A.J. cut in, "me and Montae, we got this handled. You know this. We make the runs and you do your..."

Ezra held up his left hand to silence him without taking his eyes off Montae. He waited for his oldest brother to answer his question.

"Yeah, you're right Ezra, you still got it. Ain't no thing, man," Montae said. "This here is just different for you is all."

"The streets are different, so I have to be different. I see it, even if you two can't. I have to make sure we stay tight. No trust issues here though, just foresight; me covering all angles."

"All right, Ez," Montae said. "Like I said, ain't no thing."

"Then it's all good. Have we heard anything from Detective Grimes? Everything still on as scheduled?"

"Yeah, everything is still on, lil brotha," Montae said. "We're supposed to meet him in about an hour."

"Good deal. Well, let's get on with it," Ezra said, knocking back the last of his drink and gathering his coat and hat off the coatrack. “It’s late, I’m tired, and I told Liv I wouldn’t stay out too much longer.”

*Always business to handle.*

## *Chapter Twenty-Three*

Sixty minutes later, Ezra Harrell began his meeting right on schedule. He and his brothers met Detective Grimes downtown in the basement of the Beans Knows Best coffee shop and lounge.

The coffee shop's doors had been closed to the public for more than two hours, affording Ezra all the privacy he needed. As a favor to a close friend, he'd bankrolled the start-up costs for Beans Knows Best. In return, the owner volunteered the use of his establishment whenever Ezra needed it. No questions asked.

"So, what we have here is someone rocking our boat, Grimes. And more than just a little bit, too," Ezra said, sitting straight up at the large round table where he and the detective sat. "I'm talking major waves being made here. Now, you tell me, what the hell is going on?"

"Yes, I know Mr. Harrell, I've seen the bodies myself," Grimes said as he fidgeted in his seat. "Some real nasty stuff too, but we don't know where it's coming from just yet."

The man didn't make much eye contact, which meant he was scared. Ezra sat directly across from Grimes while Montae and A.J. flanked him on either side. He should be scared. AJ didn't pose much of a threat, but Montae was a pit-bull waiting to attack.

"Well, since you *know*, Grimes, then you also know what we're up against here. This type of shit is bad for business, so I need you to find out who's responsible. Do what you gotta do and get me some answers. My people are working this, but I want to know what the MPD has. Another war is the last thing I want, but believe me, I have no problem taking this to the streets if I have to."

"Whoa, whoa, hold on for just a minute, Mr. Harrell," Grimes said with both hands raised. "No one wants a war. You can trust me with this one. I'm on it. Working overtime on this. Give me a chance to take care of this problem for you, Mr. Harrell. No need for heads to roll. We'll find whoever is kicking up dust and take care of them."

Ezra cracked a slight smile and sat back in his chair. He knew Grimes was full of shit. This crooked cop wasn't working overtime on a damn thing except padding his pockets.

He clasped his hands behind his head and said, "Yeah, you do that, Grimes. But you need to be quick about it. I don't want any heat coming my way on this. This is what we pay you for, right? So, get in the streets and find me some damn answers. I don't want to have to call you in like this again."

He dismissed the detective with a wave of his right hand, signaling the end of their meeting.

Grimes got up from the table and exited the room without saying another word. Ezra watched the snake slither from his sight. He could think of a hundred better things to do with his money than continuing to bribe the city's corrupt police force.

There was no doubt he'd put many a policeman's child through college over the years. But he needed the law in his pocket. So, for the time being, they remained a necessary expense.

The Harrells would retain the services of the MPD at least until they found a way out of this life altogether. But until that magical day arrived, Ezra would be hunting for whoever had made the mistake of messing with his business.

# *Part III*

# *"TIME ENOUGH FOR CHANGE..."*

# *Chapter Twenty-Four*

At 10:00 a.m. Monday morning, the Avalon Towers apartments in Northwest D.C. had fallen into a temporary state of peace and quiet. The commuter rush was over, and parents had ushered their children off to daycares and summer camps on their way to work. The neighborhood's teenagers weren't out and about yet. Now would be the best time to make a move.

MPD Detective Darius Cole and his team had staked out this neighborhood for the last two days without any sign of their suspect. The only action they saw came late last night when two homeless men scuffled over a shopping cart of junk. Since then, zero, no movement out of the ordinary. Their watch had remained uneventful until just before dawn when their suspect and a second man entered the complex's rearmost building. Darius had wanted to take them down right then and there, but hadn't received the green light to go until just now.

Alleyway surveillance confirmed that the two men hadn't exited the building since they first appeared. Having seen most of the residents leave for the day,

Darius knew this was his best chance. They could wait for the men to exit, but there was no telling when that would happen. Whenever the men did show their faces again, they would be strapped. No doubt about that. Darius couldn't afford to lose control of the situation and risk putting innocent bystanders in harm's way.

Five months' worth of police work hinged on the next few minutes. Time for it all to pay off. Their suspect was wanted on various charges ranging from narcotics trafficking, armed robbery, assault, and homicide. He was a big fish that Detective Cole had every intention of reeling in once and for all.

* * * *

The nine-man team of plainclothes officers took their designated positions in and around the building. Two secured the front entrance, and two more guarded the rear of the building. Darius and three detectives approached the entrance of a second-floor apartment leased by the suspect's girlfriend. She had left with their three children earlier that morning, leaving the two men alone in the apartment. The last remaining team member maintained a surveillance position on a rooftop across the street from the target building.

Darius and his team positioned themselves in the dark hallway just outside of their suspect's apartment door. Each man made sure his weapon was hot and his bulletproof vest was strapped on tight. After receiving radio confirmation that everyone was in place, Darius used his fingers to give a silent three count to his team. *One...two...three...*

Detective Devin Jordan, a broad-shouldered linebacker look-alike, swung the sledgehammer he held in his large hands towards the door. A loud boom echoed throughout the narrow hallway as the metal door bent like cheap tin beneath the big man's assault. From one solid hit, the flimsy door groaned, folded inward, and snapped free of its hinges, ripping away from the doorjamb.

"Police!" Darius yelled as he and his team took quick but cautious steps into the apartment, their pistols extended in front of them.

"Police!" he yelled again. "No one move!"

The cramped living and dining rooms were both empty. Drawn window shades blocked the mid-morning sun from penetrating the thick shadows covering the apartment's front rooms. Darius didn't hear a sound and nodded to his fellow officers to fan out and secure the rest of the apartment.

Crouched low, he eased deeper into the darkness, sweeping his pistol's muzzle from side to side, searching for any movement. He squinted and blinked as his eyes adjusted to the darkness.

*Too damn quiet,* he thought as the other officers secured the kitchen, bathrooms, and two bedrooms sitting beyond the living and dining room areas. All were empty.

Darius began to believe that somehow his suspect had slipped past his team's surveillance for the third time in five months. Then the pungent scent of burning marijuana filled his nostrils, drawing him towards the bedroom at the end of the hallway.

He stepped towards the closed door of the third bedroom, wondering if his suspect could be in hiding in there. He touched the doorknob, half expecting it to burn his fingertips as if the door stood between him and a raging fire. His expectations weren't that far off.

Inhaling a deep breath and tightening the grip on his Glock 17 9mm pistol, he felt his throat go stone dry. He doubted he held the element of surprise over anyone hiding in this bedroom. Was Death waiting for him on the other side of this door? He turned the knob and edged the door open. Silence greeted him once again.

Then, like a jungle cat surprising its prey, the rapid-fire burst of an assault rifle exploded out of the darkness.

Dozens of rounds ripped into the bedroom door and nearby wall. Darius dove back into the hallway, wood and plaster debris from the door and wall raining down on him.

Instincts and training kicking in, he twisted and returned fire. He rolled backwards onto his feet, fired several more shots and charged forward. He kicked in the splintered door, sidestepped and dropped into a kneeling shooter's stance.

To his left, he spotted the first perp holding an AK-47. Without thinking, he leveled his weapon on the man's chest and squeezed the trigger. His Glock spat out three shots, each one hitting the man center-mass and sending him crashing into a tall wooden dresser. He was down and wouldn't be getting up. Darius's eyes searched the shadows for the second man.

The *rat-tat-tat* of automatic gunfire rang out to Darius's right and several rounds burrowed high into the wall behind him. The second shooter, hiding in the master bathroom, had him in his sights. He returned fire and dove behind the nearest corner of a king-sized sleigh bed. The gunman sent another hail of bullets in his direction, shattering the dresser's vanity mirror and showering him in broken glass.

When Darius stole a glance, he saw the man ducking out of the bedroom window and onto an outside balcony. He fired another shot that missed wide. The darkness of the room and the sleigh bed obstructed his view, but the fleeing man looked to be his primary suspect.

The other detectives rushed into the bedroom and tried to help him up, but he waved them away.

"He's gone out of the window," he shouted, his words riding hard breaths as his lungs grasped for fresh air. "Go around and try to cut him off. I'll follow this way."

He scrambled to his feet and rushed out of the same bedroom window the gunman had raced out of seconds earlier. The small balcony didn't have a fire escape, so his man must have jumped to the ground below.

*Shit and goddamn.* They were two floors up. Darius saw his man sprinting down the alleyway and knew he couldn't lose him again. He wouldn't lose him again. It had taken a month and a half to get a fresh lead on his suspect this time around.

He tucked his pistol in its holster and grabbed hold of the balcony rail. He swung both legs over the edge, hung onto the bottom rail for a second, and then dropped to the pavement below.

On the way down, the sleeve of his black sweatshirt snagged on the balcony's rusted corner throwing off his balance. He collided into a couple of metal trashcans as he landed on the ground. Pain ricocheted throughout his body. A slick stream of blood leaked from a gash on his left hand and at least one of his ribs felt broken.

He pulled himself up without checking his injuries, drew his pistol again and sprinted down the alley behind his suspect. He ignored his body's pain, knowing he would feel every bit of it times ten later on. Detective Darius Cole was a professional angler and his prize catch was getting away.

*There's no crying in crime fighting.*

# *Chapter Twenty-Five*

The trash-littered alleyway behind Avalon Towers ran into Georgia Avenue, one of the busiest streets on this side of town. In the middle of the day, crowds of cars ferried up both sides of the two-lane avenue.

Darius saw his prey up ahead about fifty yards in front of him running up the sidewalk. He'd turned left out of the alley and headed north up Georgia Avenue where the D.C. and Maryland borders met. He ran in the direction where he thought he would be able to lose his pursuers.

"No chance you are getting away, not today," Darius thought and pushed himself to close the gap.

The man ran at a fast pace, but trying to avoid pedestrians slowed him down enough for Darius to get closer.

"Police! Stop! Stop goddammit!" he yelled, dodging an old woman and her white poodle.

He jumped over the dog, almost tripping on its pink leash. The poodle's annoying yip-yap barking followed him as he kept moving up the street.

Darius didn't want any of the bystanders to intervene and hoped they would clear a path for him and his suspect. The last thing he needed was for the man to bump into a possible hostage. He figured the man wouldn't duck into one of the carry-outs or stores lining Georgia Avenue for fear of getting trapped. But, he may try to carjack someone or hold them at gunpoint to assist in his escape. That couldn't happen.

A few of the pedestrians cleared out of the way, but the rest were too busy rubbernecking to remember to move. The suspect crossed at Georgia and Hobart Place and was damn near flattened by a Kia Sportage running through the red light.

The small SUV braked hard and swerved, its rear bumper clipping the man. He bounced off the lime-colored Kia like a rubber ball off a playground wall. He spun around and somehow kept his balance enough to keep running, but could no longer muster a full out sprint. Fatigue and the impact of the car had regulated him to a fast-paced jog slowed by a noticeable limp.

Three more cars sideswiped and rear-ended each other in a failed attempt to avoid the Kia stopped in the intersection. Darius witnessed the four-car pileup, but couldn't stop to offer any help to the injured. He continued his chase, darting in and out of the halted traffic, no more than a couple of blocks behind his man.

In desperation, the suspect fired a few blind shots behind him, forcing Darius behind a parked car as the bullets whizzed by. This asshole had opened fire on a crowded street full of innocent bystanders.

Darius prayed, *Dear God, please don't let anyone have been hit.* He had to put an end to this.

The gunman fired again and ran into an alley with Darius close behind. In this empty side street, Darius found the opening he needed.

"Police! Stop!" he yelled one last time.

His suspect kept running. Darius got down on one knee and took aim. He squeezed off one shot and then a second. The perp stumbled and then belly-flopped face down onto the pavement. Darius ran up to the fallen man and kicked his pistol away.

"Don't you move! Don't even twitch!" he said, out of breath.

He kept his pistol trained on the man as he checked him for other weapons.

"Rashaan Strouse, you should've stayed in the wind. You come home just to get a couple of bullet holes in your legs. Not a good look for you."

Short pain-filled gasps escaped the man's mouth. The gunshots had taken him down, but he was alive.

"I-I need a damn doctor man," the man cried, his voice filled with agony. "My legs man, oh shit, man, I need a doctor."

"Shut up. Don't even worry about that," Darius said as he closed a pair of flex cuffs around the man's wrists. "You'll get medical treatment where you're going. There's a little matter of drugs and murder we need to talk about. And, oh yeah, how about we add assault on a police officer too, just for good measure?"

He used his cell phone to call dispatch for a blue and white to take custody of Rashaan Strouse. Then he called the rest of his team for a pickup. His tired and bruised body had no intention of letting him walk all the way back to the Avalon Towers.

Despite his wounds, he felt good about the success of today's stakeout and raid. After all the man-hours logged over the last few months, he'd finally hooked a big one.

## *Chapter Twenty-Six*

After making his marathon arrest, Detective Cole turned over his suspect to two MPD patrolmen who would transport him to central lockup. There, Strouse would receive treatment for his gunshot wounds under maximum security watch.

Darius then received much-needed medical treatment at Washington Hospital Center before heading to the Third District Station.

After he debriefed and filed his required reports, he hurried through a shower and jumped into his clothes. He was running late and needed to move as fast as his sore body would let him.

Next up on his plate was a scheduled appointment with the MPD's chief of police. He had suffered bruised ribs, a sprained ankle, and a sprained back, but would've preferred a second stakeout and chase to this meeting.

At the request of Chief Walters, he was to report to the Metropolitan Police Headquarters on Indiana Avenue at 7:00 p.m. sharp. He had less than half an hour. With the normal rush hour headache, he would be lucky to make it there in double that time.

When the chief had called him personally, he mentioned the word informal and how Darius should come in his normal clothes. So, he didn't bother with his dress blues, but he did wear a suit: a charcoal two-button, white shirt, and blue tie. This was the chief of police he was going to see, and Darius believed in first impressions. He didn't know why the chief had requested to see him, but he would at least look the part.

The digital clock in the dashboard of Darius's midnight blue '92 Nissan Maxima read 7:43 p.m. when he parked near the Henry J. Daly building. Traffic had been stop-and-go throughout the city, and the weather hadn't helped matters any. Heavy raindrops pelted him as he limped across the street and up the steps towards the entrance of the gray stone building.

Just about all of the personnel, including the deputy chief and their assistants, had gone home for the evening. When he made his way to the fifth floor, the chief's office light was still on. After checking himself over and wiping the last droplets of water from his blazer, he knocked on the closed door and waited.

"Come in," Chief Walters answered after half a minute.

"Sir, Officer Cole reporting for our 7 p.m. appointment," Darius said after opening the office door and stepping into the office. "My apologies, sir, for being late."

Chief Walters looked up from whatever he was reading and smiled. "Detective Cole, come in please," he said, standing and offering his hand to Darius.

"And no apologies are needed. I know traffic was really bad this evening with the rain and all. Plus, Detective, I understand you were busy closing a long-standing case today?"

"Yes, sir," Darius said, shaking the chief's hand in one firm motion. "It ran a little longer than I expected, sir."

Darius didn't believe for a minute he'd been called to headquarters this late just to discuss his caseload.

"Yes, sir, I remember those days myself, and hey, I have no problem with our officers doing what it takes to get the job done. The report says you actually chased down the perp on foot?"

"Yes, sir," Darius said, "something like that. I had some help from the traffic moving along Georgia Avenue. I was just happy to hear that no innocents were harmed today."

"Fine job, Detective Cole. Fine work indeed, son," Chief Walters said. "Matter of fact, I hear through the grapevine you're doing plenty of good things for our force and our city."

"Thank you, sir," Darius said, still standing at attention in front of the chief's desk, "I'm just doing my job."

"Please, have a seat, son. There are a couple of things I'd like to discuss with you," Chief Walters said as he came from around his large desk and closed the door to his office.

Darius took a seat in one of the red leather chairs sitting in front of the chief's desk. Scanning the large office, he noticed the many commendations adorning the walls. None of them appeared to belong to the chief. Rather than display his personal achievements, and Darius knew there were many, Chief Walters preferred to display the accomplishments of his officers.

*Leader* was the first word that popped in Darius's mind.

The chief returned to his seat, folded his hands in front of his face, and took a long look at Darius. Then he picked up the file he'd been reading when Darius first entered his office.

"This is your personnel file, Detective," Chief Walters said, holding up the file, then setting it back down on his mahogany desk. "A lot of good work in here for such a short career."

"Thank you again, sir," Darius said, still wondering where the chief was going with all of this.

"Five years on the job, numerous commendations, top three in your academy class, made detective first time out," the chief said as he flipped through the file. "You're what we call a fast-burner, Detective Cole, a hard-charger."

Darius didn't relish being in the spotlight, preferring to stay below the radar as much as possible. He always chose to be on a team versus chasing the glory that many of his peers seemed to crave. Personal stats, awards, and making rank never mattered to him.

"I just try to do the best that I can, sir," he said, clearing his throat. He felt a bit embarrassed at hearing his accomplishments read out loud. "You know, do my part to make a difference."

Chief Walters smiled again. "Modest. Humble. That's good. I hear you about making a difference, Detective, which is why I asked you to meet with me this evening."

*Okay, here we go,* Darius thought. Had he missed something, neglected procedure somewhere along the line? He didn't think so. Maybe he was getting a long overdue reprimand? No record stays spotless forever, right?

Then he thought of the car accident he'd helped cause on Georgia Avenue. There would be some kickback from that. Maybe someone had gotten injured and would be suing the city? Either way, shit flows downhill, and he would be at the bottom waiting to catch all of it.

"I did some looking into your background," the chief continued. "Rough beginnings for you and your family?"

The question made Darius uncomfortable, and he shifted in his seat. He'd always tried to keep his past buried as much as possible.

"Somewhat rough, sir, but no more than most, I guess."

"I see. Well, although we're here to discuss the future, your past will play an important part in all of this. I understand that the neighborhood you grew up in has long served as a hotspot for narcotics trafficking, even allegedly playing home to the humble beginnings of this city's organized narcotics cartel, The Syndicate I believe it's called?"

"Yes sir, I believe that's where they started. Maybe not under that exact name, but I think that's where they began. But all of that happened before I was born. By the time I came along, they were already running that part of the city."

"Right," the chief nodded. "Well, son, over the years numerous attempts have been made to try and bring down The Syndicate and each attempt has either failed or produced nothing more than minimal results. It's time for all of that to change."

"I agree, sir, but change how?"

Chief Walters removed his wire-rimmed glasses. In the dim lighting cast from his shaded desk lamp, he wore a grim expression. "We are losing control of our city, Detective. Inch by inch, corner by corner, these thugs are starting to overpower us."

"Yes, sir," Darius said, "it's been an uphill battle. And it's pretty ugly out there."

"What's worse, Detective, is that I believe many of my officers have taken up the stance of 'if you can't beat them, then join them,' I'm sad to say."

"You mean dirty cops, sir?" Darius asked with surprise. He'd heard the rumors about many of his fellow officers throughout the force being on the take. Tough times, bad economy, and low salaries made the dirty money real attractive.

He considered himself lucky. He didn't have a family to feed and never thought about taking anything he didn't earn. He knew when he took his oath that he wouldn't get rich on this job.

As far as dirty cops running wild, he'd never given any merit to those rumors. He didn't work for internal affairs. He was a narcotics cop. His job was catching drug dealers, not worrying about which of his comrades wasn't living right.

He got the feeling that he wouldn't like the outcome of this conversation with the chief. Did the man expect him to become some kind of snitch? If so, Darius wouldn't do it. Period.

"That's exactly what I mean, son," the chief said. "Corrupt, dirty, whatever you want to call it. But yes, dirty-ass cops."

"Well, I'm sorry, sir, I wouldn't know much about anything like that."

"I haven't been able to prove anything solid just yet," the chief continued, skipping over what Darius said. "But I'm working on that. I'm also working on taking out the bigger problem at its roots, and that's where you come in, Detective Cole."

"I'm not quite sure I follow, sir," Darius said, but he suspected he had an idea of where the chief was headed with this.

"This is about more than just dirty cops, son. It's about more than just drugs. We've always had both, probably always will. But, the two are feeding off each other in a way I've never seen in all my years. The combination of the two has created a monster that's overrunning this city. There are individuals in important places acting on behalf of the city's criminal minds, making some of them virtually invisible and untouchable if you can believe that."

"I'm not really sure what to say, sir," Darius said. "I guess I've never had the opportunity to see it from that broad of a viewpoint."

"Most people haven't seen it that way, son. Unfortunately, we all get so caught up in just getting the day-to-day stuff done that the big picture has a way of creeping up on us. So, it's the big picture here that I'm looking to attack and break down. The mayor has approved my latest request to assemble a new narcotics taskforce. We've tried taskforces before, but not quite like this. In the past, it was big and bulky, you know? It had way too many moving parts and way too many hands in it. This time around I'm thinking about a more streamlined and covert approach."

"How streamlined and covert, sir?" Darius asked.

"Just the two of us, that's how streamlined," Chief Walters replied without the slightest hint of humor in his voice. "You undercover and me as your sole link to the outside, that's how covert."

"I'm sorry, sir, did you say just the two of us? That's it? No tactical team, no outside intel support, nothing?" Darius asked, hoping this was all a joke that would soon be followed by a hilarious punch line.

"How will that work, sir? That's major gang warfare we're talking about diving into out there. I know about the house burnings and the bodies. It's starting again isn't it, sir?"

"Yes, Detective, it's starting again. That's the look of it, and I want to put a stop to it before it becomes another full-scale war. Chop it down from the inside. As far as the two-man team goes, I'm not sure who can be trusted outside of this office. Like I said, corruption is spreading like a cancer throughout our force, hell, throughout our city. I just don't quite know where and how yet."

"So how do you know you can trust me sir? With all due respect, you don't know me from a can of paint."

"You're right, I don't know you on a personal level, son. But I know your type; I know where you come from and I know what this city, what this fight means to you. I know enough of your history to know this is personal for you. That's why you jumped at the chance to join the frontline of narcotics. Every stakeout, every major bust, you try to be right there. I believe that's the reason you wanted to make detective. You don't give a damn about the money or rank. You want to make a difference; you've said that much already. But all of your street-level arrests aren't making quite the dent you hoped they would, are they? Well, I'm offering you the chance to make a real difference here, Detective. I'm offering you the chance to take down this monster from the inside out at its highest level."

The Chief's words had hit home. He was right on all accounts, no doubt about that, but his plan sounded like suicide. A two-man team? How do you put that up against an entire drug cartel?

"Well, what do you think, son? You ready to kick it up a notch and dive in the deep end? You want a shot at making a real difference out here in this jungle?"

For the last year and a half, since making detective and transferring to the Narcotics squad, Darius had taken every tough case. He'd requested to be a part of every task force and had gone after each and every one of the hard-core criminals. He'd seen plenty of success in a short time, but the chief was right. For every dealer and corner he helped shut down, new ones popped up in their places.

The chief had also been correct about something else: this *was* personal for him. Drugs had stolen his youth and were controlling his adulthood. For him, common sense didn't matter much anymore. What mattered was bringing down The Syndicate. His decision was a no-brainer.

"Yes sir, I'm in," he said, leaning forward and looking the Chief in his eyes. "I want to help bring this monster down, and I'm willing to do whatever it takes to make it happen."

# *Chapter Twenty-Seven*

Ezra Harrell sat in the rear passenger seat of his silver Cadillac Escalade ESV while Donnie drove him on his daily commute. It was 7:00 a.m. and the morning was shaping up to be a beautiful one.

As usual, Ezra obsessed over the details of his day and ignored the view outside the Escalade's tinted windows and armored exterior. Running two businesses required his constant attention, but as Ezra typed away on his phone thoughts of retirement invaded his mind.

This life he led still amazed him. He'd gone from working corners in the projects to running not one, but two lucrative corporations. That GED course and the courses at UDC had paid dividends for him, hadn't they? He gained his business degree by sweating it out in night school while his brothers celebrated their lofty criminal status.

But it was so much more than the academic lessons that had groomed him for where he stood today. The dealings with professors and students from very different backgrounds than his had changed his way of thinking. He'd absorbed every conversation, circumstance, and interaction. The experience as a whole in that new world had jarred Ezra to his core.

His brothers had been unable to understand his need to go to school or start a legal business. They couldn't see things how Ezra could see them. He'd gone from thinking that the world revolved around the Palisades to using his criminal involvement to escape the projects. Now, he dreamed of the day when he could live without worrying about police capture or death from enemy bullets.

He wondered if that's all his new life would ever be: a distant dream. He'd made promises to Olivia, but despite the growing success of Harrell Enterprises, his other life continued to latch onto his coattails. Ezra knew it wouldn't be much longer before that life dragged him and his family off a cliff.

"I've been doing some thinking, Don," he said, looking up from his phone for the first time that morning. "Thinking maybe it's time for us to get out of this game, maybe start a new life? How would you feel about that? You know, if we left all of this behind and maybe started over somewhere else, outside of D.C.?"

Donnie didn't answer right away. Instead, he stared straight ahead, keeping his attention on the traffic as he maneuvered the king-sized Cadillac along I-395. He usually took his time to answer, appearing to weigh his thoughts before relaying his opinion to Ezra.

"Well, Mr. Ezra," he said after a few moments, "to be honest, you've been doing this for a long, long time. And you've been the man in this city almost since you started. Hell, you've made selling drugs safer and more profitable than it's ever been.

"But," he continued, "when a man has done all he can do in one place, he can't be afraid of making a change. A man never wants to be forced to move on, especially when he has the power to make that choice on his own."

Donnie didn't need to say anything else. Those few words he'd spoken weighed a ton. He always looked serious to Ezra, never smiling much or wasting words, but always sharing his great wisdom. He'd survived as long as he had by being smart and by taking his time. Ezra had tried to adopt this same philosophy in his lifestyle.

Donnie always watched his back with both his pistol and his insight on life, and Ezra loved him for that. The Family employed plenty of drivers and bodyguards, but Donnie was more than just an employee. He was a dear friend. Even with Donnie in his mid-sixties, sporting gray hair and deep-set wrinkles, Ezra's trust in him never wavered.

"Yeah, I hear you, Don, and you're right, but this here is all I know. D.C. is all I've ever known. This life, this money, all of this is me. I don't know shit else, ya know? Even the legit side of what we do is tied into our illegal operations. This is all one big hustle, all of it, and it's what I'm good at. Damn good too. So, what else can an old-ass hustler do if he isn't hustling anymore?"

# *Chapter Twenty-Eight*

Detective Darius Cole drove his Maxima up North Capitol Street on the northeast side of D.C. The stoplights and heavy push of cars on the two-lane street had traffic crawling along at a snail's pace. During the morning rush, he could see many of the ingredients that made up this melting pot of a city he loved.

He saw the people in their cars and at bus stops hustling to keep pace in the everyday rat race. There were the homeless men and women at their normal spots on the corners and at the intersections looking for spare change. He watched the children making their way to school, the youngest of them oblivious to the madness all around them. The thought of these kids trying to reach adulthood in this city saddened him. He'd grown up on these evil streets and knew firsthand of the uphill struggle most of these kids would face.

Thinking of his past, Darius thought he should be dead or in an alley sucking on a crack pipe. But he had beat the odds, outlived the CNN predictions, and managed to become an exception to the rule of these streets. He was a young black man who'd made it past the age of twenty-five and out of the Pruitt Palisades Projects.

After making it out, he'd decided to come home to try and heal the plague of pain infecting much of D.C. He made it his purpose in life to help put an end to the madness wreaking havoc throughout his city.

Darius had been a member of a narcotics division that had made just mediocre progress in the war on drugs. It succeeded in taking down a few mid-level dealers, but had failed to crack the upper echelon of the narcotics flow. Chief Walter's formation of this new task force had come with perfect timing.

After yesterday's meeting with the chief, he hadn't done much else but think about getting to work on his new assignment. The chief had taken care of the transfer from his division, wanting Darius to get started right away. After just a couple hours of sleep, he'd risen at five thirty this morning to report in at his new duty location.

Darius would transform his entire life. He would move from his small apartment downtown to an upscale condo the chief had set up for him in Columbia, Maryland. He would live and work out of the two-bedroom as part of his cover. The chief would provide everything needed to make his identity as a high-level trafficker stick. He would get new clothes, a new car, a new name, a new background, and new money: the entire package.

The chief also provided him with another very important tool: a laptop containing classified files on the city's top-tier narcotics organizations. He would study these files until he knew all of the major players like the back of his hand. Then he would become one of them.

He would begin by observing and studying, finding a weak point, and then inserting himself into the Underworld. He didn't have any family to worry about, no relatives, no kids, and no girlfriend, not even a dog. He'd been alone since he was a teenager. His entire adult life had revolved around the job. Now, he would have to learn a different way of living to fit into his new assignment. He would learn to live and breathe as a high-rolling drug dealer. Fast women, fast cars, and life on the edge. Chief Walters had stressed the importance of him remaining in character for as long as he could. Darius wasn't sure where this new life would lead him, but he'd do whatever was needed to see this through.

The chief appeared to have done his research on him. He knew about his background, including his rough upbringing. He'd told Darius how he could help right the wrongs of his past by working undercover. He'd also warned him that he would be alone in the streets.

The two men would talk and meet often, but otherwise, he would be flying solo. They would report their progress to the mayor and no one else.

Taking this assignment meant he would embrace the monster he'd spent his entire childhood running from and his entire adulthood fighting. He would immerse himself in a world that had taken so much from him. Defeating this beast required him to live within it, to breathe it, to love it. He understood that from the outside looking in, he was limited.

Drugs and crime had overwhelmed his city, and he was determined to help take it back from the animals. But he couldn't help but wonder if there would ever be enough tears to shed for the lost lives of the innocent.

## *Chapter Twenty-Nine*

Art Grimes mashed down on his car's horn trying to hurry along the cement truck inching along in front of him. That idiot didn't have a clue how much he was holding up rush hour traffic by carrying his load in I-295's fast lane.

"Move your ass!" Grimes yelled as he stuck his head out of the open window. "Get the hell out of the way!"

He reached for the switch that would turn on his car's siren, but instead, knocked over his cup of hot coffee. The small Styrofoam container flipped out of the flimsy cup holder and onto into his lap. Its steaming contents soaked through his tan Chinos and burned his right thigh.

"Aw damn! Shit!" he yelled when he felt the sting of the scalding liquid. "Dammit! Goddammit!"

He stomped down on his car's brake pedal as he reached for napkins and wiped at the wasted coffee. Behind him, a red Toyota had to slam on its brakes, which drew an angry horn from its chubby blonde driver. He started to give the fat lady the finger, but she'd already beat him to it.

What the hell was wrong with him? He'd allowed himself to lose all of his focus after his meeting with those fucking lowlife thugs. Who the hell did Ezra Harrell think he was to talk to him like he was a peon? He was *Art Fucking Grimes,* for Christ's sake, a senior inspector in the MPD, and no one talked to him like that. He wished he could've put two bullets in that arrogant asshole, one in his chest and one right between his beady eyes.

He hadn't planned on making his move this soon, but Ezra Harrell had just forced his hand. For all of his big talk, the old man had to be more scared than he'd been in a long time.

Grimes could either waste time tracking down whoever was hitting the Harrell family or he could play his ace in the hole. He offered his services to multiple clients in the Underground, but The Harrells were always his highest paying employer. Maybe now was the time to lean more towards the next highest bidder.

A shakeup appeared to be on the way, one that could lead to a major power shift within the Underground. Grimes would align himself with the winning side when all of the dust settled. This was all about survival. Someone had been hitting the Harrell Family hard and meant to topple them from their throne. A war was coming, and it was no longer a sure bet that the Harrells would hold power once the mayhem ended.

It was time for him to reassess his loyalties. There was no question that he would investigate these killings, but not for Ezra Harrell's benefit. He would seize this opportunity for himself and begin the financing of his next big payday. With a little bit of dirty work and showmanship, Supercop Grimes would steal the headlines once again.

*Carpe Diem...*

# *Chapter Thirty*

"Ezra-Baby, are you sure about this?" Olivia Harrell asked her husband as she sat a plate of hot food in front of him.

Tonight's dinner consisted of a heaping mound of scrambled egg whites with cheddar and provolone cheeses, mushrooms, and red and green peppers. On the side were plump Italian turkey sausages, buttered cinnamon toast, and chilled orange and cranberry juices. The crazy hours Ezra kept had long ago expanded his culinary tastes, and he often preferred to eat breakfast late at night.

It was midnight and Olivia was wide awake, her internal clock in tune with Ezra's, who'd just gotten home from work. After all these years together, she'd grown used to his fickle food tastes and odd hours. Just like she'd grown used to so many other things in her life that came along with being Ezra Harrell's wife. Tonight, he'd given her one more thing that she would need to get used to in a hurry.

"I'm not sure about much these days, baby-love," Ezra said, taking a sip from his glass of orange juice. "I just know it's time for us to get out. Out of D.C. and out of this life. It's just time, baby, that's all. Past time."

Those were the words Olivia had waited years to hear. Now that she'd heard them and they were sinking in, she didn't know how to react. She was speechless.

She looked into her husband's brown eyes from across the black marble counter in the kitchen of their five-bedroom Georgetown townhome. He hadn't been sleeping well.

Puffy bags the color of coffee stood out against his caramel complexion. The gray hair around his temple had spread past the edges of his ears. He slumped as he sat back in his chair. For the first time that she could remember, the wear and tear was beginning to show on him.

"Everything's changed," he continued, "and I don't know for sure what will happen next. But, we have to leave this life behind for good, while we still can."

It took a minute before Olivia found her words again.

"Well you know I'm behind you, baby, all the way and always," she said, the unsteadiness of her voice betraying her efforts to calm the fear quaking in her heart. "But what will happen when you announce your plans to everyone?"

She knew this wasn't a lifestyle that you could just up and quit. It didn't work that way. The rules of this game were bigger than all of its players, including her husband.

"I don't know how everyone will react. It won't be good, I'm sure, but I've held onto this life for too long. Been trying to own something that never belonged to me in the first place. No one can own this kind of life; the best any of us can hope for is to just try and survive in it for as long as we can, but we gotta know when to get out. And I think now is our time."

Ezra rose from his seat. He stepped behind her, pulled her close to him, and whispered in her ear, "Liv, I promised you a better life, and what we were doing here was just a means of getting to that better life. You know I never meant for this here to actually be our better life."

Olivia looked back and smiled at the man she'd loved for what seemed like a thousand years. She remembered their days together in high school and all of their years since leading up to this point. Through the good and bad, they'd always had each other's back.

She felt his strong arms wrap around her waist. He kissed the back of her neck, his mustache tickling her and sending a chill down her spine. *He felt so good.* She'd missed him. She always did. His scent, his touch, the sound of his voice in her ear. Whether it was for a few hours or a few days, whenever they were apart, she missed him.

"So how do we do this, baby? This life is all we've ever known. What will we do? Where will we go?" she said, turning to face him. "Don't get me wrong, Ezra. You know I want this, I always have, but how do we start over after all these years?"

"Yeah, that's the thing about it. It won't be easy. I know it won't, but we won't take any chances with this," he said. "I plan on making the announcement very soon, but before I do, I want you and D to go to the estate down south and wait for me. I'm putting you, him, and a few of our best soldiers on a private plane so you can be with the family while I take care of business here. Cuttino will take care of everything down there until I can wrap up everything in the city. He's ready to step up and be a man. It's time, so I don't want you to worry about a thing."

She shook her head. "No, I don't want to leave you here. Don't make me do that. I've been by your side and we've seen tougher times than this. Do you remember when we first started out? Remember how crazy that was? All the time never knowing what would happen next? Having to worry about the police or somebody taking a shot at you? I think I used to get high off the thrill. I still do."

She winked at him and laughed, "After all, I was dating the baddest dude walking. I still am."

Her husband used to be so headstrong in his younger days, full of risk, believing he was indestructible. He'd grown so much wiser since then. So had she. They both had grown to understand that this wasn't a game.

"Liv, I need you to trust me on this one, like you always have," he said. "Everything will be fine. I'll make sure of that. We just need to be careful, that's all. This is all brand new for us, and I don't want to have to worry about my wife and my son. I gotta admit, I don't know how this will play out, and it's the not knowing that scares me."

He pulled her close again, wrapping her five-foot-three-inch body into his six-foot frame. She felt tears beginning to form and buried her face into his chest.

He squeezed her and bent to kiss her forehead. "Besides, Donnie, Montae, and A.J. will watch over me; they always have and always will. Everything will be cool, trust me."

Olivia didn't agree with what Ezra was asking her to do and he had to know that, but she would do it. She always did what he asked of her, always the good wife. Not out of fear, but out of love and trust. It had always been this way, since the beginning before they were even married.

She'd known then that she would be with Ezra forever. Soulmates. He'd shown her what it meant to be a real man. It didn't matter what was going on; he always made her feel safe, and she believed in him. She needed to believe in him, needed to trust him, and so she always had. And she always would.

# Chapter Thirty-One

"Okay, fellas, there is a pretty simple reason why I asked you both here this early," Ezra Harrell said as he began to break the news of his decision to his brothers. "You see, I've been sitting back and watching what's been going on around us. Things are changing more and more every day. Hell man, the times are changing, like they always do. Not a whole lot you can do about that except to adapt and make some changes as well. And that's my point here, the time's come for the Harrell family to make a change."

After his talk with Liv, he'd slept a few fitful hours before deciding there was no reason to wait any longer. First thing in the morning, he'd called both of his brothers and asked them to meet him at his Virginia office.

He planned to tell them flat out that the family was ending its life of crime in the nation's capital. They would have to see things his way, and there wouldn't be any negotiation on the matter.

"So, here it is: I've decided that we're pulling out of The Syndicate and out of D.C. I think it's about time that our family move on."

He paused, checked for his brothers' reactions and then continued, "Now, I know that D.C. is our home. I know this. But there are some better things waiting for our family outside of this city. I've put plenty of thought into this decision, and it's the best thing for all of us."

Montae and A.J., who sat on opposite sides of a large camel suede couch, stared at him from across the room. Their faces remained expressionless as they waited for the punch line to what had to be a bad joke.

From behind his desk, Ezra returned their stares and waited for a response, but both men remained silent. He could almost feel the heat from his oldest brother's glare. A.J., on the other hand, avoided eye contact and pretended to focus on the picture hanging behind Ezra's desk.

"You hear what I'm saying to both of you, right?" he asked, breaking the long silence. "Hey fellas, this isn't a joke. I'm dead serious about this, never been more serious. It's time for us to get the hell out of here."

Montae looked at A.J., who maintained his eye-lock with the wall, then he returned his stare to Ezra. "Man, what the hell are you talking about, Ez? What do you mean it's time to get out of here?"

"I'm saying it's time for me to retire, time for *all of us* to retire. The Harrells are pulling out of The Syndicate and out of this way of life."

Montae stood and walked around the side of the couch.

"So you're talking about quitting, Ez? Is that what you're talking about here?"

Ezra let his eyes fall to the melting ice cubes swirling towards the bottom of the glass he held. He knew how this conversation would go. The ice in his glass reminded him of what D.C. had become. A once proud city dwindling down to nothing because of him and the men just like him.

"Just like I said, Montae, I want out. Completely out. It's time for us to get out. I'm shutting down the Harrell's interests in D.C., everything. All of it."

"Shut it down? Get out? How?" A.J. finally spoke up. "There is no getting out of this life, little brother."

"Wait. Just wait a minute here," Montae cut in. "You mean to tell me that after we built this shit from the ground up, got it all correct and running exactly like we want, you wanna just up and leave it? Let it all go, just like that? After all of our hustling and hard work?

After all these years, Ez? You can't be serious, man. You gots to be fucking kidding me here."

His brothers had reacted just as he thought they would. He had no delusions about how they would accept his decision.

"Okay, look, why don't both of you pipe down for a minute and just listen to what I'm saying here? For one thing, this isn't up for discussion. My mind is made up, so *this right here is* final. Second, you two act like you don't see what's going on out here, how out of hand things are getting. Just what the hell do you think is going on out there in those streets?"

"There's a new war starting up, and yeah we've been through plenty of those, but this time we don't even know who's on the other side of that battlefield. Somebody snatched five of our boys the other day," Ezra said, holding up his left hand in the number five to emphasize his point. "Five, man! And then they burned them inside one of our stash houses!"

"And to make things worse, I just got word that four more of our scramblers got hit. Shot up right on their corner this time. That makes nine of our people dead and gone in the last few days. Now rest easy, 'cause we will handle this. But after we do, we'll be looking at another war, and that just isn't worth the risk to our family anymore. We're moving elsewhere. California or down south maybe, we'll see. Either way, the Harrells are leaving D.C."

"Ezra, come on man, have you lost your mind?" Montae said. "That's it, right? Seriously, tell me something bro, 'cause you got me worried here. How do you think this will play out? We just up and move? Retire from the game, right? Okay, so we do that. What about our partners?"

"Yeah, Ez. How do you think that will go over?" A.J. said, still sitting on the couch. "Do you think the rest of The Syndicate will let us out with no static? Let us up and walk away? You know just like I do what they'll think and then what they'll do."

"Ez, come on man; think about it for a second." A.J. continued. "You worried about a war starting? There will be a war if we just up and bail out. We'll really have one on our hands if we run. Yeah, I know, I know, you got us this. But you a fool if you think we can just up and walk away. We try to leave, they think we're weak or we turned on them, and they'll come at us with everything they've got."

Ezra swiveled in his chair and turned away from his brothers. He folded his hands in a prayer that they would somehow understand this new direction in which he was leading them.

"Yeah A.J., I know what everyone will think and what they *think* they'll be able to do about it," he said when he turned to face them. "And you're right. They'll think we've cut a side deal with the Feds or somebody and we're leaving them to take the fall. And yeah, they'll come at us with everything they've got, but don't you see that's what's already happening? You think them corner hits were random, right? You think it was just a couple of freestylers looking for a quick payday? Open your eyes, man. Those were execution-style hits. Somebody was delivering a message to our doorsteps loud and clear."

"And let me go a step further with this. I'm hearing that the police are preparing to tear us down once and for all. Our money ain't talking as loud as it used to, is it? Nah, not anymore, not in this city. We can take care of our partners, but not with the law on our backs. We do it my way and we get out while the getting is still good. We go elsewhere and start over. Maybe even start completely legit, you know? The most important thing is that our family will be safe. That's all that matters. But if we make the mistake of staying and trying to fight this war, our family will bleed worse than it ever has. And in the end, we'll lose everything."

"Ez, I hear you," Montae said, "I do, but I don't see it that way. I can't see it. Man, I don't know shit about running away."

Ezra pointed a stiff right finger in his brothers' direction. "I guess growing older hasn't made either one of you any smarter, huh? No, see, you two are the fools for believing we can get through this untouched. We won't come out clean, not this time. Nothing is more important than the Family. *Nothing before family.* Both of you remember that, right? Make damn sure you never forget it."

The large office fell silent again. None of the Harrell brothers spoke. Ezra hadn't wanted it to go this way. He hated having to talk to his brothers like this, but they didn't understand. They didn't see. He would have to make them.

"Things have changed. It's different," Ezra began again. "I can't explain it all the way, but I just know it's different and not in a good way. Feels like our time has come and gone, you know?"

"Different? Different how?" Montae said, the agitation evident in his voice. "Ain't shit different around here, Ez. Just new bullets need shootin' is all. We just need to answer back. We drop the right bodies and then everything goes back to how it's always been: cool and under our control."

"That's the thing about it, I don't want to shoot any new bullets. This is about more than droppin' bodies. We do that and then what? Things return to normal, right? No, I don't think so, not this time."

"Well, I *do* think so," Montae said. "I think if we take care of this like we always have, then everything will go back to how it's always been, like I said. Period. Easy."

"You aren't listening. I don't want any more bodies, Montae. Hear me on that. No more bloodshed on our account. I'm tired of that shit."

"No more bloodshed? Come on, who do you think you're talking to, Ez? You forget we've seen you end dudes like it was nothing."

"I know what I've done, and that's what I'm saying to both of you, I don't want to do that shit anymore. There's no need for us to do any of *that shit* anymore."

"Oh ok, I see, I see. So, you've got a conscience all of a sudden? What they call it? Scruples? Morals? Or are you scared? That it, Ez? You scared, man? Tell me something. 'Cause, I have to be honest with you here, you're sounding like a bitch, little brother."

"Watch your mouth, Montae," Ezra said, his voice dropping into a low rumble. "Remember who you're talking to."

"Watch my mouth? Remember who I'm talking to? How about you remember that I'm your *older* brother?"

"And what the hell has that meant since we were kids? Not a damn thing, jack shit to be exact," Ezra said, his words like viper venom.

"You know what? I did some checking on some of those bodies," he continued. "All of them were kids, some even younger than we were when we started out. Kids, man. I didn't even know they were working for us."

"Ezra, please, man. Who are you trying to fool? Don't try and get all holier-than-thou on us. You know how this shit goes. We get it done, whatever it takes. You're the one who stopped giving a damn about this side of the house. You got yourself so wrapped in the corporate side of this shit that you forgot all about the grunt work down in the trenches, the dirty work that makes this machine run. You think that dope sells itself? We still make most of our money at the street level, but you wouldn't know shit about that anymore."

"You just keep pushing, Montae, don't you? But you don't see the big picture here. Neither of you do. You never have."

"Ez, look man, maybe it was one of our partners, you know?" A.J. said. "Maybe one of them or all of them even. Wouldn't surprise me at all. We just need to find out who it was and hit 'em back. We hit 'em and put 'em down quick. Set this mess straight."

"Okay, but tell me why? Why would they do it? Why now?" Ezra said. "Why do it all out in the open like some kind of show? Why risk bringing down the heat on everyone, including themselves? Why risk messing up the money? That shit doesn't even match up. None of it does. Either of you ask yourselves any of that before jumping up ready to go set the streets on fire? Have you?"

"And A.J.," he continued. "Since you're talking about getting some payback, are *you* ready to pick up a piece again after all this time? You finished partying all of a sudden? Finished living the life of a rockstar? You ready to handle business now? Ready to take a life or two or three? Are you? I seriously doubt that, Arthur James."

His words shut A.J. down and forced him to resume his silence.

"The why and how of this shit don't much matter. And neither does any big picture, Ez," Montae said. "All that matters is that we find out who did it and put some fire in their asses quick, fast, and in a fuckin' hurry. Outside of that, I don't know a damn thing about any of that other shit you're talking about."

"I know you don't, big brotha, and that's why I'm making this decision, not just for me, but for the entire family. Something bad is coming and I don't know from where. I just know it's coming our way. Could be the law or something else or both. Either way it's time for us to pull out while we can. Now, I'm asking both of you to trust me. I've never once steered us wrong, have I?"

He was done talking, and although Montae and A.J. continued to protest, he didn't budge on his decision. He wouldn't continue to justify his reasoning to anyone, not even to his brothers who'd helped raise him as a child. They had stood by his side all these years and always trusted his leadership, until now.

What had happened to them? His brothers acted as if they couldn't exist without this lifestyle. He'd always preached how this life couldn't become all that they were. How the Harrells always had to be bigger than the game. *Make the game, don't let it make you.*

Ezra used to look up to Montae and A.J., but that was a long time ago. This was *his* family. He'd built the Harrell Empire and was its undisputed king. He led them into this hell and he would lead them out, kicking and screaming if it came to that.

He was focused on the future and nothing else. Not the past. Not the present. Not what his brothers or anyone else said or thought. He was doing the best thing for his family. He had to hold onto that belief if this move had any chance of succeeding.

# *Chapter Thirty-Two*

Lucas Meadows had been built to end lives. Through an extensive and intense regimen of training and programming, he'd been constructed to hunt and eradicate any target. Everything prior to his life as The Clean had been just a preliminary, and now he was living the main event.

"I could wrap up this job right now, collect my money, and go home," he thought as he watched Ezra Harrell through the sight of his riflescope. "Two bullets would put him in the ground real easy like."

The five-block distance combined with the city's landscape concealed his location and his high-powered scope zoomed in on Harrell's every move. Lucas also kept a close eye on the older man sitting in the driver's seat of Harrell's black Cadillac SUV. He was Harrell's personal driver and bodyguard and went everywhere with the drug kingpin.

For the past two weeks, The Clean and his crew of shooters had tracked Ezra Harrell's every move. It was easy to see that the crime chief ran a very organized operation and was well guarded at all times.

In addition to his driver, a full cadre of guards stood watch over him, his family, his home, and places of business. Wherever Ezra Harrell and his family went, armed escorts followed close behind. Getting close to Mr. Harrell would not be an easy task.

Of course, he'd known this would be the case. His employer had provided him all of this info in his initial intel package. He'd known from the very beginning how tough this job would be, but the hefty payday would make it all worth it.

As he always had, The Clean would find a way to finish this job exactly as his employer had requested. Each and every detail culminating in the desired bloody finale. That's how it always went. He'd been doing this too well for too long for it to go any other way.

* * * *

Colonel Lucas Meadows had devoted 20+ years of decorated service in defense of this country as a U.S. Marine. As a member of the Marine's elite recon battalions, he'd endured combat tours in Southwest Asia, Kosovo, and Somalia. He even commanded a small unit responsible for conducting dozens of black ops missions all over the globe.

Having survived those nightmares, Colonel Meadows had looked forward to retirement when he hit the twenty-three-year mark. He'd planned to stay in North Carolina where his wife and child had settled over the last part of his career. But even the best-laid plans can go to shit, the Marines had taught him that all too well.

The landscape of Lucas's entire world shifted forever when his wife revealed that their ten-year-old daughter wasn't his biological child. Rayne Meadows had been the product of one of Ivy's multiple affairs during their seventeen years of marriage. While he'd rotted away on foreign soils fighting this country's battles, his wife had been back home getting her freak on. His baby girl, whom he loved more than anything, wasn't his baby at all.

After learning the truth, a deep, hateful darkness consumed him. He wanted to choke the life out of Ivy with his bare hands or put a bullet in her head. But his darkness soon gave way to absolute clarity. Lucas Meadows realized then what he was and the life he was meant to lead. He was a warrior, a hunter, and a killer.

He immediately put in for retirement and filed for divorce. He cut off all contact with Ivy and even Rayne, who hadn't deserved the pain her mother had inflicted on their lives. He loved his little girl, but she wasn't his and he couldn't deal with that hardest of truths.

Leaving the Marines and his heartache behind, he headed west to California where he began his new life.

For Lucas, the typical nine-to-five meant stuffy offices, stuffy suits, and, worst of all, stuffy people. All of these were all a no-go for a man like him. He went another route and looked up many of his former military contacts seeking employment that would utilize his unique skill set. Some of his so-called friends had acted as handlers for Lucas. They introduced him to a whole new way of life, one fueled by death and cash.

These middlemen connected him with people who were willing to pay large sums of money for the use of his extensive talents. The corrupt and wealthy hired men like Lucas for jobs requiring discretion, detachment, and the deadliest of intentions.

He all but dropped his God-given name in this new world and immersed himself neck-deep in his alter ego, The Clean. His nickname stuck, not so much for his bald head, but more for the thoroughness of his work.

For each target, he studied backgrounds and habits. The Clean became their shadow up until the moment when he extinguished their lives. No loose ends left behind and no evidence pointing to him or his employer... *Clean...*

After getting his feet wet as a subcontractor, Lucas used his knowledge and new contacts to begin solo freelancing. After a few years in San Diego, he moved a couple of hours south to the resort town of Rosaritos, Mexico. There, The Clean began contract killing for an extended list of new clientele.

Anyone from local drug cartels to politicians to Vegas casino owners seeking to force out local competition sought his services. He despised the majority of his clients and their motives, but he loved their endless money flow. If nothing else, he was good at taking lives. Damn good.

At first, he'd taken simple contracts for hits within the states and Mexico. But as his reputation began to spread, larger, more complex contracts requiring travel abroad began to come his way. The Clean began stacking up frequent flyer miles from his trips all across the globe.

He left corpses like business travelers left wrinkled sheets in their unmade hotel beds. He collected the souls of the dead like vacationers collected souvenirs. He was the end of the road, the chill down your spine, the bad dream you wouldn't wake up from.

*The ghost and the shadow...*

# *Chapter Thirty-Three*

A headache pounded its way up from Ezra's neck towards his temples, leaving a trail of pain in its wake. He and Olivia were at their estate in Bushwood, Maryland. This small fishing town was located an hour south of the city and was the perfect getaway from life's everyday chaos.

As he stood in front of a bay window overlooking the mouth of the Wicomico River, his thoughts revolved around tonight's agenda. The tide was headed out for the evening, and the action looked slow for the fishermen on the nearby dock. Ezra's tide would be heading out too and if he had his way, it wouldn't be returning to this shore.

He knew tonight would be a huge risk for him, but he didn't see any other option. After breaking the news to his brothers, he'd contacted the heads of each of the other three families within The Syndicate. He'd arranged a no-notice meeting where he would reveal his plans for retirement. He knew there could be trouble, but he wanted to inform his partners of his decision to retire face to face. He owed them at least that much.

For years, they had showed patience and trust in his leadership. They had even showed a measured amount of respect and loyalty to the boss of crime bosses. He hoped he could minimize any concerns the other families would have about their futures in D.C.'s narcotics trade.

He was nobody's saint and had no thoughts of trying to spread his newfound conscience to anyone outside of his family. He planned to hand over his majority share of The Syndicate, which included his legal contacts and narcotics supplier. All of his illegal assets, his corners, safe houses and other holdings, would be divided between each family. He'd leave with what he'd stashed away and the profits yielded from the sale of his various legal business interests. That would be plenty to last his family for a long, long time.

According to his plan, he would move his entire family out of the D.C. area for good. Then the remaining families would be free to run the show however they chose.

After making his final decision, Ezra had begun making preparations for tonight's meeting and everything that would take place afterward. He'd started contacting his legal system payroll and his supplier to inform them all of his plans. In today's economy, he had no worries of his legal contacts turning down The Syndicate's money after his departure. His supplier also wouldn't care who they dealt with as long as their product kept moving.

Above everything else, age and time were his biggest enemies. Ezra felt stretched and thin, like peanut butter spread over too many slices of bread. Stress had taken its toll. It was like a heavy anchor pulling him downward. The joints in his body hurt and he didn't sleep much anymore. He was flirting with the thin line between urgency and desperation. This entire ordeal needed to come to an end before his body quit on him.

Tonight's meeting would be held in one of the Harrell-owned warehouses to ensure his personal safety. Harrell soldiers would be posted throughout the building and, as always, Montae and A.J. would be right beside him watching his back. The king of D.C. was prepared for anything that might happen tonight.

# *Chapter Thirty-Four*

Ezra Harrell had created The Syndicate Narcotics Cooperative as a peacemaker to calm the storm that had been threatening to tear the city apart.

When the '90s began, the Harrell brothers had already made their play to take over the streets of D.C. Before the Syndicate, the city's illegal narcotics trade had been dysfunctional and chaotic.

With the Harrells standing atop the food chain, the remaining dealers were left to fight it out amongst themselves for the leftovers. The power struggle to become the underground's *second* strongest family had begun to collapse the already fragile infrastructure of the city's Underworld.

Ezra had managed to minimize his family's losses over the years and had been determined to keep it that way. The creation of an umbrella cooperative that would organize and oversee the city's narcotics flow had become a necessary evil. Under the SNC, a few other families had been allowed to have a minor say in the D.C. narcotics game. But, most importantly, the violence had been curbed.

The Mellwood Family, the biggest threat to the Harrells, had emerged as the second largest crime family in the SNC. Their lack of numbers and territory kept them regulated to a strong second and forced into taking orders from the Harrells. If not for the looming presence of the other families, Ezra would've channeled all of his energy into eradicating the Mellwoods.

Squatting more than standing at just over five and a half feet, Buster Mellwood made up in girth what he lacked in height. At close to three hundred pounds, Buster was a sloth of a man who always moved in slow motion. Ezra and Buster didn't agree on much of anything, never had and never would. And Ezra would've taken a special pleasure in putting two bullets in the back of Buster's bloated head.

The two men had been in competition since they were both teenagers, but Ezra had always maintained the upper hand. When he approached the Mellwoods about joining the SNC, he knew Buster would have to give in or risk going to war. Ezra's soldiers and his many legal influences would pick the Mellwoods apart, but at great loss to both sides. By that time, neither family would have control of the city's narcotics trade, and both men would be either dead or in jail.

The head of the Mellwood clan had agreed to join the SNC, but Ezra never forgot Buster's main goal. He knew that one day, the fat man would make his play to have sole control over D.C.'s Underground.

* * * *

True to their street name, the Fifth Street Hardheads was a crew of knuckleheads with juvie records from the northwest side of town. None of their members were older than thirty. They were stickup kids and corner pushers trying their hand at organized crime as if it was a fashion trend. These youngsters had made enough noise and gathered enough numbers to earn a small spot at the table. Always the forward thinker, Ezra could see the times changing. Against the wishes of the other SNC families, he'd pulled The Hardheads into their ranks a few years ago.

Their leader was a tall, lanky boy named Bernard. He talked tough, but had proven to be street smart and patient during his time in The Syndicate. He'd even impressed Ezra a little, if such a thing was possible. The boy was hungry, ambitious, and smart. While the other families argued over every small detail, he would sit and observe, listening and learning and speaking only when he should.

Despite his distaste for today's younger generation, Ezra acknowledged the sign of the times. He'd allowed

Bernard a seat at the table hoping to pass on the respect and tradition that should always accompany this lifestyle.

It was about more than just hustling and making money. It had to be about more than just survival. To achieve greatness *and* longevity in this life, the game had to be learned at its purest level, like an art form.

* * * *

Cleo "Smitty" Watkins had been around as long as both the Harrells and the Mellwoods. He'd been a small-time gunrunner in Cleveland before catching his wife in the arms of another man. Smitty shot his unfaithful spouse and her lover and dumped their bodies in the Ohio River.

Afterwards, he dragged his three sons east to the nation's capital during the 1980s drug boom. Smitty and his three sons had succeeded in carving out a small piece of D.C.'s drug trade. Like the Mellwoods and the Fifth Street Hardheads, Ezra decided to use the Smittys to his advantage.

A street-wise old man in his late sixties, Smitty Watkins preferred to stay below the radar. He hoped to live a comfortable lifestyle for as long as he and his sons could. He had no interest in being in charge of anything so long as he continued to get his fair share.

According to Smitty's skewed logic, he'd left his violent past in Cleveland to enjoy life in D.C. as a peaceful, honest businessman. It was funny how things worked. One man's heaven was another man's hell. Well, at least that's how the saying went.

# *Chapter Thirty-Five*

At just after 11:00 p.m. that evening, Ezra entered the warehouse room with his two brothers flanking him on either side. Each family's head was seated around the long wooden table, accompanied by one of their bodyguards.

Ezra had arranged for a buffet style midnight meal consisting of deli sandwiches, fruit, an omelet chef, and an open bar. By the time he arrived, everyone had a plate in front of them and a drink in hand. In a legitimate environment, The Syndicate Narcotics Cooperative could function as a powerful financial, real estate, or technology corporation. Its members were all shrewd businessmen who'd helped make the SNC into a criminal enterprise larger than any other in D.C.'s history.

When the meeting began, Buster Mellwood spoke first. "So, what's this all about, Ezra? It's the middle of the damn night, and it's raining like all hell outside."

Ezra scanned the faces of the men he'd made truckloads of money with over the years. Whether he considered these men friends, foes, or just plain business partners, the exact parameters of their relationship didn't much matter. In the end, the bottom line remained clear and unwavering: together these men had gotten rich off this city's lost and addicted. And it was time for the Harrells to move on.

He took his usual seat at the head of the table. After exhaling a deep breath, he took a giant leap of faith and crossed the point of no return. The city's most powerful criminal began laying out his retirement plans to the heads of the city's major crime families. The chips would fall whichever way they chose.

* * * *

The meeting didn't go as Ezra had hoped it would, but of course he hadn't truly expected any favorable results. His retirement announcement caused an uproar among the other members of the SNC.

Each crime boss expressed their strong opposition to his decision to divide his share of the co-op among the three remaining families. Each family also feared the possibility of losing the legal protection and the narcotics connection Ezra brought to the table. It was unanimous that Ezra's departure would reduce The Syndicate to nothing more than an unorganized group of drug dealers and gangsters.

Even Buster Mellwood agreed that now would be the worst possible time for Ezra to leave the SNC. Ezra knew this was a front and that Buster was licking his fat chops at the prospect of him vacating his seat. He knew that as soon as the Harrells left, Buster Mellwood would attempt a hostile takeover to assume control of The Syndicate.

Maybe Buster was already making his move. Maybe he'd been behind the recent bloodshed. Ezra still had no idea who hit his safe house and corner, but the Mellwoods were the logical choice. With a potential change of mayoral administration on the horizon, Buster could see now as do-or-die time for his family. The same way Ezra saw now as do-or-die time for getting out of The Syndicate. He didn't believe The SNC could survive a new administration promising to do whatever was needed to eradicate the organized narcotics trade. Maybe Buster somehow saw a new mayor as a golden opportunity for him. Those dead bodies could represent just the start of his bid at a hostile takeover.

Despite Ezra's assurances that he would do whatever he could to ensure the SNC's future after his retirement, the debate continued. The meeting ended four hours later more out of frustration and exhaustion than resolution. A new day was dawning, in more ways than one, but no progress had been made from the midnight meeting.

Ezra stood beside his decision and left the meeting with an increased urgency to leave this life behind as soon as possible. He'd always trusted his instincts. They had guided him this far and kept him alive. Now, his instincts told him his family wouldn't be safe another day beneath the dark shroud of The Syndicate.

# *Part IV*

## *"LOVE AND WAR..."*

*"See the Storm Comin'..."*

**It's the thoughts I shouldn't have**
**that come with ease...**
**Invading heart & mind**
**like life's worst disease...**
**And I can see the storm risin'**
**yet I embrace the rain...**
**Knowing the thunder & lightening**
**forecast future pain...**
**And I can feel the heat**
**but still I reach for the flame...**
**Longing for a slow burn**
**but unwilling to accept the blame...**
**Pushing wisdom to the side**
**off the cliff I dive...**
**Falling towards my heart's death**
**never feeling more alive...**
**Forsaking past regrets**
**& healing old scars...**
**walking thru the rain into the sun**
**searching for the stars...**
***'cause it's the little things that count...***
**I can see the storm comin'...**
**but I ain't runnin'...**

# *Chapter Thirty-Six*

***Fuquay-Varina, North Carolina...***

The smoky, spiced aroma of cooked food rescued Cuttino Harrell from a fitful sleep. Thoughts of home had filled his dreams, causing him to toss and turn for hours. When he edged his eyes open that morning, the first thing he did was check the time and date on his phone. The phone's digital display read:

**7:10 a.m.**

**Tuesday, July 31**

One month had crawled by since his father had sent him to stay with their family in North Carolina. For Cuttino, the last month had felt more like a prison sentence or an exile to some remote island.

As he eased out of bed and his surroundings came into focus, Cuttino reengaged with reality. He wasn't home and probably wouldn't be anytime soon. His father had put him on a private plane in the middle of the night with his two personal bodyguards. He'd been shipped off like a package to the middle of the boonies in North Carolina.

Iran and Taurus Beasley had been watching over Cuttino since they were nineteen and he was seventeen. Some might mistake the identical twins for a couple of Mack Trucks. Each man-mountain towered at six-feet-nine-inches, wore clean-shaven heads, and weighed in at about two hundred and fifty pounds of brick-hard muscle. Neither man smiled or said much from behind their full-bearded, dark-skinned faces. They'd been brought up through the Harrell Family ranks from a young age, starting off as Harrell corner muscle. After earning Ezra's trust, the twins were assigned to be Cuttino's personal guards.

Like Cuttino, neither man had married nor had kids. Their lives revolved around The Family, and both men had uprooted their lives with just a word from Ezra Harrell. Cuttino trusted both men with his life. The three men had become close friends in their years together, and Cuttino knew he would need them now more than ever.

There hadn't been time for packing or discussion, just quick goodbyes to his mom by telephone and his father at the airport. Cuttino had gone from the fast lane in D.C. to a slowed-down existence about six hours south in sleepy North Carolina. He stayed with family—

aunts, uncles, and cousins on his father's side—but he itched to go home. He missed his parents. He hadn't heard much of anything in the way of news since he relocated down South.

Each day, he spent hours in front of his laptop scouring the Washington Post and other websites for any news from home. He spoke with his mother a couple of times each week, but with his father even less. When father and son did speak, they talked about everything but the family business.

Cuttino always asked, but his father dodged his questions by telling him something like, "Don't worry about things up here, son. I'm straightening all of this mess out."

"Yeah, Dad, I know you are, but I also know you need me up there. I could be helping you get everything straight on that end," Cuttino would counter. "And I'm ready to come home. You know I've been down here too long."

"Listen to me, son, where I need you is right where you are, you hear me?" he would say, ending all talk of Cuttino returning to D.C. "Just do what I ask, boy. And don't worry about it, your uncles are here watching my back just like they always have."

"Besides, I need you to have all the best fishing spots scoped out by the time I get down there," he would add, lightening the mood. "We'll have plenty of time for that, once we close all of this business out up here."

Each conversation went that way. Cuttino would hang up with his father, feeling powerless to do anything more than sit back, watch from a distance, and wait.

## *Chapter Thirty-Seven*

At the urging of his growling stomach, Cuttino hurried through a shower and headed from his third-floor room towards the kitchen. He used the same spiral staircase he'd played on as a child whenever he and his parents had visited the Big House. The huge Harrell Family estate in North Carolina had always been called the Big House for as long as he could remember.

He'd always carried happy memories from this house, such as playing and fishing with his cousins. And he remembered his Grandmother's cooking. Grandma Mimi could've made dog food taste like chocolate cake. He smiled whenever he thought of his grandmother. She'd passed away after a two-year bout with cancer when he was just a teenager, but he remembered her loving nature. All of those fond memories offered minimum comfort now as his thoughts drifted towards home.

The Beasley twins were seated at a black marble table in the family room, playing dominoes with his cousin, Boom. The three men were seated at separate rounded ends of the table, guarding their game pieces like treasure. Each man wore a scowl. The stakes had grown high in this game. Cousin Boom looked up, winked at him, and flashed a thin smile. That smile meant he was in the process of relieving the twins of all their pocket change. Cuttino's favorite cousin was known as the Harrell Family card and domino shark.

Cousin Boom's real name was McNeil Harrell, and while he took pride in his last name, he'd always hated the name McNeil. Boom had earned his nickname as an eleven-year-old little league linebacker. Each time he laid a crushing hit on one of the other kids, his mother yelled, "boom!" from the sidelines.

The name stuck, and Boom continued to live up to it all the way through high school and three years at UNC. In the final game of his junior year, a blown-out knee ended Boom's college career and NFL aspirations. Cuttino's father had paid the best doctors to repair Boom's knee to the point where he could resume playing. He tried, at first, but he never regained his raw animal lust for the sport. Boom held onto his nickname, but he left the game of football behind forever.

At the urging of his mother, Boom finished his four-year marketing degree and began working for the Family. He became Ezra Harrell's eyes and ears down south. Cuttino's father relied on Cousin Boom to keep a close eye on the family's dealings in that part of the country. He made sure the Harrell payroll in and around North Carolina remained intact and extensive. All Harrell shipments pushed up through the Carolina I-95 gateway en route to D.C. fell under his watchful eye.

Boom also ensured that Fuquay-Varina would always be a safe haven for the Harrells. He prevented any sizeable narcotics activity from being conducted within the borders of the peaceful country suburb. Any dealers that tried to set up shop in or around the small town were dealt with quick, fast, and in a hurry.

Cuttino knew his father trusted Cousin Boom and always had. The two men remained close to this day and spoke on at least a weekly basis.

"Mornin', baby!" Cuttino heard his great aunt Cecelia sing when he entered the kitchen.

She was at the stove with her back to him, but somehow, she'd known it was her youngest nephew entering the room.

"I thought I was gonna have to send one of the boys up to get you. You hungry?"

"Good morning, Aunt CeCe," Cuttino said, stooping to kiss the old woman on her cheek. "Where is everyone?"

"Well, you saw my crazy son out there hustlin' the twins as usual, and 'Nessa already left to take the kids to their day camp," Aunt CeCe said, referring to Vanessa, her daughter-in-law of the last seventeen years.

"The kids' camp is doing a daytrip to that Carowinds amusement park over in Charlotte. She volunteered to chaperone, so I expect they'll be gone until this evening."

Vanessa and Boom had four beautiful kids and had managed to build a happy family here in Fuquay-Varina. Feelings of guilt jabbed at Cuttino for having disrupted the peaceful environment they'd crafted for their children. For the last month, the kids had seen three strangers roaming around their house without even knowing why they were there.

Cuttino followed his aunt into the family room, helping her carry several large dishes piled high with a good, old-fashioned country breakfast. Like her late sister, Aunt CeCe knew how to throw down in the kitchen.

Crispy bacon, tender sausage, and fried and scrambled eggs with cheese filled a couple of the dishes. The remaining plates carried buttered biscuits, home fries, beef scrapple, grits, and stacks of Belgian cinnamon waffles with hot pecan syrup. It amazed Cuttino that even in her mid-seventies, Aunt CeCe could still cook like she did. At Ezra's insistence, she allowed a staff to manage the house chores and estate maintenance, but under one condition: she would continue to do all of the cooking herself.

"Damn, man," Iran said and slammed his dominoes on the table as Cuttino and Aunt CeCe brought in the plates. "Broke again."

Aunt CeCe cleared her throat and glared over the top of her thin glasses at him. "Iran, Taurus, or whichever one you are, what did I tell y'all about your mouths in this God-fearing house? Boy, don't think I'm too old or you are too big for me not to give you a taste of my switch."

"I'm sorry, Aunt CeCe," Iran apologized, "but I, we...well, Boom has been beatin' the brakes off me and Taurus since we got down here, you know? I mean we ain't won a game. Not one."

Aunt CeCe laughed because she knew what the big man said was true. "Well, you just watch your mouth and never mind all that anyway. Y'all clear this table of all this mess, it's time to eat."

She threw a sly smile in her son's direction. "I'm sure Boom will give y'all the chance to win back some of your money later on. Y'all shouldn't be gambling anyway in this house. Lord don't like all that mess. And that's why you losing all your chicken change. Lord have mercy on their souls, thank you, Jesus."

"Any news from home?" Cuttino said, taking the seat next to his aunt. "You talk to Dad, Cousin Boom?"

"Yup," Cousin Boom answered in his slow and deliberate drawl, "spoke to him last night for a few ticks." He stopped speaking as he scooped deep spoonfuls of cheese-eggs onto his plate.

Cuttino wanted to tell Boom to put down the damn eggs and spit out the news, but he respected his older cousin. He held his tongue and maintained his patience for the slowed down pace of the south.

"He told me thangs are gettin' worse back home, lil cuz," Cousin Boom said and grabbed a couple of biscuits.

"We lost more people in another stash house hit. Eight this time around. Whoever did it burned this one too. Left all the bodies inside again."

"Mm-mm-mm, Lord knows," Aunt CeCe said, shaking her head and covering her mouth with her hand. "Lord knows ain't no good can come from this mess."

"Ez also said he met with the other families again," Cousin Boom continued. "Nobody knows anything about who's droppin' bodies."

"So they say," Iran said.

"Somebody knows something," Taurus said, finishing his twin's thought.

"I should be home," Cuttino said. "Dad say anything about me coming home?"

"He left standing orders," Boom said. "Said he wants you to stay put. Wants you to wait till he gets down here. Said you won't be going back to D.C., period."

"Wait and do what?" Cuttino said. "Keep hearing day old news about our family's dead bodies? I should be home helping Dad fix this."

"And what you gon' do, lil cuz?" Boom said and pointed his fork at him. "What can you do that Ezra, Montae, and A.J. ain't already doing? No sir, what you need to do is cool out and follow your father's orders. He'll take care of this. He always has."

"Cuttino," Aunt CeCe said, "please listen to your cousin. And listen to your father too, baby. You're safe down here with us. It's what your father wants and you know we don't go against what Ezra wants."

An uncomfortable silence stretched across the next few minutes as Cuttino digested what his aunt and cousin had told him. They were right on both counts. There was nothing he could do, and no, they didn't go against his father's wishes. No one did.

"Ok, Boom, you and Aunt CeCe, both of you are right," he said. "It's just hard, I've never been away this long. Not like this and not with this kind of mess going on back home. I just feel like I should be doing something, you know?"

"We all feel like that," Boom said. "All of us. But we gotta stay the course on this and do our part. Ez knows what he's doin'. It'll work out. Trust in that."

"Yeah, I know it will. It's just tough sitting on the sidelines, but I know what's right and I'll stick with it."

"Cool. So wha's up cuz?" Boom twanged. "You want the next game or what? I don't have any pressing business till the afternoon and I'm sure you got a few chips I can snatch out of your pockets? Maybe losing your dough will help take your mind off that mess up north."

"Hmm. Maybe I'll steal your money a little later on, Boom," Cuttino said, allowing his attitude to shift some. "But I was thinking that it's about time for me to get out of this house and have a look around town. Since I'm stuck here and all, I might as well get reacquainted with the place."

# *Chapter Thirty-Eight*

Although the suburb of Fuquay-Varina was just a short drive from Raleigh, it seemed to exist in a world all by itself. Its population registered below twenty thousand, and much of its natural landscape had been well preserved. Fuquay-Varina's small-town, slowed-down pace made it the perfect nesting spot for the extended part of the Harrell family.

Each day crawled by at a snail's pace just like the one before in an uneventful and flat-out boring manner. After spending the first month milling around the Big House, Cuttino had begun to grow stir crazy.

With the Beasley brothers and his family watching his back around the clock, Cuttino started doing some exploring. He fished with his older and younger cousins when they weren't at work and summer camp. He also watched the summer "two-a-day" football practices at the local high school, remembering when he'd played for his high school's team. He even found a country diner named Melvin's that he began to frequent a couple of times a week. He enjoyed the food, but always made sure never to eat too much there so as not to offend his aunt.

One afternoon, he sat in Melvin's typing away on his laptop when he heard the diner's door open. He raised his head for a look when his nose caught the sweet scent of a perfume he couldn't place. The fragrance pulled his attention away from the computer's screen. What he saw made him forget what he'd been reading on his laptop moments earlier.

Walking towards the rear of the diner where he sat was a woman. But not just any woman, this one was absolutely stunning. She looked to be about five-foot-seven, with a slender, curvy build and the sexiest pair of legs he'd ever seen. Her brown shoulder length hair sported honey highlights and her mocha skin was smooth and flawless.

The mystery woman wore a linen pinstriped summer blazer with a white linen blouse underneath. Her toned legs flowed from beneath a tight brown skirt and into a pair of stylish chocolate-colored heels. She looked way out of place in this tiny suburb, and that was a damn good thing.

As she made her way to the table in front of his, their eyes met for a brief second. Cuttino thought he saw a slight smile escape from her otherwise all business expression. She placed a brown leather portfolio and her Louis Vuitton bag beside her as she slid into the booth facing his. Again, their eyes met; this time for a second or two longer. He was searching for something to say when she beat him to the punch.

"You know, it's impolite to stare without at least saying good morning," she said and smiled through full glossy lips. Cuttino could've sworn he felt electricity passing between their tables.

Cuttino returned her smile and nodded. "You're right, good morning," he said. "Sorry, I'm used to people moving too fast to even think about speaking."

"Wow, is that so?" she laughed. "Then you must not be from around here? Because everyone moves slow and says good morning in Fuquay-Varina."

"That's funny, because I was thinking the same about you. The not being from around here part, I mean."

"Good guess," she said, removing her glasses and placing them on the table. "No, I'm from the west coast, but I've made this my home."

"Well, I'm brand-new here and don't know too much about how things work down here in the South," he said, "but maybe you can teach me a little bit about southern hospitality?"

He knew he shouldn't be doing this. The last thing he needed was to be getting involved with a woman. He was supposed to be lying low until everything at home had been resolved. He, Iran, and Taurus had even picked up local cell phone numbers as part of their isolation. No one outside of the Harrell Family could reach them. But he'd gone without female interaction for far too long.

"Maybe. I might be able to show you a thing or two, you never know," she winked and laughed. "So, what's your name, Mr. Tourist?"

He wondered if he should give his real name, but he couldn't come up with a believable alternative, so he said, "It's Cuttino, and yours?"

"Cuttino? Ok, Mr. Cuttino, and what is it you do for yourself? You aren't with the circus that just rolled into town, are you? I'm not a big fan of clowns."

He laughed. She was beautiful and funny. "No, no, nothing like that. I don't sing, juggle, or perform magic. I'm down here on family business. Looks like I'll be here for a while."

"Well, aren't you lucky that I believe in southern hospitality, even though I wasn't born and raised in the south?"

"You know what? All of a sudden, I do feel extra lucky today," he said. "So, can I join you Miss, um...you never told me your name?"

"My name is Sidney, and I have a confession," she smiled her electric smile again and cast another wink in his direction. "I would love for you to join me."

## *Chapter Thirty-Nine*

For Cuttino and Sidney, their meeting at Melvin's diner had been just the beginning. Over the next three months, they spent every available moment of their time together. While she was at work, he hung with the family and the twins, doing everything he could to pass the hours. Their time apart crept along like a sputtering, broken down Pinto. When he was with her, the hours zoomed by and he tried to cling to each and every minute.

Before Sidney, Cuttino's investment in the area of love hadn't gone any deeper than temporary infatuation. The fast-lane life he'd loved since he was young had always trumped matters of the heart. That was why he and Michelle hadn't worked. Any woman who tried to get next to him had been pushed far to the right and into the slow lane. What he found himself experiencing now felt like tasting fresh water for the first time.

Sidney amazed him with her mind as much as her sheer physical sexiness. He'd never met a woman like her, and even more amazing was that he'd met her in this country suburb. But the timing for this couldn't be worse. In D.C., the family was fighting for their survival and here he was in North Carolina chasing a woman. He knew better than to be doing this, but against his mind's warnings, Cuttino Harrell had fallen in love.

More than four months had passed since he'd left D.C. His time with Sidney had helped him to all but forget about home. Almost. Truthfully, the troubles of his family never traveled far from Cuttino's thoughts.

* * * *

Shadows danced on the wall. The dull, blue glow from a nearby television cast dark images all around Cuttino's head. He lay alone in his bed, his thoughts busy and restless and keeping him from sleep. That evening, he'd had dinner with Sidney as usual and then dropped her off at home afterwards. His agreement with Cousin Boom made sure he returned to the Big House each night.

The clock on the TV screen showed 2:00 a.m. He was considering popping in a movie when his cell phone jumped to life. The screen's display read: **SIDNEY Mobile** and showed a picture of her smiling face. He snatched his cell off the nightstand and hit the green button on the touch screen to receive the call.

"Hey," he spoke into the phone, "what you doing up this late?"

"Cuttino?" she whispered. "Where are you?"

"I'm home." She sounded different than usual. "Why do you sound like that? Is everything alright?"

"No, everything isn't okay. I need you here with me."

"Sid, where are you?" he asked, sitting up now. Something was wrong. "Are you okay? Sid, do you hear me?"

"I'm at home, baby. Please come over. Hurry. Just come over right now, please!"

Before Cuttino could speak again, the line went dead. He looked at his phone:

**call ended**

*Hell, no...*

A feeling of terror began to suffocate him. Cuttino jumped out of his bed and pulled on jeans, a t-shirt, and sneakers. He dialed Sidney's number, but the call went straight to her cell phone's voicemail. His hands began to shake. Had his family's enemies found him despite all of his father's precautions and warnings? Had they been watching him with her? He'd known all along that their relationship was a bad idea. How could he have been so stupid and careless? There was no time for love when you were fighting your way out of hell.

He grabbed a loaded Berretta M9 and two extra magazines from the nightstand drawer at his bedside. He stuffed them into the waistband and pockets of his jeans and rushed down the stairs without waking Iran or Taurus. He could be running into a trap and knew he should wake them but pushed ahead without his two friends. Sidney's condo wasn't more than twenty minutes from the family's property. He'd call them on the way.

Frantic, he rushed out the dark house and sprinted to his black BMW 6-series parked in the driveway. He was a damn fool. He'd involved an innocent soul in his family's madness, and she would wind up paying the ultimate price for his selfishness.

Who the hell was doing this? How had they found them? Were they just trying to lure him out in the open? Maybe if he showed, they wouldn't harm her.

*Bullshit.*

He had to stop them or she would be dead either way. And so would he.

Cuttino started the BMW's ignition, threw the car in gear, and sped towards the main entrance of his family's estate. He stopped the car just long enough to signal the gate guard to let him through. The man looked as if he wanted to question him, but saw the look in his eye and thought better of it. He activated the necessary controls and opened the tall iron gate. Cuttino sped through the gate, made a quick right turn, and headed for the local highway.

"Just a few minutes," he told himself, "she's not that far away. Just a few quick minutes."

As soon as the car hit open road, he mashed down on the BMW's accelerator. The luxury sports coupe lurched and shot forward like a rocket on the wide stretch of road. The sheriff's department in Fuquay-Varina held a lucrative spot on The Harrell payroll, so he didn't think twice about being pulled over. He also didn't consider calling for their assistance either. The less attention he drew, the better.

Darkness enveloped the empty roads this time of night, and the lone worry was of deer crossing the roads. The car's headlights would hypnotize a stray doe or buck and a collision at ninety miles per hour would send them both into the afterlife.

He gunned the car through the pitch-blackness and almost flew past his exit. Veering the 6-series to the right, he exited the highway and two minutes later, turned into Sidney's condominium complex. He switched off the BMW's headlights and pulled up near her place where he saw a light glowing inside. Her green Toyota Camry sat in its assigned parking spot in front of her condo. He didn't see any movement in or around her place and as expected, the rest of the neighborhood was quiet.

The smartest move would be to call Iran and Taurus, but they would want him to wait outside until they arrived. There was no time. He sent a text message to their cell phones. They would read it and come right away, but he couldn't wait that long.

Sidney could be in serious trouble or worse. He wouldn't be able to live with himself if he could've saved her but had decided to play it safe and wait. Anything could be happening inside her home, and each second could mean the difference between her living and her dying. He made his decision. He was going inside.

Cuttino parked his car across the parking lot next to a dumpster and got out with his pistol in hand. Crouched low, he ran across the parking lot towards the single-story condo. He stopped just short of the walkway leading to Sidney's front door, hid behind two large bushes, and looked around again. Nothing. No movement and no noise.

Cursing, he stepped toward the left side of the front door. His damp t-shirt clung to him. The North Carolina summer yielded a harsh humidity even at night. Sweat trickled down his neck, back, arms, and face. He raised his hand to knock, but stopped when he noticed the door was already cracked. Bad sign.

Cuttino remembered the lessons his father had given him on how to use a pistol. He edged the door open with his left elbow, pistol high, expecting to be shot at or jumped on as he entered. The white fluorescents in Sidney's small fish tank provided the dim light he'd seen from the outside. There wasn't anyone in the living or dining rooms. He gripped the Berretta in both hands and swept the muzzle towards the kitchen; it too sat in an empty silence.

"Sidney? Where you at, baby?" he called out, worry tweaking the edges of his voice.

The only sound came from the flow of water running from the aquarium's filter into the tank. Cuttino cursed himself again for allowing this to happen. He should have never put Sidney in this position, knowing what he and his family were up against. He stepped towards the hallway leading to the two bedrooms and two bathrooms. There was a faint light creeping from under the closed door of the master bedroom.

"Sid?" he called out again in a hushed voice. "Where you at, girl?"

Again, there was no answer. She was dead, had to be. Someone had killed her, and he would find her body somewhere in her home. He opened the door to the bedroom, still aiming the weapon. Nothing. She wasn't there either. The bed wore fresh linens and looked as if no one had slept in it tonight. Had she been snatched?

Every muscle in his body tensed when he heard muffled music coming from the bathroom. He hesitated, afraid of what he would find, and then he reached for the doorknob.

The bathroom door swung open and a rush of warm air and glowing light greeted him. What he saw made his knees weak and forced him to lean his right shoulder on the doorjamb for balance.

# *Chapter Forty*

What looked like a hundred candles burned all around the bathroom, on the sink and the edge of the bathtub. The sweet aroma of burning incense mixed with the fragrant candles teased Cuttino's nose. The sound of Raheem DeVaughn's "Believe," floated from a nearby speaker and in the bathtub sat Sidney.

She wasn't dead, as he'd expected to find her. It was just the opposite. Instead, she sat with her back to him in a steaming bubble bath. Her hair was pulled up, and the candles cast a shiny outline on her slim neck and shoulders.

She turned halfway and smiled at him, "Surprise."

He managed to tuck his pistol in his waistband before she turned all the way around to face him. His chest tightened, and he struggled to catch his breath as she rose out of the water to greet him. Her perfect body glistened as the hot water dripped from it. Bubbles slid their way over her round breasts, across her flat stomach, and down past the magnificence between her thighs. In the short time they'd been seeing each other, he'd never seen Sidney like this. They had never even spent a night together.

"Damn, girl. I, I thought something was wrong over here," he stammered, trying to clear his throat. "Thought something might have happened to you."

"Oh, I'm sorry, baby," she said and smiled at him. "I wanted to surprise you, but I didn't mean to worry you. Don't be mad at me. I mean you can forgive me, right?" She winked just like she had the day they'd met.

"Woman," he said with a smile, "what am I gonna do with you? You know you scared the hell out of me, right? But seeing as how you went through all of this trouble, I guess maybe, I might be able to forgive you. Maybe."

"Well, I thought three months was definitely long enough for both of us to wait for this, and to be honest, I just didn't know how much more I could stand," she said and extended her hands out towards him. "So, for starters, why don't you come on over here and wash my back for me?"

Cuttino licked his lips, feeling a wave of relief wash over him, followed by a stirring in his crotch. It had been a long time since he'd felt the soft warmth of the opposite sex. Too long since he'd smelled the scent and savored the sweetness of a woman.

"Hold on, wait just a sec. I left the front door wide open," he said, backing out of the bathroom. "Let me get that locked up. Be right back."

He secured the front door, returned to the bedroom, and hid his pistol in between the mattresses of Sidney's bed. He also sent a text message to the twins telling them what happened and that he was okay. They would still come, but at least they wouldn't kick in Sidney's front door.

He came back into the bathroom and took Sidney in his arms as she walked towards him. She felt warm, slick, and soft, her body fitting into his shape just right. He kissed her lips and thought he might have just learned what the saying "heaven on earth" meant. As she removed his clothing and began kissing her way down his body, his world briefly stopped spinning on its troubled axis.

Right here, right now, everything felt just right. Keeping his lips glued to hers, Cuttino scooped Sidney into his arms and stepped into the large Jacuzzi style tub. He reached for the condom she was holding in her hand.

For the first time, they made love, exchanging a heat that put the burning candles to shame. Then, they enjoyed each other again for a second and third time in her bedroom before allowing sleep to consume them.

And for at least one night, as they lay in each other's arms, everything was just how it should be.

# *Chapter Forty-One*

Sidney hummed a Corinne Bailey Rae tune as she tapped away on her keyboard. The words on her flat-screen monitor flew by in a blur as her mind drifted away from the activity report she compiled. Cuttino Harrell occupied her thoughts.

The handsome man who'd fallen into her life still remained a mystery to her. She couldn't quite place it, but she knew there was much more to him than what he told her. He didn't talk much about his family or their business. He preferred to listen to her drone on and on about her business, life, hopes, and dreams. It all felt so different from what she'd experienced in the past, in a very, very good way.

Still, she'd tried to take her time getting to know Cuttino, using caution as she swam into deep waters with him. But in the short time they'd known each other, he'd stirred something in her. Something she hadn't felt in a long time. Something she'd believed was long dead. Feelings buried so deep she'd forgotten just how high they could make her float.

The phone on her desk rang, and she reached for it without bothering to look at the caller ID. The clock on her office wall read 11:40 a.m. She was expecting Cuttino to call when he was ready to pick her up for lunch. Butterflies fluttered in her stomach, and she felt like a teenage girl experiencing her first high school crush.

She snatched up the phone's receiver before the first ring ended and said, "Gannes and Chase Investment Management, Ms. Barnes."

"Hey, pretty girl," she heard a man's voice say.

She felt herself blush and started to reply, "Hey you" before her mind halted her tongue. Her girlish grin faded as she recognized the voice on the other end of the phone. It didn't belong to Cuttino. To her surprise and disgust, it belonged to an unwanted blast from her past.

Sidney wanted to hang up the phone, slam it back down into its cradle. She wanted to disconnect the line as if that would once again disconnect this part of her past. She could do it, too. That wasn't the problem. But the memories would still be there. That wasn't the problem, either. She'd learned how to cope, how to deal with the memories, how to lock them away enough to allow her to function. The problem lay on the other end of the phone she held in her hand.

Her past had found her, despite how far she'd run from it. If she knew anything, she knew hanging up the phone couldn't make this go away.

With a loud sigh, Sidney exhaled what felt like a lifetime's worth of misery. Her eyes watered, and her stomach began to churn. In an instant, all of her nervous excitement had deteriorated into a familiar feeling of dread.

"Rico," she said, all of her morning joy gone, her smile replaced by a frown. "How did you find me, and what do you want?"

"Damn baby, don't sound so happy to hear from me," Rico Pettysworth said. "Don't I get a better hello after all this time?"

He couldn't be serious. After everything he'd done to her, he had the nerve to call her and act like they were old friends playing catch-up?

"I said, what... do... you... want?" Sidney repeated her question through gritted teeth this time as she tried to maintain her composure. "I'm at work and can't talk. Why are you calling here? How did you get this number?"

"Yeah, I know you at work baby-doll, but you ain't gotta be so damn rude, girl," he said, ignoring her question. "And who the hell is Sidney Barnes? Your name is Cheri Granger, girl. I mean, this is Cheri, ain't it?"

"Don't call me that."

"Call you what?" Rico said with a laugh, "Your damn name? I swear that's what's wrong with our people today. We always tryin' to forget who we are. Finally had a brotha for President and still can't act right. Mm mm mm... make no damn sense. You see he didn't change his name to please no damn body, and he still won. Your momma named you Cheri, so your name is Cheri to me. Forever. How about that?"

"I know what my mother named me, Rico. But I can't go by that name anymore, can I?" she said, lowering her voice into a whisper. "Your evil ass made sure of that, didn't you? What the hell do you want, Rico?"

"I missed you, baby," he said. "I want to see you. It's been way too long. Eight long years."

This was a game to him. How did he get out?

"I'm hanging up, Rico. You can go to hell. Don't call me again."

"Go to hell?" Rico laughed. "I just spent the last eight years in hell because of your ass! If it wasn't for my damn good behavior and my rehabilitation to become an upstanding citizen, I would still be in hell."

"Well, you can go back there. I'm sure they miss you. Goodbye."

"Cheri!" Rico's voice boomed, all of the playfulness evaporating from his voice like water beneath the hot sun. "Don't you hang up this damn phone on me, girl!"

Sidney flinched, but remained determined to stand tall. "I'm not scared of you anymore, Rico. Them days are long gone. Things have changed, and that shit don't work over here anymore. I'm not the same little girl I used to be."

"Look here, Cheri, I don't give a damn about all that change shit you talkin' about," he said. "But I know you had better not hang up this damn phone. That wouldn't be a smart career move for you Cheri, Sidney, or whatever the hell your name is these days. That wouldn't be too smart at all, and I think you know this."

She stopped herself from hanging up the phone. There was no point in it. He obviously knew where she worked and maybe where she lived.

"How did you find me?"

"Hell girl, I ain't ever lost you." Rico said, laughing again. "You can run, but you can't hide. You should know me better than that. All this new ID shit you got working don't mean nothing. Hell, you think going by your middle name and your mom's maiden name could help you hide? Yeah, maybe it threw me off a lil bit, but not for too long."

"What do you want from me, Rico? Why are you contacting me? Why? Why can't you just leave me alone?"

"What do I want? Hell, I want you, girl. Always have and always will. But for starters, I need some money. Some cheese, moolah, dollar-dollar bill, goddammit! Shoot, seeing as how I just got out and all. Hell, I'm broke as a joke."

"I'm not giving you anything, Rico."

"Oh, yeah? You not giving me anything, huh?" Rico chuckled. "Yeah okay, well how about I come around and start creating problems around some of them uppity-ass folks you work for? Would you like that, baby-girl?"

"No," she whispered, feeling cornered. "No, I wouldn't like that."

"Good. That's good to hear," Rico said. "About time you stop tripping and get some act right in you."

"What do you want from me?"

"I already told you. Damn, girl, I see you still don't listen, huh? Look here, I'm gonna call you real soon so we can talk about the future. Our future."

"Future? We don't have a future, Rico. All we have is a raggedy past. One that I thought I'd gotten rid of."

"Whatever, Cheri. There ain't no getting rid of what we got. You just be ready for my call. Don't think about not answering, and don't think about changing your numbers or going anywhere or any of that shit. And *do not* contact the police, girl. Don't do it. We got business, me and you."

"Rico, don't do this. Just stop, please."

"Don't do what? Come on, Cheri, this is me. You know me, and you know how we do. So, I'll talk to you soon, baby-doll. Real soon."

The line went dead, and Sidney sat in her seat, too shocked to move, frozen by fear. She wanted to scream. She should call the police, but she couldn't. She wanted to call Cuttino, but he didn't know about this part of her past. Not many people did. She never spoke of Rico and the things he'd done. He was the last person on earth she ever wanted to hear from. She'd run, but he'd found her. Somehow, this psychopath had tracked her down.

Five minutes ago, she'd been humming a song about falling in love. But after Rico's surprise phone call, her world felt as if it was falling apart all around her.

From sunshine to torrential rain in the blink of a damn eye, life always has a way of turning itself upside down. The worst part? You get taken right along for the rollercoaster ride each and every time.

## *Chapter Forty-Two*

Sidney Barnes had been born Cheri Sidney Granger. She'd grown up as the middle child with two older sisters and one younger brother. When she was born, her father had been an Air Force pilot stationed at Los Angeles Air Force Base in California.

During the first ten years of her childhood, the Grangers moved up and down the west coast and overseas. The family lived all over before settling down in Los Angeles after Major Gregory Granger retired.

Cheri finished up high school in the City of Angels and then enrolled in the University of Southern California. It was there where her life had been flipped upside down for the first time.

She met Rico Pettysworth at USC during her sophomore year. He was a junior at USC taking the same management course as Cheri. The two connected right away although Rico was her polar opposite. He was bold and brash, having been raised on the streets of South Central. His grit and good looks excited Cheri and drew her in like a moth to a flame. He came into her life and swooped her out of the rigid, sheltered existence her parents had always imposed on her. Growing up in a military family had kept her disciplined, but also shy and naive when it came to men.

It wasn't long before her life existed around Rico. She stopped going home on weekends and soon enough, her grades slipped. Near the end of the summer after her junior year, she found out she was pregnant. She was too scared to tell her parents about the news, afraid of disappointing them. Rico pressured her to tell her family about the pregnancy and their plans to drop out of school to begin a family. When she refused, a whole new side of the man she loved raged to the surface.

She considered abortion, but when she tried to talk to Rico about it, he became furious and lashed out at her. He accused her of trying to kill his baby. She tried to explain that while she wasn't sure what to do about the baby, she couldn't drop out of school. He hadn't wanted to hear any of it. He told her to stay away from him and to do whatever she wanted with the baby. Pain, confusion, and sadness attacked her heart.

Cheri's relationship with Rico came to a horrific conclusion three weeks later. She hadn't heard from or seen him around campus until he showed up drunk at her apartment late one evening. He forced his way into her apartment demanding to have sex with her. When she asked him to leave, he pulled out a pistol. He forced her into the bedroom where he raped and beat her.

After he was done, Rico left the apartment, leaving Cheri battered, violated, and in serious need of medical attention. The next morning, a neighbor noticed the apartment's front door standing wide open. He peeked his head in and found her unconscious and bleeding on the living room floor.

When she regained consciousness the next day, she was in the hospital. The doctors told her about the miscarriage. Her baby was gone. She never had the chance to tell Rico about her decision to keep their child.

The police arrested him a week later hiding in his old neighborhood. At her parent's insistence, Cheri pressed full charges against the man she'd thought she would marry one day.

The subsequent trial proved to be a test of her sanity as the lawyers forced her to relive that awful night. After eleven long months, a jury found Rico guilty, and a judge sentenced him to serve time in the state prison. He received fifteen years for rape, assault with a deadly weapon, and attempted murder.

Despite California's fetal homicide law beneath the U.S.'s Unborn Victims of Violence Act, the jury had failed to convict him of feticide. The defense brought up the lack of evidence supporting the time frame surrounding Cheri's pregnancy. The lawyers contended that the embryo hadn't reached the week nine fetal stage, which by California law prevented prosecution for homicide. The jury had been forced to cast the charge aside.

Rico's arrest, conviction, and jail sentence were the beginning of Cheri's recovery. She needed more than a year of therapy, physical and emotional, to begin moving on with her life. Part of her healing included the decision to alter her name and move away from the west coast. Rico was locked away, but she needed more than that to begin feeling safe again. Her family protested, wanting her to move back home, but she insisted this was the best thing for her.

After changing her name, Sidney relocated to North Carolina where she finished her degree in business management. Upon graduation, Gannes and Chase Investment Management Corporation offered her an entry-level position. She spent the next four years rebuilding her life and climbing the corporate ladder. She was now a regional manager at Gannes and Chase.

Things had gotten so much better for her. She'd healed herself and had even found a man who loved her. Now, eight years after that terrible night, Sidney's nightmarish past had forced its way into her peaceful present.

# *Part V*

# *"BAD INTENTIONS…"*

**For man also knoweth not his time: as the fishes that are taken in an evil net, and as the birds that are caught in the snare; so [are] the sons of men snared in an evil time, when it falleth suddenly upon them.**

- *Ecclesiastes 9:12*

# *Chapter Forty-Three*

***Rosslyn, Virginia...***

Death had finally decided to play its trump card. The entire thing happened so fast that the memory of it would seem like nothing more than a dreadful blur. In the span of a few short minutes, the untouchable became the touchable. The hunter became the hunted...

A harmony of rain fell from the bellies of a chorus of dark clouds gathered overhead. A killer's rain. Swollen drops rushed from the heavens in mass, stripping away the humidity clinging to the nighttime air.

The downpour penetrated the layers of oil and grime coating the blacktop and washed it away in a rainbow-tinted rinse. Thunder clapped and fingers of lightening stretched and wiggled their way through the blackness. This summer storm set the table for tonight's meal: an appetizer of panic, a main course of pain, and for dessert? A few last breaths, one or two last words, and maybe one final prayer of repentance.

* * * *

It was just after 10:00 p.m., and Ezra Harrell was concluding today's business and preparing to leave his office for the night. He'd put in another long day and retirement couldn't get here soon enough. As always, he and two of his guards would leave through his private exit. The trio would go down a set of stairs and come out into a rear lot. Donnie would be waiting there to meet them.

Heavy thoughts of the failed talks with his brothers and the members of The Syndicate bogged down his mind tonight. Questions about his family's future also loomed. What had he allowed his city to become? Rather, what in the hell had he helped make his city into? He was, after all, responsible for the madness surrounding him.

His search for a better life for his family had led them all down a path of destruction. He couldn't change the past, but he'd hoped to control the future. So far, his attempts to leave this life behind were being blocked by two of the people he wanted to save.

What could he do to convince his brothers that this was the right move for the Harrell Family? He needed to make them see things the way he did. It was too late in the game, and as much as he loved his two brothers, they left him with no choice. If he had to, he would dismantle the *entire* SNC. He would leave Montae and A.J. with nothing and force them to come with him.

Ezra's troubles pulled him inside his head and monopolized his thoughts to the point where he did something he'd never done. And would never have the chance to do again. For the first time in years, he allowed his guard to drop.

As he and his guards exited the building, he failed to notice that the parking lot was much darker than usual. The nearby streetlights that always cast a dull orange shine throughout the alley all seemed to be malfunctioning. Some flickered while others cast distorted shadows. His bodyguards, feeling fatigued and caught up in the monotony of their routine, had also allowed their awareness to falter. By the time Ezra's natural instincts warned of trouble, it was already too late.

* * * *

Donnie Gainsford had known something was wrong when he couldn't reach the two guards assigned to watch the outside of the building. Mr. Ezra always called when he was ready to leave his office. The call had come at least twenty minutes ago, and the guards should've returned by now.

Each night, when the call came, the two outside guards would leave their posts to perform one last perimeter sweep. Meanwhile, the two inside guards would escort Mr. Ezra down to the rear parking lot. Then all four guards would follow behind Donnie and Mr. Ezra in a second vehicle.

This had been the normal routine for years, four men plus Donnie watching Mr. Ezra's back. No problem. But with recent events, Donnie had wanted to add extra security. He'd made sure a mobile rover carrying five more guards stood on standby a couple of blocks away.

Everything had been going according to routine until the two outside guards hadn't returned from their area check. Then, his cell phone had stopped working. For the second time in the last ten minutes, he tried each of the men on their cell phones.

Again, neither call connected. When he tried the inside men and Mr. Ezra with the same result, a shudder of anxiety rippled through him. He'd received the call from Mr. Ezra, but now his phone wasn't working at all. Something was for damn sure wrong. All of a sudden, he felt isolated and alone.

*What the hell was going on here?*

Donnie drove the Cadillac Escalade from its normal parking spot out to the alley opening. If someone was coming, he didn't want to be a sitting target or risk being boxed in the parking lot. The building's parking garage offered a better hiding place, but he didn't want to risk being trapped in there, either.

No, he would secure Mr. Ezra first, and then he could come back for the Cadillac. If he had to, he would hustle his boss up the alley to where he'd left the Escalade parked. Worst case, if there was trouble, everyone could wait inside the building until the rover arrived. If he didn't call within the next thirty minutes, the five extra guards would make their way to the building.

The longtime Harrell driver and bodyguard looked both ways down the deserted main street. There was still no sign of the two guards. He tried to use his phone again. Still no signal. He wanted to believe, as he always had, that no one would be stupid enough to come after Ezra Harrell. That belief no longer felt rock solid.

After parking the Escalade, he exited the vehicle and pulled off his navy-blue suit jacket and burgundy tie. Tossing both onto the driver's side seat, he hurried around to the passenger side. He checked his Ruger LC9 and retrieved a Taurus .45 ACP from a concealed compartment in the SUV's dashboard.

Donnie's heart began to thunder in his chest. Perspiration saturated his white dress shirt. All of his years on these streets told him something bad was on the way. He could feel it, damn near smell it.

With both pistols drawn, he started back down the alley towards the rear exit of the office building. He wasn't sure if someone waited to ambush them and knew it was best to remain as hidden and quiet as possible. The two guards still hadn't returned. It wasn't long before he knew why.

Midway down the alley, he found their lifeless bodies beneath a stack of trashcans, garbage bags, and cardboard boxes. An ugly bullet wound scarred the forehead of each man.

*Goddammit…*

He wanted to double back for the Cadillac, but there was no time. Mr. Ezra would come out of his entrance any minute, and Donnie wouldn't let his boss walk into a trap.

He scanned the area surrounding the alley. Darkness covered all directions, but everything appeared to be clear. The secluded alleyway leading up to the private entrance also looked deserted. The heavy rain continued to fall. He checked his cell phone again. Nothing.

He had to find a way to contact his boss and warn him to stay inside until he could secure the area. Mr. Ezra wouldn't need to call again unless he had a change in plans and needed to stay upstairs a while longer.

Time was almost up. He picked up the pace and moved deeper into the alleyway, ready to open up on anyone he didn't recognize as friendly. There was nothing there. But there had to be something. Someone had killed those two guards and dumped their bodies.

He reached the end of the alley and saw the door to the rear entrance slide open. The first guard stepped into the parking lot followed by Mr. Ezra and the second guard.

*Out of time...*

Donnie managed to yell, "GET BACK INSIDE!" just before the unthinkable happened.

# *Chapter Forty-Four*

A barrage of gunfire rang out and ripped through the first bodyguard, chopping him down with shots to his midsection and head. Then four, maybe five, shooters emerged out of the shadows at the opposite end of the large parking lot.

Donnie's previous feeling of alarm launched into all-out horror; he should've seen this coming. But he'd missed it. He failed in his duties, and now they were trapped on the target end of a damn shooting range.

Dropping into a firing position, he clicked on the LC9's laser sighting and fired several shots at the gunmen. He'd been a decent marksman since his days in Uncle Sam's army. Two of his 9mm rounds found a home, hitting one of the shooters square in the chest. The man tumbled backwards and buckled to the ground.

The other gunmen ducked for cover and began returning fire in his direction, pinning him against the brick wall of the alleyway. Kneeling behind a dumpster to his right, Donnie returned fire at the gunmen with both of his pistols. He had to find a way to get Mr. Ezra to safety. This quiet alleyway in Rosslyn had disintegrated into a shootout scene straight out of a Hollywood movie script.

From where he crouched, Donnie could see his boss and the remaining guard. They were both alive but pinned down behind a wall about ten feet from the entrance of the building. The guard had stepped in front of Mr. Ezra, but both men took turns firing at their attackers.

The gunmen were fanning out in a half circle to gain a wider target range. This maneuver would make it impossible for the wall to continue shielding Mr. Ezra and the guard from the gunfire. Donnie also knew that the wider the gunmen spread-out, the harder it would be for him to reach the two men. He needed to do something fast. Or they would all die right here in the next few minutes.

Donnie waited until the gunman closest to him needed to reload. Then, he made his move. With as much strength as he could muster, he tried to push the dumpster towards the parking lot. He pushed, grunted, and pushed some more. The dumpster's wheels squealed and began turning as the oversized trashcan began to budge.

The falling rain made the ground slippery, but he managed to steer the dumpster away from the wall. He angled the dumpster lengthwise so it rolled between him and the shooters as he pushed it into the lot. Mr. Ezra and the guard must have picked up his idea because they began making their way towards him.

The gunfire continued to spray from both sides of the parking lot. Donnie's ears rang from the harsh sound of bullets slamming into the metal dumpster. He continued to return fire as he made his way closer to Mr. Ezra's location. It was slow moving, but he pushed the dumpster until his senior citizen body all but quit on him. He was about twenty feet from the two men and signaled them to make ready to move.

He and the bodyguard fired at the gunmen while Mr. Ezra made his way towards the dumpster. He stopped to try the building's entrance again, but the sliding doors wouldn't open. Gunfire had damaged the entrance's electronic mechanism.

Donnie caught Mr. Ezra's eye and waved him towards him as he kept firing at the gunmen. He saw a second gunman go down, but then he saw the last bodyguard fall a minute later. The guard had taken multiple hits and lay unmoving in a puddle of rain. Dead.

"What the hell, Don?" Donnie heard his boss ask after he'd made it behind the dumpster. "Where did they come from?"

"Don't know," he wheezed, still out of breath. "But we gotta move. All of our guards are dead. I found the bodies of the other two. I'm damn near out of bullets here, and them boys are closing in fast."

He continued to return fire and had to yell over the loud gunfire and drumming rainfall.

"We won't be able to hold 'em off much longer," he said. "We gotta get you outta here."

"Okay, Don. What's the move?" Mr. Ezra said, tossing aside his empty pistol. "Where's the rover?"

"I got the Cadillac parked past the opening of the alley towards the right side," he said. "We gotta get to it and get the hell outta here. Ain't been able to reach the rover, phones ain't workin'. Hoping they will come soon, but we can't afford to wait."

He reached into his pocket and handed his boss the Escalade's keys.

"Here you go, Mr. Ezra," he said, looking him in the eye. "Just in case."

"I'm not leaving you behind, Don," Mr. Ezra said, "that's not how this goes. We're getting outta here in one piece, and then we'll deal with these dudes after we go get some help."

"Okay, boss. We gotta move. You get down that alley, keep your back pressed to the left wall, stay in the shadows. I'll cover you. Then, I'll be right behind you."

For the first time, he'd lied to his longtime employer. Truth was, his old body had carried him as far it could go. Even under normal circumstances, he would slow Mr. Ezra down. And these circumstances were far from normal. He was tired, and worst of all, he'd been shot. The excruciating pain from the bullet lodged in his left knee told him following his boss would be impossible.

"Don, you can't walk on that leg," Mr. Ezra said when he noticed Donnie's knee. "I'm helping you get out of here."

"How long have we been doing this, boss?" Donnie asked. "I ain't never once left your side, and I don't plan on doing that just yet. We got retirement staring us in the face. But if you try and help me, these boys will be all over us and shoot us dead for sure. Does the family no good if you get killed. No good at all."

"Okay, Don," Mr. Ezra said after a long hesitation.

He placed a hand on Donnie's shoulder. "I'll be waiting for you at the beginning of the alley. You come right behind me, and I'll cover you."

"Yes sir, I will," Donnie said and put the last of the magazines in each of his pistols.

He handed the .45 to Mr. Ezra. "Go on, boss, take it. I'll make sure you're clear. Then, I'll see you in a few."

He struggled to stand, exhaustion and pain causing him to grit his teeth with every move. He propped himself up on one leg and looked over the top of the dumpster. The three remaining gunmen had advanced to within thirty feet of their location.

"Go! Go now!" he yelled and started firing again at the gunmen. "Get out of here!"

Mr. Ezra didn't budge at first, and then he turned and headed up the alley. Donnie watched him for a second. Then, he said a silent prayer and gathered the last bit of his strength.

## *Chapter Forty-Five*

Ezra heard the dueling gunfire erupting in full competition, Donnie's pistol fire versus the rat-tat-tat of automatic gunfire from the shooters. Why hadn't the police been notified? Ezra would have welcomed police intervention at this point. And where was his mobile rover? Shouldn't they have been here by now? How the hell had this happened?

Just as he reached the middle of the alley, he looked back and saw something that froze him in his tracks. Donnie wasn't following him. Instead, he was still trying to fight off the gunmen. Ezra watched as his friend fired the last of his ammunition. He'd hit another of the gunmen, but there were still two left.

The remaining gunmen closed in from both sides. Donnie staggered and looked as if he'd taken a couple of bullets himself. Ezra started to go and help him when he saw one of the gunmen fire several bullets into his friend's chest. The force of the gunshots slammed Donnie up against the dumpster, and then his limp body slumped to the ground.

Ezra felt his heart stop. The stabbing pain in his chest made him feel as if he'd taken those bullets himself. Tears blurred his vision, and he clenched his teeth so hard his jaws ached. His hands formed into fists, and he reached for the pistol Donnie had given him. He wanted to charge back down the alleyway and blow as many holes in the two gunmen as he could.

It didn't matter who they were anymore. He wanted to kill them. He wanted to spill their blood and watch it mix with the rainwater falling from the sky. They had attacked him and executed one of the few men he considered a friend.

Donnie had been a mentor and an advisor. He'd been a father figure and had just sacrificed his life for him. Ezra wanted revenge, and he would have it. But he knew he couldn't do it this way. If he went into that alley and came up dead, then Donnie and his guards would've died for nothing.

They had sacrificed their lives for him. Ezra would avenge their deaths, but he would have to be as smart as he'd always been. Whatever it took, however long it took, he would find whoever was responsible for this and put them in the ground.

He ran out of the alley towards where Donnie said he'd parked the Cadillac. The gunmen would be coming his way. He saw the Escalade waiting in the shadows and reached in the pocket of his suit pants for the SUV's keys. The rain penetrated his suit just as the pain of watching his friend die had penetrated his heart.

The vehicle's engine started, and its doors unlocked when he pushed the button on the keyless remote. He didn't want to leave his friend's body, but he had no choice. If he didn't leave, he knew he would end up beside Donnie on a steel slab in the city morgue.

He reached for the door handle but was yanked backwards by what felt like a vise grip locked on his left shoulder. He tried to turn, but couldn't move. A strong arm locked around his neck. He reached for the .45, but something smacked his hand away. Then, a fist, as heavy as a dumbbell, pounded into his chest. The air blew from his lungs and was replaced by a throbbing agony.

As he struggled to catch his breath, Ezra felt himself being jerked off his feet. A blistering pain seized him as a white-hot current of electricity surged and ran wild throughout his entire body.

He heard himself cry out. His body went rigid and then began to spasm just before he collapsed to the rain-soaked ground. His vision blurred, his face went slack, and his convulsing arms and legs went limp. So, this was what death felt like.

As he slipped into darkness, Ezra saw a husky, powerful-looking man standing over him.

He heard the man say, "Good evening, Mr. Harrell. I've been waiting for you. We have some serious business to tend to, deadly serious, I'm happy to say."

Ezra had to struggle to keep his eyes open. He saw his attacker smile and heard him laugh. After that, he couldn't see or hear anything.

Then, Ezra Harrell's world faded to black.

# *Chapter Forty-Six*

"W-whoever...you...a-are..." Ezra said, his words slurred as he tried to shake the grogginess from his head. "You...must...be...c-crazy...do you know who the hell I am?"

His swollen and sore mouth felt like it was filled with cotton balls. From head to toe, his entire body hurt. He felt his heart jack-hammering in his chest as fear tightened its grip on him.

The blindfold across his eyes and the handcuffs anchoring him to a chair made sure he couldn't see or move. But lack of sight and mobility didn't stop Ezra's sense of feeling. The pain ravaged him, making him nauseous and dizzy.

The bullet wounds in both of his thighs and arms felt like hell. The oozing blood from the wounds combined with his sweating had worked to soak through his clothing. He was surprised he hadn't bled all the way out. It felt like a couple of his ribs were cracked, and each breath he drew in felt like a gut punch. Stinging cuts and raw bruises molded his bloated face and would have made clear vision difficult even without the blindfold.

Consciousness had visited Ezra, left him, and then visited him again. He had no real concept of time and no idea how long his kidnappers had been holding him. The first time he'd come to, they had kicked, punched, and even shot him until he blacked out. Then, when he'd regained consciousness again, they had started up again. This had happened at least twice so far, but Ezra couldn't be sure. The craziest thing was that they weren't asking him for anything. They were just beating the hell out of him.

Today's hip-hop songs all talked about dying like a real gangster, going out in a storm of gunfire, and meeting Death head-on. But in real life, when Death tapped you on the shoulder, even the hardest man would start singing a different song. He didn't want to die, not tonight, not like this.

Ezra could hear the footsteps and talking of the cowards who had ambushed him outside of his office. The last thing he remembered was the electroshock from what had to be some sort of stun gun or taser. His attackers had tossed him in the back of a van and sped away before he knew what happened to him.

*Where are my guards? Where's Donnie?* he'd thought as he rolled around semi-conscious and helpless on the filthy floor of the van. Then, it all came back to him.

He'd seen Donnie and his guards die in the rain-drenched alley outside his building. He'd seen his friend and his guards slaughtered, and he hadn't done a thing about it. Donnie hadn't deserved that type of death. His soldiers hadn't either. He'd watched, but he'd failed to act.

"What the hell you want from me?" he asked now to anyone that was listening. He received nothing but silence as an answer.

"Say something, man. I know you know who I am. You gotta know my folks will be coming for me. You gotta know that, right? What's this about? Money? Dope?"

Silence. They were enjoying this, hearing him beg and watching him squirm like a fish on dry land.

After a few long minutes, he heard one of the cowards speak. "Let 'em come, Mr. Harrell. It'll make our job that much easier. Either way, you're a dead man. All of your money and power don't mean shit at this point."

Right then and there, Ezra knew it was game over for him. Despite all of his clout and money in and around D.C., he had nothing left to use as a bargaining chip.

Someone had put these killers on a mission, and that someone carried way more juice than even him. He tried one last time to free himself, hoping for a miracle, but the sting of his wounds killed that idea. His broken body had nothing left to give.

In his remaining minutes, he remembered all of the people and the things he loved. He thought of Liv. She was his wife, lover, and partner in life. Against his better judgment, he'd allowed her to remain in D.C. instead of sending her away with their son. What would happen to his angel with him gone? Had they already gotten to her? What would happen to his boy? His brothers? How would the Harrells survive now?

The best memories of his family and the sights, sounds, and smells of his city flooded his mind. He remembered better times than now and tried to forget his list of regrets.

He thought about the lives he'd destroyed by being who he was and by living the way he had. There was nothing he could do about those who were dead and gone. It was all part of the game.

A game he'd wanted to quit. You live this life until you can't live it anymore. Then you get out, before the life gets you. He'd tried to get out, but this life wouldn't let him go. All part of the game.

Right before his life came to an end, he managed one final thought: "What's going to happen to my family?"

He would never know the answer to his question. The last thing he heard was the click-clack pump-action and ear-shattering roar of what sounded like a shotgun being fired at close-range.

The last thing he felt was the searing pain.

The 12-gauge buckshot tore into his upper-body, neck, and face, destroying bone and muscle and creating an explosion of blood and tissue.

And then there was nothing. No more sounds, no more thoughts or feelings. His blindfold had come loose.

In death as in life, Ezra's eyes remained wide open, but now they were vacant, soulless windows.

The life of D.C.'s underground king had come to the harshest of ends without any of the ceremonious celebration befitting of royalty. He'd been met with the most ruthless of judgments parallel to the way he'd lived his life. And now that life was over, and Ezra Harrell had joined the ranks of the dead and gone.

*Live by the gun and breathe your last breath on the business end of one.*

# *Part VI*

## *"HERE IS GONE..."*

*"Touching GOD"*

**Life lived fast until life runs out...**
**Reclaimed by its origin...**
**and erasing all doubt...**
***...Touched from above...***
**From beneath the big light**
**into the shadows**
**an end to the fight...**

## *Chapter Forty-Seven*

Everything was coming together just as Lucas Meadows had planned. He'd completed the first part of this assignment with nothing more than a few minor hiccups.

He'd lost a few of the shooters he'd subcontracted but he didn't give a damn about them anyway. If the idiots had followed his instructions with the same preciseness with which he'd relayed them, they would've survived. But they hadn't listened, had they?

Those amateurs were too slow with their positioning, too inaccurate with their shooting; just too imprecise all the way around. So, they got what was coming to them. Let it be a lesson to the rest of their crew to follow orders exactly as they were given.

What he wouldn't give to have a few of his Devil Dogs from the last battalion he'd commanded. Now, those were some headhunting, no shit-taking, motherfuckin' killers if he'd ever seen any. With a couple of his Marines in that alley, there wouldn't have been any mistakes. But that wouldn't happen, would it? His life as a Marine officer was long over and best left in the past. That life carried far too many anchors and held too steep of a price to remain connected to.

All in all, it had been a good showing considering what he'd had to work with personnel-wise. At least the equipment supplied by his contact had worked just as he'd been promised it would. The automatic rifles, night vision goggles, and military grade cell phone and GPS jamming device had all worked to perfection. Even the stun gun had come in handy. He'd snatched Harrell and gotten out of dodge before the police or anyone else could get there.

His contact had also told him that he wouldn't need to worry about Harrell's back-up crew. Another promise kept. He hadn't seen any sign of them the entire night. Not that he couldn't have taken care of them himself if they had showed up.

He'd known Harrell would be well protected, but his driver had surprised him. *Pleasantly, in fact.* He'd thought the old man would be the first to go. He should've known better. Wisdom and experience had a way of trumping youth and energy most times.

Harrell's driver had been a pretty good shot, too. He'd managed to take out two of the shooters before the rest of those clowns got to him. Minor losses. The job had gotten done just as his employer had requested. That was what mattered. The Clean had hunted and killed the big game once again, but this wasn't over. Far from it.

There were many more bodies to drop before this contract would be fulfilled. This meant plenty of cash funneling in his overseas accounts. The more the better. Money paved the road to his second retirement and the real life he deserved. But first, there was work to finish, then a few lingering debts to settle, and then the enjoyment of life in earnest.

The 747 took its cue from the tower, taxied down the runway, and began the 6 a.m. flight from Dulles International Airport. In a few hours he would be home.

At last, Lucas let himself relax just a little. He'd rid himself of the disguise he'd worn for the past few weeks only to don another, less complicated one. He wouldn't allow his true self to shine through until he was in his domain, safe and sound.

Since he'd been forced to work with outsiders on this job, his disguise had required much more detail this time around. The team he subcontracted needed to remain unaware of his true identity for his sake and theirs. His normal sunglasses, baseball cap, and facial hair hadn't been sufficient. He'd used all of those and more.

The silicone prosthetic mask and the body shaping gear had served their purposes in excellent fashion. He was sure no one could tell his true physical appearance. He'd even feigned a Caribbean accent.

*Good shit all the way around,* he thought and allowed himself to feel pleased with the job's progress up to this point.

Lucas was also happy to be leaving D.C., at least for the time being. This trip had been his third one in the last few months. After the first two hits on the corner boys, he'd left D.C. right away. A month or so later, his employer had requested a similar operation. Lucas had done that op, left D.C. again, and waited until he received his next set of orders.

After completing this latest hit, he was following the same routine: get the hell out of D.C. Fly home and wait. The waiting part was tedious, but well worth the money.

His employer had yet to send the details on the next stage of the job, which forced Lucas to again be patient. Like the previous two times, he'd paid the amateurs and told them to lay low until he made contact again. He was paying them an excellent rate and had no doubt they would be ready when he called.

They were clumsy, but the crew had done as well as could be expected. Their methods were far from flawless, but they had at least gotten the important parts correct. Was he accepting something less than perfection? He must be getting softer in his old age.

*No, the end justifies the means, right? Hell, yes.*

As the plane reached cruising altitude, he checked his watch again. He was sure someone had discovered the bodies by now. His planning had been flawless and more than made up for the imperfect execution. The precision of the battle plan and exit strategy had been the truly beautiful part.

While he'd driven away with an unconscious Ezra Harrell, Lucas had ordered the shooters to remove the bodies of their dead. Only the bodies of the driver and the guards remained.

Per the details of the job, he'd tortured Harrell before putting him out of his misery. Not wanting to risk returning to the scene, he'd dumped the mangled corpse a few blocks from the original kidnapping. News of the carnage would dominate the day, just as his employer had wanted.

The equipment and weapons they'd used all rested at the bottoms of different parts of the Anacostia and Potomac Rivers.

It had been a tight squeeze, but Lucas made his flight with just a few minutes to spare. He would return to the east coast as soon as his employer called.

Today, he was soaring through clouds and time zones to the treasured seclusion of his Mexican hideaway. Time enough to relax and allow The Clean to recharge and prepare for his next performance.

## *Chapter Forty-Eight*

Olivia Harrell dreamed of bells. She didn't know what kind of bells, but she could hear them. They sounded far away, but very loud at the same time.

*Ding-dong...*

Church bells? No, not quite.

*But they sounded so familiar. Ding-Dong...*

Wedding bells? No, no, that wasn't it either.

*Ding-Dong...*

Doorbells maybe?

*Yes! That was it!*

Of all things, she was hearing doorbells, but why? She had no idea. But in the vast, white emptiness of her dream, the doorbells kept ringing. She tried to find them and knew she was getting closer when the bells grew louder.

*DING-DONG, DING-DONG, DIIIIIIINNNNNGGGGG DOOOONNNNNGGGG!*

Then there was darkness. Her white dreamland had vanished. She was awake and lying in her bed.

Olivia had been dreaming of doorbells. But the bells had been more than just a dream, because even in the darkness, she could still hear them ringing.

*It was her doorbell that was ringing. Someone was at her front door.*

She forced herself completely awake and blinked through sleepy eyes at the clock near the bed. Its red digitized numbers read 6:36 a.m. The doorbell continued to ring, accompanied by an insistent knocking. The house phone was also ringing off the hook.

The space where Ezra slept next to her was empty and undisturbed. Her husband hadn't come home last night. He wouldn't have gone down to the Bushwood estate without letting her know. So, where was he?

Olivia reached for the phone, thinking it might be Ezra, but the knocking and ringing doorbell possessed an urgency that demanded priority.

She slipped out of bed, pulled on a robe over her nightgown, and called out to whoever was at the front door, "I'm coming, I'm coming, just hold on just a minute. *I'm coming!*"

Normally, Serena would've answered the door, but it was Saturday morning, and the Harrells never asked their housekeeper to work on weekends. She had two little boys, and they wanted her to spend as much time with her family as possible.

The urgent knocking and doorbell ringing continued. Olivia hurried downstairs and through the family room towards the front door.

She squinted through the peephole and saw a group of men she recognized, two were Ezra's older brothers. She rushed to disengage the locks on the front door, unable to fight the feeling something was very wrong.

Questions lacking answers flooded her mind. Where was her husband? Why wasn't he here or with his brothers? Had something happened to him? Was he sick and laying up in somebody's hospital bed? Or worse?

*No. No. No.* She couldn't think like that, she wouldn't. Ezra had said everything would be fine, and she believed in him. So, everything would be fine. That was it.

She opened the door and stepped to the side allowing Montae and A.J. to enter. The other three men remained outside to stand watch. Her assigned guards were also out there watching over the house as always.

Olivia glanced up and down the street. People were already beginning their weekends. Last night's rain had stopped and given way to a Technicolor sunrise cast against a clear blue sky. All the makings of a beautiful day.

"Liv, are you okay?" Montae asked as he looked around. He held a pistol in his hand. She noticed that the other men, except A.J., had drawn their guns as well.

"Yes, I'm fine, Montae. I was asleep. You all woke me up ringing the bell and banging on the door like that. What's going on?" she said, trying to read their eyes.

"What's wrong? Why are you here this early? And where's Ezra? I don't think he came home last night. Is he with you?"

"Hey Liv, why don't we go sit down?" A.J. said.

"Sit down for what? Why would I need to sit down, A.J.? What's happened? You're starting to scare me. Please just tell me what's going on."

"There's a problem, Liv," A.J. said, and exhaled a deep breath. He couldn't look Olivia in her eyes, and his words were shaky as he spoke them. "Liv, s-something's happened."

"What kind of problem? What do you mean, A.J.? What's happened?" she said, afraid she already knew the answers to her questions. "Talk to me, please. What's going on? Where's Ezra? Oh God, is it... is it Ezra? Has something happened to him? Is it Cuttino? Has something happened to my family, A.J.?"

A.J. opened his mouth to speak again. His lips moved, but no words came out. She saw tears form in his eyes, and he turned away from her. Her heart began to hurt.

*No...this can't be happening...please don't say it...*

"Olivia, Ezra's dead. He's gone. He's gone, Liv. I'm so sorry," Montae said, his words hard and flat like an open-handed slap. "Someone murdered him."

Olivia's entire existence crumbled. The first thing that happened was a slight shaking of her head from side to side. Immediate denial. Followed by the rapid blinking of her eyes and the furrowing of her brow. Failed comprehension.

Finally, her jaw went slack, allowing her mouth to fall wide open. Her beautiful facial features twisted and reflected the shocking realization of her brother-in-law's words. Had he just told her that someone had killed her husband? That she would never see him alive again?

*No, that couldn't be what he'd said. Couldn't be.*

Because that would mean he was trying to play some kind of sick joke on her, and Montae just wouldn't do that. She must have heard him wrong.

"W-what did you just say?" she asked, her head still shaking no, her words no louder than a whisper. Her knees were turning to jelly, and her left hand reached out for something she could use to steady herself.

"I said he's gone, Liv. Ezra's gone."

She managed to catch the tail end of her breath as it flew from her chest. The grief was instant and felt like a dropkick to her stomach.

"No! No! Oh God, no! NO! Don't you say that! Don't ever say that! Ezra has to be okay. He has to be. *Where is my husband, Montae*?"

She felt A.J. catch her just as her knees buckled and gravity snatched her towards the wooden floor. He held her up by her arms and guided her to a nearby couch.

"Police patrols responded to a call about a shootout near his office in Rosslyn. They found him, Donnie, and four of our guards, Liv," Montae said, his words sounding far away and dreamlike now. "They were all dead. Somebody got to him. We don't know how; we don't know who."

"I'm so sorry, Livia," A.J. whispered in her ear and hugged her close. "I'm so sorry."

"Oh no, no, no, no, *noooooooo*!" she screamed and pounded her fists into A.J.'s chest. "Not Ezra! Not my husband! He said everything would be okay. He promised me! He promised! Oh my God! I –I can't breathe. Oh God, Ezra!"

"We'll find them, Liv," she heard A.J. say. "We'll find whoever did this to Ezra. I promise you we *will* find them. But first, we have to get you out of this city. Cuttino's fine. We'll get you down there to him."

Olivia let out an agonizing, inhuman sounding howl. She shrieked at the top of her lungs until she felt them burn. There were no more words left, just screams and uncontrollable sobs as she struggled to catch her breath. There was no sense of time for her, no connection to anything except the reality that her husband was dead and gone.

She felt A.J. wrap his arms tighter around her, but his embrace offered no comfort. Her screams continued. The earth seemed to shake beneath her feet. In a matter of seconds, her world had fallen apart. Olivia Harrell's deepest fears had fast become a horrible reality.

# *Chapter Forty-Nine*

"Looks like an open and shut, so to speak," District Attorney Graham Robertson said as he set the morning edition of the Washington Post on the mayor's desk. "A slam dunk, wouldn't you say, Chief?"

Chief Walters picked up the newspaper and reread the headline of the Metro Section's lead story for the umpteenth time that morning:

**Killings Continue in Latest Gangland Massacre**

The homicides were nothing new, not with the recent influx of violent crime in the city. It was the sub-headline that had D.C.'s DA in such a good mood and had Chief Walters equally disturbed:

**Local entrepreneur Ezra Harrell among the dead**

From the outside looking in, this would appear to be a good thing. The most powerful suspected drug dealer in D.C.'s history had been put down. But that was on the outside. Things always ran deeper than the surface story. The chief knew this fact all too well.

"No, I wouldn't call it a slam dunk, DA Robertson," Chief Walters said, folding the newspaper in half. "Not at all."

"And why is that, Quinn?" Mayor Dunbar asked from behind his desk. "With Harrell in the ground, his entire criminal organization should come tumbling down, shouldn't it?"

Chief Walters had expected these two idiots to miss the big picture and the new crisis they were facing now.

"Well, Mr. Mayor," Chief Walters said, "to be honest, Ezra Harrell's assassination presents more of a problem than it does a solution. The structure of today's narcotics cartels resembles something like a terrorist cell. It's not like the old days where you could kill the head and expect the body to wither and die. It doesn't work that way anymore. You kill the head, and a new one takes its place. Then, the new head stands to be smarter and stronger after witnessing the mistakes the last head made. This new head learns and adapts. Makes our job harder. So, no, I don't see Ezra Harrell's death as a slam dunk. His death is only going to make things worse. As a matter of fact, we don't know much of anything about the Syndicate Narcotics Cooperative beyond its name. That's why we needed to bring Harrell in. We were just getting to the point where we could do that and have a good chance of the charges sticking.

These murders add further ambiguity to an already ambiguous situation."

"Furthermore, Mr. Robertson," the chief continued, turning to face the DA, "we needed to prosecute Harrell to try and force him to give up his associates, his connections, and his entire payroll. That's how you topple a criminal organization these days. You attack it and force it to turn on itself."

"Under these circumstances," Chief Walters said, holding up the folded Post, "his death washes out years of police work spent building a viable case against him. It also nullifies all prospective new cases that could have stemmed from squeezing him and forcing him to talk. Cases that would have served to help subdue the monster that is the D.C. narcotics flow."

DA Robertson didn't respond right away, but it looked to the chief like the DA was struggling to suppress a smile. *Like this was all some damn game.*

*Of course you are smiling,* the chief thought, *because you already knew all of this didn't you? You corrupt, shortsighted, simple-minded sonofabitch.*

"Well, Chief, I understand your frustration," DA Robertson answered after the silence mounted to an uncomfortable level, "but how many years has your department wasted chasing Ezra Harrell and his family? Way too many, in my opinion. The man couldn't be arrested, let alone convicted. Period. I don't know how or why that was the case, but he's gone. Dead. So, arrests and convictions, or lack thereof, are really a moot point. He's out of our hair. You say you had a case this time? Well, I'm sure you did, but at least we don't have to find out while wasting taxpayers' money in court. This is a good thing here, Chief. At least we have Harrell off our streets. If he's in the ground, it won't matter if the charges stick or not. Come on, Chief. That right there is at least a little bit of a silver lining."

*Shouldn't you be worried about who'll be lining your pockets?* the chief wanted to ask him.

*But you already know the answer to that, don't you, Mr. District Attorney? There is a reason why your office has never been able to make anything stick to Ezra Harrell.*

"Yes, well, I'm not a big fan of street justice," Chief Walters responded. "Didn't think you were either, District Attorney Robertson."

"No, Chief, I'm not a fan of street justice or vigilantes running around playing judge and jury," DA Robertson said, bristling at the chief's insinuation. "In fact, I graduated from Howard University's School of Law so I could administer the type of justice driven by the laws we are sworn to uphold. I despise street justice. However, with *your department* unable to provide sufficient evidence enough for my office to mount a legitimate case, I'm forced to take it as I can get it. I can no longer afford to suffer through a lack of evidence or a failure to follow the letter of the law that results in these criminals getting off on a technicality."

"My department?" the chief said, his calm tone growing razor sharp teeth as he shot forward in this chair. "My officers are busting their tails out here in these streets! You have no idea how much..."

"Gentlemen, please!" the mayor interrupted. "This is neither the time nor the place for this. Let's do away with the heavy-duty sparring and try to stay on point here. We are on the same side, remember?"

Chief Walters clenched his fists and gritted his teeth in an effort to maintain his composure. He wanted to snatch this smooth-talking punk clean out his chair.

His designer horn-rimmed glasses, custom-tailored suits, and expensive Italian leather loafers were all paid for by drug money. The chief would bet money on it. D.C.'s district attorney was no different than the men he was supposed to be prosecuting. He was serving as their unofficial defense lawyer.

Every lead, every shred of evidence his officers presented, the district attorney's office found a way to discount it. He was in bed with these criminals, Chief Walters was sure of it. He just couldn't prove it yet.

The corruption in this city's law system didn't rest at the police level. It was born of greed and deception and possessed long legs on which to climb. And it wouldn't stop climbing until it reached the top.

Mayor Dunbar cleared his throat to break the tension building in the room. "Okay, gentlemen, so what's the next move?" Mayor Dunbar said. "Where do we go from here?"

"Well, sir," DA Robertson spoke up first, "I think this is a great day for our ongoing effort to combat the organized crime and narcotics flow in D.C. Unlike the chief, I'm of the belief that if you cut the head off a snake, it will die. And while I'm not foolish enough to think one death will solve all of our problems, I do think Ezra Harrell's death will diminish his organization and force it to degenerate into an unorganized state. At that point, I believe the remaining criminal element will be easy pickings for D.C.'s finest."

"And what happens up until that blessed day comes?" Chief Walters started up again, returning to his calm demeanor, but unwilling to let go of his original argument.

"You ever think about who took Harrell out and why they did it? It's a safe bet they weren't doing it as a favor to us. Maybe they knew we were getting closer to him and wanted to take him out before we could close in on him. What if this was just an old-fashioned coup? Whatever the reason, last night's events mean we could be looking at more bodies stacking up real soon. I'm telling you this much: someone will take Ezra Harrell's place, either by choice or by force, but it will happen. Our immediate concern should be how it happens."

The chief paused long enough to let his last few statements sink in before continuing. "It's suspected that the Harrell Family controlled the lion's share of the organized narcotics flow in and around the city. It is also suspected that Ezra Harrell was sitting pretty as the king of the hill over an extensive network of dealers. If all of this is true, we could be looking at a major gang war for control of the criminal underground. We haven't even mentioned the payback his family will be looking for after last night."

"Wait a minute here. That's just a theory, Chief," Mayor Dunbar said. "We can't prove anything yet. Not beyond a doubt anyway, according to the DA. Hell, maybe Harrell isn't even the man we all thought he was. Or maybe there isn't anyone to take his place and without him, his organization will cease to function. We don't have any clear-cut proof of a Syndicate Narcotics Cooperative even existing. Maybe we are sitting here getting all worked up for nothing."

Mayor Dunbar glanced over at the district attorney for confirmation. Robertson nodded his agreement with the mayor, and Chief Walters had to restrain himself again. It was all he could do not to throw a right hook to the side of the DA's inflated head.

"With all due respect, sir," the chief said, "this is much more than just a theory. It's a fact that a gang war could spawn as a result of last night. At a minimum, we need to consider the revenge factor. Whatever role the Harrell Family plays in all of this, do we really believe they will sit by and let one of their head members get gunned down without exacting some kind of retribution?

And if by some chance a war doesn't break out and the next boss is allowed to assume control without any sort of conflict, we find ourselves right back at square one: trying to mount a case against a brand-new kingpin. As crazy as it sounds, last night was the worst thing that could have happened in the big picture of what we are trying to accomplish here."

"I understand your position, Chief, really I do," the mayor said, "but my question remains, where do we go from here?"

"Well, sir," Chief Walters said, "to answer your question, we stay the course. In fact, it would be best that we gear up for a war. It could get messy in our streets. I need more money towards OT for my officers, sir. And we need to outsource this to outside agencies and bring in federal help to assist on the ground and with intel gathering. There's a slight chance The Syndicate could be weakened for a short period of time, but that will be a small window at best. We need to use that window to continue infiltrating their ranks and start wrecking this thing from the inside out. I need a bigger budget for wire taps and surveillance as well as for a few more undercover officers and informants."

"Chief Walters," DA Robertson said in his normal condescending tone, "I can appreciate your enthusiasm, but we don't even have the slightest indication that what you're saying is true. For the mayor to sign off on such significant budgetary allocations would certainly be overkill, would it not?"

"Sir," DA Robertson said, addressing the mayor, "I recommend that we do maintain our current course, but that we also adopt more of a wait and see posture with this. Let's see if and how this *alleged* Syndicate reacts to the death of Ezra Harrell. It's my personal feeling that our city's narcotics flow is not as complex and organized as the chief thinks it is. I think one man ran the show, and that man is gone."

"*It is* organized," Chief Walters said, his frustration returning. "There can be no doubt about that. We may not know all of the players, but it is organized. Very, very organized. Why else do you think we haven't been able to stop it so far?"

DA Robertson ignored the chief's question.

"Quinn, I'm not sure about the overtime just yet. Let me think about that," the mayor said. "We're coming up on the fiscal year budget review, and I have everyone from the schools to each of the public services beating down my door bidding for budget increases. Everyone's hands are in the cookie jar. And as far as the Feds? No, it's not gonna happen. Under no circumstances do I want them in here nosing around. This is our town, our business. We'll handle this our way. Anyway, the war on terror is keeping them plenty busy. Bad enough I got the President right up the street. No sir, I don't want any external agencies in here. Something happens in Maryland or Virginia, fine. You go liaise with them on an as needed basis. But we don't need federal help."

"I want both of your offices to maintain your present postures," the mayor continued. "No need to start running additional undercover and surveillance just yet. Graham, you keep building our cases. Quinn, you and your people keep attacking this beast. Bring it down. Make your arrests, good arrests, and get Graham and his people something to work with. I want this done yesterday. Let's keep the blood off our streets."

Chief Walters left the mayor's office in an even worse mood than when he first arrived. As he headed for his car, he mentally replayed his meeting with the mayor and the DA. How could they be so stupid? Unfortunately, the chief knew there was more than stupidity at work here. He took out his cell, opened a saved file, and made a one-word entry:

**Robertson**

Then, he saved and closed the file. The DA was more than just an egotistical jackass; he was dirty, and the Chief would prove it.

Next, he made a phone call to his undercover operative. The phone rang once on the other end before Detective Cole answered.

"Chief, how we looking, sir?"

"Just leaving the mayor's office," Chief said. "We need to meet ASAP. We have some... adjustments to make in light of what happened last night."

"Sounds good, sir," Cole said. "Location number three? Thirty minutes?"

"See you then," Chief said and disconnected the call.

*He could feel himself getting slapped upside the head.*

# *Chapter Fifty*

Location number three wasn't some high-tech secret site hidden from public view. It was just the opposite. The Crisfield Seafood Restaurant on Georgia Avenue in Silver Spring, Maryland was one of Darius Cole's favorite places to eat. He hadn't been far from the area, so Crisfield was an easy choice when the chief called wanting to meet.

He could hear the stress in the chief's voice, and he knew the cause of it. All of the local news outlets ran the shootout in Rosslyn as their lead story. Today's intelligence reports had confirmed the death of D.C.'s alleged crime chief.

Given Ezra Harrell's demonstrated ability of imitating Teflon when it came to beating criminal charges, this should've been seen as good fortune. Darius and the chief couldn't see it that way. This wasn't a win for the home team. They had put in long hours and felt like they were making headway in building a case on Harrell and his family.

Obviously, so had someone else. That someone had taken out the king of D.C.'s underground before the

MPD could arrest and prosecute him. It could all be a coincidence, but none of this sat well with Darius. Someone with plenty of backing must have gotten to Ezra Harrell.

Prior to going undercover, he'd tracked dealers, made arrests, and sent the criminals to jail. On this current assignment, he'd been trying to become one of the people he'd always hunted. For the past few months, he'd lived in the Underworld using a different name and an altered appearance. The objective was to get on the inside without getting himself killed.

Working as an undercover operative meant he wasn't subject to the same rules or confinements of the everyday officer on the MPD. He didn't fill out paperwork, attend morning roll call, or respond to the everyday calls of disturbing the peace or domestic violence. In fact, undercover work forbade Darius from answering any emergency calls that could jeopardize his fabricated identity. He ignored anything he saw that fell outside the scope of his mission.

This made life pretty simple for him: infiltrate, always play the part, and then eliminate the threat. On the downside, he was also in the wild without the same safety net regular police enjoyed. There was no backup, no shift relief, and no normal life whatsoever. Chief Walters served as his lone outside contact.

Darius had made contacts he was sure would lead to the top tier of the narcotics ring, but Ezra Harrell's murder changed everything. If Harrell was the main man, as Darius and the chief suspected, the city's main supply could be cut off.

Before, he'd been trying to work his way in as a low-level dealer. With the sudden death of Ezra Harrell, he'd need to tweak his identity and establish himself as a viable high-level connection. One that could offer high-grade product and step in to become The Syndicate's new narcotics supplier. Whoever killed Harrell would be trying to do the same thing.

Darius knew Ezra Harrell's assassination could prove to be a major setback in his investigation. It could also serve to start a gang war with everyone vying for control of the city's drug trade. D.C.'s law enforcement would have its hands full trying to contain the insanity as the battle for control of The Syndicate raged. The amount of bloodshed and dead bodies filling caskets would be incredible.

Darius needed to find the other members of The Syndicate and take them down. He wouldn't have much time to make something happen before the entire city was set on fire.

# *Chapter Fifty-One*

***Fuquay-Varina, North Carolina...***

The house where Cuttino Harrell had spent the past four months was a custom-built mansion. It sat in the middle of a vast forty-acre estate that had been in the Harrell Family since the early 1900s.

Today, the entire property looked like something out of a magazine about the rich and famous. Cuttino had begun to get used to the peace and tranquility of living on the family's estate. Just by being here, he'd come to better understand his family's rich history and tradition.

Lincoln Arthur Harrell had come to own the property after the Civil War Reconstruction era. Given the climate in the South during that time, it had been a miracle that Lincoln had maintained his ownership. As it is documented throughout history, black people were subjected to unimaginable cruelties during that time, despite the war and the Emancipation Proclamation.

The land had been given to Lincoln as a debt of gratitude from his former employer. This white man, named Ben Montgomery, had been a rich businessman who owned several large properties in North Carolina. Lincoln's parents had worked for Montgomery years before Lincoln's birth in 1862. His father had been killed shortly after his second birthday fighting for the Union Army in the Civil War.

When the war ended in 1865, the destruction in the South had been widespread. Mother and son stayed on with Montgomery to help with the rebuilding effort after the Confederacy's defeat and subsequent surrender.

Upon his death in 1900, Montgomery left Lincoln the wooded property in his will as thanks for his years of loyal employment. Great Granddad Lincoln constructed a small three-bedroom home with his bare hands. He took a wife, and they had children. Those children became adults and started families as well. The Harrell family tree grew and branched out, but the property had stayed in the family through the generations.

The original house also remained standing as a memorial on the estate. Cuttino's great-great grandmother, great-grandfather, great-grandmother, and grandmother, along with other family elders, were all buried on a secluded part of the property. There was also a large pond full of largemouth bass, crappie, and channel catfish, as well as bluegill, sunfish, and yellow perch. For years, this pond along with the property's crops and hunting resources served as the staples of the Family's diet and income.

Cuttino's father had financed the building of an eight-bedroom house and four other smaller homes on the property. Cousins, aunts, and uncles resided either on or near the gated compound. They ran their everyday existence as if they weren't tied to one of the biggest drug cartels operating on the East Coast. His father moved about in and out of their lives at his discretion, supplementing whatever their legal incomes couldn't manage.

When Cuttino had arrived in Fuquay-Varina, no one asked why he was there and how long he would be staying. Everything had been prepared for his arrival: bedrooms for him and his guards, new cars, and clothes. His father had briefed the rest of the Family on the situation before he'd told his son.

His father maintained strict control over the dissemination of information regarding the true nature of the Harrell family business. He allowed regulated access to those relatives with direct involvement in The Syndicate and held all others at arm's length. Everyone in and around the Harrell Family, whether they were involved in the business or not, knew silence was the number one policy.

Cuttino hadn't seen his extended family in years, but everyone had treated him and his guards like they'd been here all along. That's how the Harrell Family was: one big unit, undivided, regardless of distance or the passing of time.

His meeting Sidney had blindsided him and yoked him in an all new direction. Since he'd met her, he'd spent less and less time around the big house on the hill. He was falling harder than he ever had in his life.

This new feeling scared and excited him at the same time. He also felt ashamed for allowing himself to fall in love while his family was fighting for their lives back home. Had he become disconnected from what the Harrell Family was trying to accomplish?

After learning of his family's earliest beginnings, Cuttino better understood where he came from. The question was: where were the Harrells going?

# *Chapter Fifty-Two*

It was a breezy fall Saturday when life as Cuttino Harrell knew it, came to an end.

As if it were running late, the sun appeared to glide towards the edge of the horizon with a quickened pace. It blew a kiss goodnight to this side of the country, casting an orange-pink hue as far as the eye could see. The picture-perfect sunset reminded him of his parents' favorite band, Maze, and their song "Golden Time of Day."

He'd spent the day with Sidney at the farmer's market and the carnival that had come to town earlier in the week. Just after 7:30 p.m., the couple was on their way to Sidney's condo when he felt his cell phone vibrate. He slipped his cell from his pants pocket and saw a text message:

**Come back to the house ASAP.**

Without thinking, he began to maneuver their vehicle into a U-turn.

"What's up, sweetie?" Sidney asked when she noticed the SUV changing direction. "I thought we were going to my place?"

He looked at her and smiled. "We are," he said, "but I need to run by the house, is that cool?"

"Sure, no problem. Is everything alright?"

"I'm sure it's all good," he said, not quite believing the words himself. "I just need to stop by there real quick."

Followed at a distance by the twins in a brown Ford Taurus, he navigated the bronze Land Rover towards the highway. He hadn't told Sidney about Iran and Taurus, and so far, they had done a good job staying out of sight.

Twenty minutes after receiving the text, he drove the luxury SUV up the winding driveway to the Big House. When he parked in front of the house, he saw vehicles there that didn't belong to anyone who lived on the property.

He didn't know who owned these cars and SUVs but an uneasy feeling crept over him as he studied the vehicles. Each one sported D.C. license plates. His anxiety was validated when he saw a guard, who he recognized as part of his Uncle Montae's detail, posted out front.

"Who's that?" Sidney asked as she undid her seatbelt. "Is he related to you?"

"Something like that," he answered, also undoing his seatbelt and unlocking the SUV's doors. "He works for my family."

"Oh," she said, still eyeing the guard, "he looks, um, dangerous."

"Yeah," he said and nodded in agreement. "Yeah, he does, and he gets paid pretty well to look like that, too. Come on, let's get out."

Cuttino still hadn't told her the truth about what his family did for a living. He hadn't completely lied, but he hadn't been 100 percent truthful either. He'd skated around the subject, telling her his family ran a large construction business out of the D.C. area. That part was true. He'd also told her the family was preparing to expand, and he'd been sent south to look for new opportunities. Not the truth, not really.

He'd left out the part about illegal narcotics trafficking, knowing she wouldn't understand. He hoped, since the Family was getting out of that life, she would never need to know about that part. He hoped.

Members of the Harrell Family from D.C. were here in North Carolina. But, why? Had everything at home come to an end? Were his parents here? Why wouldn't they have called to tell him they were coming? Why the urgent text message? Were they trying to set up some sort of family reunion surprise?

Maybe, but the grim look on the guard's face told him no one would be yelling surprise as he entered the house. He gripped Sidney's hand as they walked up the stairs and crossed the large, covered porch of the main house. He nodded at the guard who didn't speak, but instead, opened the door and stepped aside as he and Sidney crossed the threshold. He could see the man carried at least one pistol beneath his suit jacket.

When he looked closer at the guard's face, Cuttino realized he'd mistaken the man's expression for one of toughness. What he really saw in the guard's eyes was fear and sadness.

*No, this wasn't a surprise party.*

# *Chapter Fifty-Three*

Uncle Montae's short, muscular frame stood before Cuttino just inside the doorway.

"Youngblood," he said, gripping his nephew's hand in his. "Long time."

The dark look on his face should've told Cuttino everything he needed to know. He should have turned around and left the house then, no longer needing to see or hear anything else. His uncle showing up here, out of the blue, wasn't a good sign. Who else did he have with him? No way this could be good news, no way in hell, he thought.

"Uncle Montae?" he said, returning the handshake as he stepped inside the house's large foyer area, "What's going on?"

He started to introduce Sidney to his uncle when he noticed five more of his uncle's soldiers. The group of men stood near the bottom of the large winding staircase leading to the upper levels of the house. He felt Sidney's hand tighten its grip around his, the sight of the more dangerous looking men alarming her. His aunts, uncles, and cousins had gathered in the dining room, each wearing similar solemn expressions. No one spoke a word.

He walked deeper into the house searching the face of each person for any sign of what had happened. He was too scared to ask for fear of hearing the answer. He let Sidney's hand go as he stepped across the wooden floors of the foyer and deeper into the dining room. She called his name, but remained behind when he didn't answer and took a seat beside his Cousin Boom.

His eyes met Uncle A.J.'s, who didn't say a word and lowered his head as Cuttino walked by him. Then, his mother's high-pitched wailing shattered the room's silence.

He rounded the corner, rushed down into the sunken living room, and saw his mother for the first time in months. She sat on the couch, elbows propped on her knees with head buried in her hands. Her entire body was shaking. The sofa's large cushions seemed to swallow her petite frame. His mother's older sisters sat on both sides of her, rubbing her back and shoulders.

"Momma?" he said, kneeling in front of her. "Momma, what's wrong? What happened?"

"What happened to her?" he said to his aunts, who shook their heads, but did not reply. "What's wrong with my mother?"

"Will somebody tell me what the hell is going on in here?" he asked in a raised voice, frustrated at the lack of answers he'd received.

But he already knew the answers to his questions, didn't he? Only one thing could cause this type of scene, and that was death.

# *Chapter Fifty-Four*

It took his mother a couple of minutes before she could gather herself enough to look at him. When she did, he didn't recognize the woman who'd given him life.

Her skin was ashen and had paled from her normal radiant complexion by at least a few shades. Thick, swollen bags sat beneath her bloodshot eyes. His mother's cinnamon and gray locks looked matted and disheveled. The sight of his mother in this haggard condition caused him to stand and take a step back.

"My baby," she whispered in a ragged voice that he didn't recognize, "come sit down here."

She patted the edge of the couch with her right hand and reached out to him with her left. Cuttino didn't want to sit down. He wanted to know what the hell had happened.

"Mom, please just tell me what's going on. What's wrong? What happened to you? Where's Dad?" He felt his chest tighten. "Why's everyone here? What's going on?"

The words didn't have to be said, but he wanted to hear them anyway; he needed to hear them.

"Cuttino, baby" she said and took his hands in hers, "your father...he, he's...gone, baby. Your father is gone."

"Gone? Gone where? Nah," he said and shook his head, hot tears already filling the rims of his eyes. The words hurt to pronounce, caused pain as they formed in his throat and left his mouth.

"What do you mean gone? Gone like, like dead? You mean dead, Momma? Nah. No. Nope. No. I'm not trying to hear that. No!"

He felt dizzy as the blood rushed to his head and his legs went numb from the floor up. He dropped down to one knee beside his mother, unable to maintain his balance any longer.

"Mom? Mom, what are you saying? Where's Dad? Where is he? Where is Dad? Mom?"

"Baby...oh, my baby. He's d-dead, baby. Somebody, somebody got to him."

His mother began to tremble again as she spoke those terrible words. "Th-they killed your father, Cuttino-baby. They took him away from us. *Somebody murdered him.*"

Cuttino heard his mother's words, but he couldn't believe them.

"Aw, nah. Nah, nah, nah. Momma, no. No, no, no. Don't tell me that," he said, his tears boiling over and burning their way down his face.

Cuttino buried his head in his mother's lap like he'd done when he was a child. "Please, don't tell me that, Momma."

Several minutes passed, and as his mother held him, he tried to steady himself. He needed to be strong like his father had taught him. His hero. His best friend. The man who taught him everything he knew, who he admired and aspired to be like, was gone. He didn't want to believe it. He couldn't believe it.

His father hadn't died in peace due to natural causes after living a long, fulfilling life. He'd been snatched away before his time. Murdered.

*Somebody got to him...*

He remembered his mother's words. How in the hell did somebody "get" to his father? His father had better protection than the mayor. How could this have happened? He was retiring, that was the plan. The entire Harrell Family was getting out of the dope game. For the first time, things were going to be normal for their family. But, not anymore. Someone had wiped out every thought of that normal life forever.

As always, the Harrell Family rallied around one another. Uncles, cousins, aunts, and friends surrounded mother and son, enclosing them in a tight circle as they embraced each other.

There would be hard questions asked followed by agonizing answers; but without a doubt, there would be vengeance.

The killing of Ezra Harrell would not go unanswered.

# Chapter Fifty-Five

Cuttino convinced his mother to take a sedative and lie down in one of the upstairs bedrooms.

"Baby, you find them," she said in a drowsy haze as the medicine took hold, and she drifted off to sleep. "Find out who took my Ezra away from me, and you make this right, baby. Make it right."

Her red-rimmed eyes closed, and her voice lowered into a sleepy whisper. "You hear me, Cuttino? You make it right. Your father would want you to do that for him, for our family. You find them, baby. Find them, and you *kill all of them.*"

He left his mother to sleep and prepared himself to face the rest of his family. Cuttino had traveled the entire spectrum of negative emotion from sadness to outrage and was left feeling numb and empty.

"How did this happen?" he asked as he came down the stairs. "Who did this?"

His uncles, their guards, and the Beasley twins sat at the large dining room table. The rest of the family had taken their cue to relocate to other parts of the property. Sidney had gone upstairs to keep an eye on his mother. He would worry later about telling her what was going on. He didn't think he could deal with that just yet.

"We don't know, nephew," Montae said. "It could've been anyone in or around the Syndicate. After Ezra made his announcement about retiring, everything went crazy, you know? It all pretty much went to shit right before our eyes."

"How did he die?" Cuttino asked. "I want to know everything. All of it."

"We downloaded the video from the building's outside surveillance cameras," Montae said. "The cameras are pretty well hidden, and we made sure MPD didn't get a copy of the video. It looks like Ezra was leaving his office and whoever did this was waiting on him. They jumped him. Killed his guards, killed Donnie, too. Police found Donnie and the guards in the alley behind the building. They found Ezra about a couple blocks up from there. He was shot close range. Shotgun or something powerful like that. One of our guys on the MPD notified us and bought us time to get the video from the building."

"Where's my father's body?"

"All of the bodies are still in custody. Our lawyers are working on a court order to speed up the release process," A.J. said. "Afterwards, his body will be flown down. We'll get him here as soon as we can. We'll also release the other bodies to each family. We got good people on that. It'll get done real soon."

"I want funeral arrangements made, whatever and however my mother wants," Cuttino said. "Take care of Donnie's people and the families of my father's guards. Make sure they know they still have the Harrells as family. I want my father's body here. Tell those lawyers to do their damn job."

He sat down at the head of the huge maple wood table.

"And I want these bastards found."

"Whatever you want, bro, we got you," Montae said. "We'll make it happen. I'm working on getting our numbers right so we can get on these streets. We got new product coming in the next couple of days. Business has got to go back to normal while we find whoever did this. You can stay here and look after your mom. I'll take care of everything back home. Don't worry about anything."

"No, I won't just stay down here anymore, Uncle Montae," Cuttino said. "I never should've left. My father might still be alive if I hadn't. And no disrespect to either one of you, but I'll be assuming control of the family's business here as well as back home. And after we find who did this, I plan on carrying out my father's plans for retirement."

"Wait a second, nephew," Montae said, "let's just think this through here. With Ezra gone and all, maybe we should rethink that whole retirement thing? The game has changed."

"There isn't much to think through, is there? We stay on track. Period. Do things how my father had planned. That's what he would want, and that's what we're gonna do."

No one at the table spoke, but both of his uncles nodded their heads in agreement. Cuttino knew the history of his family's beginnings in this lifestyle. He knew neither one of his uncles agreed with his decision or his stepping over them in the Harrell hierarchy. But his father had told him to be ready to lead the family if anything ever happened to him.

His father's murder had dealt a severe blow to the Harrell Family structure. They were at their weakest and everyone would be looking to him for answers. Somehow, he would have to be the one to pick up the pieces and put the Harrell Empire back together. There wasn't much time, either. It wouldn't be long before the vultures, hyenas, and coyotes started to circle.

Putting the Harrells back together would start with finding his father's killers. Until that was done, nothing else mattered...nothing. After he took care of them, he could concentrate on resolving the family's other affairs. Everything hinged on Cuttino making this right.

His mother's words haunted him... *Kill all of them...*

# *Chapter Fifty-Six*

After he set things in motion with his uncles, Cuttino took the long climb up the stairs to find Sidney. She was in his mother's room keeping an eye on her. When she saw him standing in the doorway, she stood and walked to meet him in the hallway.

"Sid," he said, but she cut him off by wrapping both of her arms around his neck and pulling him into her body.

"Oh God, Tino. I am so, so sorry," she said. "Who could have done this? What are the police saying? What can I do? Just tell me what you need. I'm here for you. I'm here."

This was that moment. He should tell her. Do the right thing for once and tell her the truth about his family and himself.

"Sidney," he began, "I have something to tell you." He knew what needed to be said.

"What is it?" she said, looking up at him.

He looked her in eyes and inhaled and exhaled a deep breath, but just couldn't bring himself to say the words. Not now.

This wasn't the time or place. There was too much happening, too many other things to worry about without complicating his relationship with her. She would walk away if she knew the truth, and he couldn't blame her. It was selfish not to tell her, he knew this, but he needed her and couldn't afford to lose her like this.

"Cuttino," she said, "what is it? Talk to me. Tell me."

"I have to go away for a while," he said. "I'm not sure how long, but I need to go to D.C. and square up my father's affairs."

"Oh, no," she said, shaking her head. "Do you think that's safe?"

"I'll be fine, don't worry," he said. "Whoever did this is long gone or in hiding trying to avoid the police."

"But can't that wait? Or can't you have someone else do it? I really don't think it's safe up there."

"I wish I could, but this is my responsibility. I have to take care of the family's businesses, and I'm sure the police will want to speak with me as part of their investigation. My dad would want me to take care of this. I know he would."

"I understand, I just... well, how about this? I have some vacation time coming my way. I'll go with you. I don't want you to be alone."

He wouldn't put her in danger by taking her to D.C. with him.

"No, Sid, thank you," he said, "but I couldn't ask you to do that. I'm hoping I won't be gone long. I'll miss you too much if I am."

"Well, I want to do something to help. What can I do? Anything."

He thought about his mother and her fragile emotional state. "If you can get that time off, I'd really appreciate it if you could be here with my mom. I know my aunts will be here, but if you could spend some time with her, it would really help."

"Okay. You know I'll do it. I'd be happy to be here with her. This will give us a chance to get to know each other. Do you know when you are leaving?"

"Thank you, Sid. Thank you so much," he said, kissing her forehead and pulling her into him. "I think we'll be pulling out right after the funeral. And please don't worry; I'll be back before you know it."

He felt better knowing she would be here at the house with his mother. Whoever had killed his father possessed intimate knowledge of the Harrells. They had planned that hit and may come looking for the rest of his family and anyone close to them. Having Sidney here at the house while he took care of business gave her the best chance of being protected.

# *Chapter Fifty-Seven*

Cuttino remembered the last face-to-face conversation he had with his father. He recalled every detail of their last time together and his father's final instructions to him.

They had met at Maggiano's Little Italy in Tyson's Corner, Virginia on a Friday afternoon as they did every week. His father had been bringing him to this restaurant for years since he was a small child. Besides their ever-present entourage of guards, it was just father and son and their private ritual.

He and his father didn't discuss Family business during this time together. They talked about everything from the Redskins, the Wizards, and the Hoyas to the latest fight scheduled to come on pay-per-view. His father always wanted to hear about the latest female or females his son was dealing with at the time.

They would joke, laugh, and enjoy each other's company over authentic Italian cuisine. Anyone who saw them together would have never believed their family sat at the head of the city's narcotics cartel.

Their meeting that particular afternoon had a whole different feel to it. They didn't talk about females or sports. There was no joking or laughing. The discussion centered on the state of the family's business.

"Do you understand what's going on, son?" Ezra Harrell had asked his son. "Everything is changing out here for our family. It's important that you understand me. It's important that you hear what I am telling you."

"I don't understand. What's changing, Dad? We still control the market here, right? We got product and power, what else do we need? I mean these are still our streets, right?"

"These mean streets never belonged to us, son. They don't belong to anyone; never have and they never will. We've just held the crown for the longest time. Somebody will hold it after us. But like I said, things are changing, and there isn't a lot we can do about it."

"I know a few bodies got dropped, Dad, but this is peacetime. What about the truce? I thought it was holding up?"

His father shook his head. "That's just it, son. The truce was holding. Everything was good, and everybody had a place at the table. But you know this life we lead; it's filled with greed. Somebody around us has gotten greedy, broken the truce, and betrayed the

Syndicate. I knew this was coming; nothing this good lasts for too long, and this is why I'm putting some other things in place outside of our life here."

"Other things? Like what? You talking about leaving the family business?" Cuttino said, and raised his eyebrows in surprise.

"Yeah, son. That's what I'm talking about. This mess could push all of us over the edge. More bodies mean more pressure on the police to make a move. Either way, it will be our family who takes the fall. We're the strongest, and we'll be the biggest target."

Cuttino waited a moment before speaking while a waitress refilled their water glasses. "So, what do we do, Dad? We leave behind everything you worked so hard to build?"

"Cuttino, you know I didn't want this life for you anyway. This is all me, not you. It's not for you, this life. I did what I did out of necessity, but we don't need this anymore. I wanted better things for you than to be out here poison-pushing."

"Dad..."

"No, son. Listen to me and understand something. It doesn't matter how much we've dressed it up and spit-shined it, that's what it is. That's what we do. We deal drugs, always have; and we've gotten rich selling that shit."

Cuttino remained silent while his father continued.

"Your mom and I wanted you to live a legit life, you know? Be a doctor, a lawyer, some smooth shit like that, something legal. So, I *need* our family to walk away from this life, son. It's way overdue, and with this latest mess... well, I just don't want to lose any more of our family. And I definitely don't want to see you try and become what I am."

"What's that Dad? What are you?"

"A damn monster. A heartless gangster who only knows how to survive by doing dirt."

In his twenty-six years, he'd never seen his father look his age. Never heard him talk this way. His smile and easygoing nature had always made him appear younger. Both were absent today. Deep frown lines and pronounced gray hair across his head revealed all of his fifty-three years. He didn't like seeing his father like this. It generated a whole new kind of fear in him.

After a few minutes of silence, Cuttino spoke. "Whatever you think is best, Dad. You know I'm with you, any way you want to do this."

He loved his father and would follow any decision he made. He knew full well the business his family involved themselves in, but he still wanted to follow in his father's footsteps.

"I want you to leave tonight, son. I've set up a plane to take you down to the Big House in Carolina. I want you to stay there, lay low, and the rest of us will be close behind."

"Dad, I hear you, man, but come on..."

"No buts, boy; listen to me," his father said and leaned forward in his chair. "I need you to do this for me. I can wrap up everything on this end, your uncles and me. So just do this for me."

Then he smiled for the first time that day.

"Don't worry about it, son. I got this handled easy. Our family will be just fine. Your uncles will take care of me and help get us out of here. You just do your part for me. And remember this, you'll have to lead this family one day. All of it will fall on you, but I know you can handle it. You're my boy, and I'm counting on you to always take care of business. Always take care of this family."

His father stood then and hugged him extra-long and extra tight. "I know you were looking forward to taking the lead on the family business like we discussed."

He looked Cuttino in his eyes. "And you still will. You'll be the one to lead our family into its new beginning. A new *legal* beginning. A whole new chapter for the Harrells. And it'll start in the same place where your great-granddaddy started our family. I love you, Cuttino. You're the best part of me."

"I love you, too, Dad, and I don't want you to worry. I'll take care of our family."

"I know you will. I got no worries about that. Listen, I want you to remember something I was taught: *Here is gone, but tomorrow has yet to come.* Your grandmother told me that a long time ago, and it's always stayed with me. I've never forgotten it, and I don't want you to ever forget it. We can't change the past, but we can work to shape the present and the future. Here is gone, but tomorrow has yet to come. It's time for a new tomorrow for our family, son. It's time."

Later that night, his father saw him off as he boarded a private plane bound for North Carolina. Again, his father had hugged him longer than usual.

The lunch at Maggiano's, and the brief goodbye at the airport, had been the last time Cuttino had seen his father alive.

# *Chapter Fifty-Eight*

On the day of Ezra Harrell's funeral, time seemed to stand still. The hours and minutes struggled by in a slow, painful grind. Cuttino couldn't focus enough to function in his normal fashion. The entire ordeal felt like a bad nightmare for him.

It had taken two weeks for the family's lawyers to secure the release of the bodies. It had taken another week to transport the body and make proper funeral arrangements. Now, after three long weeks, Ezra Harrell could be laid to rest.

Cuttino's black suit itched and felt too tight, although it had been hand-tailored to fit him. His black and white striped tie felt constrictive, and he couldn't stop adjusting the knot.

Every few minutes, he checked on his mother, scared she wouldn't make it through the day. She hadn't said much more than a few words since she first told him of his father's murder.

His father would be buried on the immense Harrell Estate beside the other Harrell Family elders. Although the property was fenced in, armed guards stood watch on the main access roads leading up to the estate.

As the service began, the family and a few close family friends gathered around his father's open casket. His killers had beaten the hell out of him before they had taken his life. It was nothing short of a miracle that the funeral director managed to host an open casket funeral.

Mr. Norris had been paid quadruple his normal fee to ensure all of his effort would be put into Ezra Harrell's homegoing service. He'd covered the bruises and cuts, but the swelling remained. Considering the circumstances, Mr. Norris had done an excellent job of getting Ezra Harrell's body ready.

Cuttino stood near the opening of his father's casket as family, friends, and even the other Syndicate members paid their respects. He gripped the edge of the coffin as he felt the nausea trying to build in the pit of his stomach. The man who he'd modeled himself after, who he wouldn't share another story or joke with, lay before him. He felt a tremor shake his entire body.

His father looked much older in death than he ever had in life. His salt and pepper hair appeared all gray. He looked peaceful, but deep lines of stress still snaked across his forehead and near the corners of his eyes and mouth. His mother had chosen a navy-blue pinstriped suit, white shirt, and sky-blue tie in which to bury his father.

Misery weighed heavy on him and he felt as if his body couldn't bear much more without breaking down. His children, if he ever had any, wouldn't know their grandfather. He bit his lip, trying to delay the tears he knew would find their way to the surface. As he scanned the crowd, he knew someone at this funeral was responsible for his father's death.

By the time Pastor Don Roland began his sermon, a light breeze was blowing, and a few clouds had grouped overhead. Six rows of white chairs were lined up on either side of the middle aisle. Each of the seven chairs in every row held a man or woman associated with the Harrell Family in some way.

He and Sidney sat on either side of his mother, holding her hands to comfort her, but she was a rock. She sat staring straight-ahead with her chin up, dabbing at the corners of her eyes with a tissue.

There would be no hysterics from Olivia Harrell. She'd passed that stage of her grieving and now carried herself with a quiet dignity, as the wife of Ezra Harrell should. She held Cuttino's hand tight in hers, and he could feel the deep sorrow and anger churning through her.

His uncles stood in the rear behind the seated crowd. While his Uncle A.J.'s tears flowed like high tide, his Uncle Montae's expression didn't reveal much of anything. Cuttino tried, but couldn't locate the grief or even the fury he expected to find. His Uncle Montae just stood there, emotionless and robotic.

Pastor Roland spoke words that stung Cuttino's ears. He called his father a man of honor and respect. What he left out was the part about his father being a street-hardened gangster who someone had murdered. The Pastor left out that his father had been a victim of his lifestyle.

Ezra Harrell had spent the majority of his adult life as the reigning king of D.C.'s drug trade. He'd made plenty of enemies ranging from hungry competitors to a couple of straight arrows in the law enforcement system. He carried more influence than the mayor, with some of the city's high-ranking and influential people serving on his payroll. Lawyers, judges, city council members, and half of the police force moonlighted for him.

He walked as close to untouchable as one could ever hope to walk. He'd even created a legitimate lifestyle to mask his underworld dealings. In the end, none of it mattered. Someone had snaked their way through all of his impenetrable layers to do the impossible, to perpetrate the unthinkable.

Cuttino didn't know what he would do without his father here to lead the way. He didn't know how he would keep the family together or how he could fill his father's shoes. What he did know was that his father's murder wouldn't be the last. His death was just the beginning. Things would get much worse before they would get better. This thing would end with either answers to his father's killing or Cuttino's death. Or both.

After the funeral guests departed the gravesite, he and his mother remained behind holding hands in front of his father's grave. Their assigned cadre of guards kept a watchful eye from a respectful distance. His mother removed her large black hat, and he could see the toll all of this had taken on her. She looked worn, tired, and close to death herself.

Mother and son held hands as if each were trying to stop the other from falling off a high cliff. As the gravediggers lowered the coffin into the ground, the clouds darkened, the sky opened, and a light rain started to fall. A guard approached with a large umbrella, but Cuttino put up a hand to stop him.

*"God help me,"* he thought as he looked towards the sky. *"What am I supposed to do now? I don't know how I*

*can do any of this. I can't do it. I'm not the man my father was."*

His mother moaned at the sight of her husband's body dropping out of sight for the final time. Her body quivered, and he wrapped his arm around her shoulder.

"Oh, baby, my poor Ezra. My husband," she whispered, and her tears began to freefall again. "I love you, baby. I love you so much. I will love you forever, Ezra. My sweet, sweet husband. I love you, I love you. Always, I will love you. For a thousand years."

A pitchfork of lightning stabbed the sky, followed by a crash of thunder that sounded as if the earth was breaking apart. Then, somewhere in heaven, a levee broke, and a cloudburst surged from the sky. An angry rain fell, matching Cuttino's tears drop for drop. This was a day that would forever leave a scar on his soul.

Again, and again, the lightning struck, and the thunder rumbled. There was a celebration going on in Hell. The Devil had come to collect his long awaited due.

## *Chapter Fifty-Nine*

At almost 3:00 a.m. on the morning after his father's funeral, Cuttino jerked upright in his bed. A slick layer of sweat covered his forehead, arms, and the back of his neck. The t-shirt he wore felt damp and clung to his body. His breathing came in quick, ragged wheezes. He'd slept a couple of distressed hours and awoke hoping this had all been a nightmare, but it hadn't been. He'd buried his father not more than twenty-four hours ago, and nothing could change that fact.

He eased out of bed, careful not to awake Sidney who was curled up beside him. He slipped his feet into a pair of black and white Adidas sandals and slugged his way to the bathroom. When he finished relieving himself, he stood at the sink and splashed handfuls of cold water on his face.

He stared at his reflection, focusing in on his eyes. Eyes like his father's. They had lost their usual sparkle. They were red and puffy from the tears he'd shed.

He thought he saw his father's face, even heard his voice telling him this was his time to be a man. His breath pushed out of his mouth in a rough cough as his heart banged against the bottom of his throat.

Just like at the funeral, a wave of nausea rolled through his body. He lurched and rested his arms and head on the edge of the sink in anticipation of becoming ill. A few seconds ticked by, and his stomach held. Instead, tears streaked their way down the contours of his cheeks.

"Can't cry anymore. I can't cry anymore," he said through gritted teeth, wiping his face with the palm of his hand. "Dad, I promise you I'll make this right. I promise you I will. I promise you this. If it's the last thing I do, I promise I'll make this right. I'll find them and I will make this right. I... promise... you."

Ezra Harrell's son was stronger than this. It was in his blood to be stronger than all of this. He was wired that way. He wouldn't break down. He couldn't allow himself to break down. His family needed him.

Cuttino felt a homicidal rage building inside of him. This here would be a whole new obsession for him, one he'd never experienced. He knew once he started down this path, this thing wouldn't end in peace, but he didn't see any other way. Anything less would haunt him the rest of his days, leaving him trapped and unable to move forward.

He had to finish this by finding those responsible for his father's death. He would hunt down whomever had made the mistake of crossing him and his family. Then, he would take the life of each and every one of them and leave the bodies for their families to bury. Every single one, no matter how long it took. Once he'd inflicted the same chaos and pain that they had inflicted on him and his family, it would be finished.

After he put his father's soul to rest by avenging his murder, Cuttino would lead the Harrells into their new beginning.

*Here is gone, but tomorrow has yet to come.*

## *Epilogue*

## *"HOME AGAIN..."*

*Fuquay-Varina, North Carolina...*

One week after his father's funeral, Cuttino and the Beasley twins prepared to board a private plane headed for Washington, D.C. He'd convinced his mother to remain in North Carolina while he went home to look for answers to his father's death. Sidney had taken the next couple of weeks off and would be staying at the house with his mother.

At the airport, tears filled Sidney's eyes as they said their goodbyes. He kissed her soft lips, and she hugged him with a fierceness that said she was scared of losing him.

"Be careful, baby. I love you," she whispered.

He stared at her and knew right at that moment he wanted to marry this woman. She'd been put on this earth for him and him for her.

"I'll be safe, don't worry anything. You know I love you. Don't ever think otherwise. And thank you for staying with Mom," he said. "Hey, smile for me. I'll see you soon, okay?"

They kissed again, and then he turned to leave.

He hated not telling her the truth, but this still wasn't the time. There might not ever be a time for that conversation.

His father's murder had ignited a new wave of violence in the city. The Family started hitting any and every one they suspected may have a hand in the assassination. Uncle Montae had unleashed the dogs in full force, and in a week's time, the body count had begun to mount.

Reports from home said Harrell soldiers were hitting the families in The Syndicate as well as crews outside of the SNC. True to form, Uncle Montae had skipped over the asking questions part and had taken to brute force and street war tactics.

Since the funeral, Cuttino had taken the time to think about how his father would handle this. Uncle Montae was handling this all wrong. Random bloodshed wasn't the answer. Cuttino needed to take quick action before The Syndicate gave way to absolute anarchy. In the week after the funeral, he'd spoken to his uncles once. Montae had assured him that he was doing everything he could to find his father's killers.

Cuttino and the twins spent the short plane ride in silence. This wouldn't be the typical homecoming, and there wasn't any talk of celebrations or catching up with old friends.

One and a half hours after takeoff, the plane's captain turned on the fasten seatbelt sign. He announced the beginning of their landing approach over the intercom.

The chartered jet began its descent out of the nighttime sky and into Ronald Reagan National Airport.

Cuttino half expected his plane to get delayed. Maybe it would be struck from the sky by a lightning or shook to pieces by turbulence too strong to navigate. He thought maybe God was telling him to stay away because there wasn't anything left here for him.

Maybe God was telling him that he'd been lucky, unlike all the bodies filling up graveyards and morgues, including his father's. In his heart, he knew he was coming home because it hurt too much to stay away. He needed answers.

Although the sun had long deserted the D.C. horizon, Ronald Reagan National Airport was a beautiful and welcomed sight. The lights from the airport shimmered off the Potomac River. He was home.

It was just after one in the morning when the plane lowered its landing gear, touched down, and taxied to its assigned terminal. Cuttino's palms were slick with perspiration. He didn't know where he would begin or how he could find those responsible for his father's death. The video from his father's building had yielded minor glimpses of the attackers. He had a feeling all he had to do was wait. His father's murderer would come looking for him.

He and the Beasley brothers made their way through the airport's private terminal towards their pickup location. Minutes later, the three men drove through the airport exit in a black Cadillac Escalade. Two identical Escalades driven by Harrell Family guards followed behind the lead SUV. Taurus had called ahead thirty minutes before their plane landed to make sure the guards and vehicles would be waiting.

"So, what's our first move, bro?" Taurus said and looked back at Cuttino from the front passenger seat. "We getting right to work and going after the fools who did this?"

"Yeah, big man, we are. There's no doubt about that," Cuttino said loosening his blue tie, unbuttoning his white shirt's top button, and removing his taupe suit jacket. "With everything that's going on, we have to do this quick, fast, and get out of town."

"Hell, yeah, bro," Iran spoke up from the driver's seat. "Shit is crazy in these streets. The police are gettin' nervous. Wondering where their money will come from now with the Syndicate out of commission."

"I could give a shit about The Syndicate outside of finding out who had something to do with my father's murder," Cuttino said. "Have either of you talked to my uncles?"

Both of the twins shook their heads.

"Bro, I hear you, but squaring things up with the SNC and the police might help us in finding out who did this, you know?" Taurus said. "We put everything right. Maybe then whoever did this will come out of hiding?"

"How do you figure that will work, Taurus?" Cuttino asked. "What you mean when you say square things up?"

"Well, whoever did this wanted your father out as head of the Syndicate, right? Maybe putting you in his place will force them to try again? Except this time, we'll be waiting for them. We get them before they get you."

Cuttino leaned back on the leather seat and thought about what his friend had just said. "What do you think, Iran?"

"Not trying to use you as bait or anything, but it makes perfect sense to me. Whoever did this will have to try again if they see the Harrells are still running the show. Plus, everyone is scrambling for our corners because they think we're finished. The bodies will really start stacking up if you don't pull this thing together and get it right. You did tell your uncles that you were taking over the business. I know you kind of changed your mind since then, but why not go through with it? Let's see if it helps find your father's killers? Lure them out in the open. Then we got 'em."

Cuttino thought for a minute before answering. "Okay, we'll work everything out with the cops and the Syndicate families. But I need to meet with my uncles first. Our family will have to move together on this, fellas."

He gazed out of the Cadillac's tinted windows. What would happen to the Harrell Family with his father gone? How would they survive this war? He didn't have a damn clue.

* * * *

Lucas Meadows massaged the grip of his chrome-plated Desert Eagle .50 caliber pistol. It sat nestled in between his seat and the center console in a custom mounted holster. He kept his left hand on the wood and leather-wrapped steering wheel and felt the subtle vibration of the idling Mercedes.

The Clean had been sitting in the same spot for the better part of the evening, watching and waiting. The contract killer twisted his neck and felt the pop of his vertebrae as they readjusted at the tip of his spine. He released his grip on the pistol and used his right hand to massage the dull ache in his neck. The last thing he needed was neck and back spasms.

"Damn airplanes just aren't made for anyone over six feet," he thought as he shifted his chiseled, two hundred and thirty-pound frame in the leather seat of the brand-new black Mercedes CLK.

He'd asked for a less conspicuous vehicle, but had changed his mind when he saw the beautiful luxury automobile in person.

*Let's live a little,* he'd reasoned with himself.

This subtle change from his normal routine caused concern for him at first. The normal routine didn't include frills and he had to wonder if he was beginning to lose his edge just a bit.

The car's narrow cockpit wasn't the best fit for his broad shoulders and tree-trunk legs, but he hadn't been able to resist. He was used to plain and drab, nondescript trucks and sedans and hoped his splurging wouldn't come back to haunt him.

"No, I deserve this," he concluded and dismissed all negative thoughts.

He felt the effects of jetlag combined with long hours, and just maybe his age, starting to set in on him. He was forty-seven, but The Clean kept himself in excellent shape. Although his clean-shaven face sported weathered features, his body had managed to ward off time's inevitable grip on it.

For years, he'd disciplined himself into a strict regimen of exercise and clean living. The exceptions to his rule were his regular use of human growth hormone and his indulgence in expensive cognacs. He was a damn machine. But even the fit get weary, and his aching body and heavy eyelids were begging for sleep.

The flight from LAX had taken six and a half long hours. All of this short-notice bouncing back and forth across the country was starting to get the best of him. He should've rested after his return trip from the West Coast, but his employer had wanted him to get right to work. He'd begun tracking his next set of targets as soon as his plane had landed.

The Clean had completed what he was sure would be the hardest part of the job. He'd taken out D.C.'s drug kingpin and had managed to make it look like a local hit from a rival gang. This latest stage of the job called for him to locate and eliminate the remainder of the Harrell Family's key members.

His crew of shooters was also on the job again. They knew the layout of the D.C. metro area and therefore were of great *temporary* value to him. When he finished with this job, he would dispose of them. Loose ends couldn't be tolerated in his line of work.

He ran his hand over his bald head and took a sip from the Mocha Latte he'd been nursing. The sun had dipped out of sight five hours ago. He was close to calling it a night when his patience was rewarded. Three pairs of blue-white xenon headlights pierced the darkness, and three Cadillac Escalades pulled out of the airport's garage.

"About damn time," he said, yawning as he watched the SUVs make a right and merge onto the main road. He waited for a few more seconds until the caravan's taillights faded from view before engaging his vehicle's ignition. He didn't need to see the vehicles in order to follow them. The GPS tracker installed on the lead vehicle made sure he knew where they were at all times.

For the next twenty minutes, he trailed the Escalades as they sped up George Washington Parkway and merged onto Interstate 395. To his left, he caught a glimpse of the Pentagon. The Department of Defense stronghold looked majestic at night and as invincible as ever.

*Oorah...* He still loved his country.

The trio of Escalades continued their trek over the Fourteenth Street Bridge and then exited towards downtown Washington, D.C. When the SUVs stopped, it was in front of a tall office building a couple of blocks from the Verizon Center. He slowed his car down, not enough to draw attention, but just enough to get a good look.

Two huge bodyguards got out the first truck, and then a third man exited as well. There he was, the man of the hour. Cuttino Harrell, crown prince of the Harrell Empire, had indeed made his return to Chocolate City.

Lucas remembered all three of the men's faces from the pictures he had stored in his cell phone. The information from his contact had been spot on as usual. Nothing beat good, accurate intel.

The Clean could feel his bloodlust returning. He loved the hunt. His next target was in play, but everything had to be done according to his employer's instructions.

"It is very important," his employer had emphasized, "that this assignment be performed down to the exact detail."

Although the Harrell boy was a wide-open target, he maintained his military bearing and drove the Mercedes coupe up Seventh Street. He remembered D.C.'s infamous speed and traffic cameras and resisted the urge to test the CLK's power. He couldn't afford to be pulled over or caught on camera. His adrenaline rush had to be held in check, or it would get the best of him.

*Hold on to it. Cage the monster. Lock him down... just for now.* Soon enough, it would be time to play.

He continued to drive at a reasonable speed past city limits and to his hotel in Old Town Alexandria. Yes, game time was fast approaching, but first he needed to rest and plan.

*Precision and execution...*

"I see you, Cuttino Harrell. It's your turn now. Welcome to the show," he whispered through a wide grin as he studied his target's picture on the screen of his cell.

"I see you. And soon, you'll see me."

*Like father, like son.*

***To be continued...***

Please continue reading for an exclusive preview of Tyrone Eddins' upcoming novel:

**DONE IN THE DARK**

*Available for purchase in summer 2019!*

## Acknowledgments

*Well…we finally got here…the first book of what I pray will be many…You would think in the time it took to get this book finished, I would have an entire acknowledgments page ready to go. Well…I don't. To be honest, I don't have the slightest clue of where to begin. What I do know is that I have plenty to be thankful for and plenty of people to thank for assisting me, and also dealing with me during this process.*

*Much love and gratitude owed first and foremost to GOD & the Lord Jesus Christ for all my many blessings. Thank you to the Eddins Clan for all of the love and support: my wife, Janelle, Dad, Mom, & Mom, Uncle Gerald, Danesha, Marvin, Jason, and all of my aunts, uncles, cousins, nephews & nieces, & the rest of the Eddins Family. Thank you to the Duncan, Moore, and Zamore families for all of your love and support: Thanks to The Fellas, the That's Game! Sports crew., and the Meeting of the Minds. Special thank you to my editor, Ms. Robyn Thomas, for taking Bad Intentions to the next level. Special thank you to Ms. Kedi Darby for the outstanding cover design.*

*The finishing of BAD INTENTIONS and the creation of SCRIPTED VISIONS PUBLISHING GROUP represents the realization of a dream. Thank-you to any and everyone who has had a part in making this dream come true. I truly believe that we all have a story to tell and a dream to chase.*

*It should never be a question of "if" we tell that story or "if" we chase that dream. Instead, the only question should be "how and when" we tell our story and "how and when" we chase our dream…*

*To anyone I may have forgotten, please blame it on my crazy mind and not my heart…*

*PEACE & BLESSINGS,*

*Tyrone Eddins Jr.*

# DONE IN THE DARK

*An unspeakable crime, a family left in ruins, and an act of vengeance years in the making...*
*Some demons refuse to die...*
*Some fires refuse to be extinguished...*
*And what was done in the dark will come to the light...*

More than two decades ago, a terrifying abduction shattered the lives of two young children and unleashed a tragic chain of events that destroyed a family and spawned a deadly vendetta.

Now, years later, a lunatic is wreaking havoc in the Nation's Capital and has the Metropolitan Police Department running around in circles. Cold-blooded and cunning, this unknown killer is gunning down members of the MPD, seemingly without rhyme or reason. But...these "random" shootings may not be as random as they appear. Could there be a link between these killings and the child abduction that took place all of those years ago?

MPD Detective Darius Cole is tired of watching from the sidelines and longs for a chance to crack a big case. His wish is granted when he's assigned to help investigate this recent string of murders. Now, Cole finds himself thrust in the middle of the manhunt to track down an elusive criminal mastermind who has left the MPD two steps behind his every move.

Full of darkness and raw emotion, **DONE IN THE DARK** is a story of retribution and redemption that delves deeply into the horrors of abuse as it twists and turns its way towards an incredible climax that even the most seasoned fan of fiction won't see coming.

*For the light stolen from our eyes and the memories heavy in our heart For the good and evil in us allthat brings us close, yet tears us apart...Chasing a fleeting dream that we lost from the start...*

*Standing in the darkest dark while reaching for that brightest light Witness to unspeakable wickednessas we dance the dance in this unending fightNow let all spirits rest easy because...what's done in the dark will come to the light...*

## *PROLOGUE*

## *"MONSTERS AND BOOGEYMEN"*

# ONE

*He is patience...*

Because he must be, for at least a little while longer. His patience will pay off. He's sure of it. After all this time, he is confident there can be just one conclusion to this story. An ending for all endings. One he has so meticulously scripted and now stands ready to execute.

And just like every good story needs a good ending, it also needs a bad guy. Especially horror stories. And that's what this is, a horror story. One full of heartbreak, sadness, and terror. A story with boogeymen who prey on the innocent and weak. A story full of wicked people who steal, kill, take, and abuse without retribution or guilt of conscience. They do this until a hero comes along and puts a stop to their evil ways.

But this is a real-life horror story with real-life monsters, and there are no heroes. There is just him and he's nobody's hero. He doesn't consider himself to be one of the bad guys, but he's more than willing to play that role because that's how he'll be able to finish this. He needs to become the thing he hates. That's what he tells himself so he'll see this through to the end.

The bad things he's planning will be done to very bad people. They are the true bad guys in this story. They are the monsters hiding in the closet and under the bed. Sharp-fanged and razor-clawed, these predators lurk in the shadows waiting to inflict their horrible brand of pain on those who are incapable of fighting back.

In this story, the monsters have gone unchecked and unpunished. They have committed evil acts and have walked away free and clear. Until now. Now their days are numbered, and he'll be the instrument of their punishment. He'll take it upon himself to right the wrongs no one else has bothered with. He will hold those responsible accountable for their crimes.

He doesn't expect anyone to understand why he's doing this. Most people aren't able to understand how it feels to have their entire life ripped apart while the world stands by and watches. How could they possibly understand what that's like? They couldn't...not unless they've experienced what he's experienced, seen what he's seen, and felt what he's felt.

So, he'll be the bad guy, for now, the lesser of two evils. And he can live with that, so long as he does what needs doing. He's waited for so long, and now he can put closure to this part of his life.

# TWO

The temperature outside has dropped steadily with the setting of the sun. In the fading light, he can see his breath forming small plumes of fog as he exhales it. His fingertips have begun to go numb inside the leather gloves he wears. The same can be said for his toes, the black leather work boots on his feet offering little in the way of warmth after standing outside for so long.

He's been waiting in this same spot for at least two hours, maybe more. But, in the end, it will be well worth the wait. He's been waiting almost a lifetime, so a few more hours won't hurt.

He places his hands inside the pockets of his gray bomber jacket, the fingers of his right hand finding and gripping the handle of the small pistol he carries. He doesn't expect to use the weapon tonight, but it reassures him to know that he has it with him. Just in case.

After another forty-five minutes, he sees what he's been waiting on. Across the street from where he's standing, two white men, both big and bulky, walk out of the front entrance of a building and get into a silver four-door sedan. A police-issued, unmarked cruiser. The alley where he's been waiting offers him enough cover so he can see them while remaining hidden from their view. Not that they would be looking for him anyway. These two have grown careless and lazy.

As he watches the men, the fire begins to burn inside of him again. Sometimes it simmers, but at times like these, whenever he is so close to retribution that he can taste it, the fire burns brightest. He's studied these two men for years, learning their lives inside and out, and today's watch has helped him put the final pieces in place.

He has their routine down to a science. He knows where they live and work, where they eat and drink, and now where they do their dirt. He is ready. He watches as the sedan pulls away from the curb, heads down the empty street, turns a corner and then fades from view. He wanted nothing more than to walk up to the driver's side of the car and empty his gun's clip into both men, ending their lives right then and there. But he couldn't do that. Not yet, but soon. He just needs the right opening. Until that opening comes, he'll remain in the shadows, watching and planning, waiting to inflict the hurt he's been holding onto for so long...

*He is patience... but he is also pain...*

# *PART ONE*

# *"GONE"*

# *CHAPTER ONE*

**Washington, D.C. – circa the mid-1990s...**

Beanie was gonna catch hell this time. He didn't see any way out of it. He'd messed around one too many times, and now he found himself about to get in deep trouble. He and his brother were supposed to be home almost an hour ago, but here they were still out in these streets. And, as usual, it was all his fault.

It was late in the day now and the afternoon had turned into evening. For most of the day, the sun had played hide-and-seek behind a thick cover of gray clouds. Now, it was well into its end-of-the-day retreat towards the horizon. It would be dark in just a little while, and the boys were still a few blocks from home. Beanie knew they weren't supposed to be out after dark.

If their mom hadn't started calling the house phone yet, she would soon. And when she did, they had better be in the house to answer or his parents would be pissed. If that happened, his dad would most likely kick his ass, take his Nintendo away, and not let him hang out with his homeboys for the next week or two, or maybe even three. Three whole weeks on punishment. Beanie couldn't imagine it. And he didn't even want to think about the holidays.

Christmas was a month away and with the way his grades had slipped during the last quarter, he couldn't afford to get in any more trouble. If he did, he might not get anything at all except a few pairs of socks or something like that. Maybe an ugly sweater, too. Not cool.

The thought of punishment and no presents under the tree lit a fire under Beanie, and he wanted to sprint the rest of the way home. But he couldn't just leave his brother behind. He was the oldest and his baby brother was his responsibility.

"Come on, Scoop," he called over his shoulder when he saw that his brother had lagged far behind him. "Hurry up, man."

Beanie couldn't run home, but he could at least pick up the pace. He hefted his book bag and gym bag higher up on his shoulders and began walking faster. He covered ground easier than Scoop, who was struggling to keep up on his shorter legs with his own book bag slowing him down.

Both boys were small for their ages. Beanie was eleven, but with his short, skinny frame, most people thought he was much younger. And Scoop, at just seven years old, was a shorter version of his older brother, sharing the same small build, cocoa-hued skin, and short, low-cut fade haircut. People always told them that they looked like twins and that they both would be so handsome when they grew up.

After school had let out for the day, Beanie disobeyed his parents' instructions to pick up his little brother and go straight home. They got on him about it so much that he had their speeches memorized by now. But Beanie being Beanie, always hardheaded and wanting to be slick, had hung out anyway.

He'd been unable to resist kicking it with the fellas for a bit and getting in a few runs on his school's new outdoor basketball court. He'd gone way over the thirty minutes that he'd planned on staying, making him late in picking up his little brother.

Scoop's school was at the edge of their ward's school zone, so it made for a long walk to pick him up and a much longer walk home. They could catch a couple of metro buses and make it home sooner, but Beanie liked to pocket the bus money that their parents left for them each morning.

Normally, his hustle worked if he stayed on top of his game. He got to keep the bus money and they still made it home on time. He usually skipped lunch and waited until he got home to eat, so he was able to pocket that money as well. The bus money combined with his lunch money always left him with a nice weekly stash to spend on whatever he wanted.

Scoop never gave him any trouble about them not catching the bus. His little brother preferred when they walked home because sometimes, they were able to stop at the store to grab a snack on the way. If Beanie left school on time, picked up Scoop, and they went straight home after making a quick stop at the store, it was all good. But today, like too many other days, Beanie wasn't on top of his game, and now they were rushing to get home before their parents started looking for them.

"Scoop," he called out to his little brother again. "Come on lil' bro, pick up the pace. You know we gotta get home, man. "

"Wait up, Beanie," Scoop called back to him. He sounded out of breath, and Beanie heard him coughing a little bit. The November air was chilly and wet, and it had a bite to it. Beanie hoped his brother wasn't coming down with something.

"Beanie, I'm tired and thirsty, man. Can we stop at Mr. Sam's store for a soda?"

"Nah, lil' man, we can't stop for snacks today. Remember Mom said we gotta have the house cleaned up and our homework is done by the time they get home. Plus, you know she don't like us to have all that sugar no way."

"Oh," Scoop said, "well we can just stop for a few minutes, right? I want some cupcakes. My favorite yellow ones, man."

Beanie knew what was coming. His baby brother didn't care about them being late when it came to him getting what he wanted. He didn't care if his parents found out that they always walked home instead of catching the bus. Scoop didn't care about any of that when it came to his sweet tooth. Especially since Beanie would be the one who got in trouble because he was the oldest.

He turned to face his little brother, who had already stopped walking. His eyes had narrowed into small slits and his round cheeks had spread into a wide smile.

"Come on, Beanie," Scoop said, rubbing his hands together. "I just want to get one thing. Pleeaassee?? Just one little thing. I'm extra hungry today. Can't you hear my tummy growlin' over here?"

"Didn't you eat lunch?" Beanie asked. "You ate your lunch today, right?"

Scoop hesitated before answering. "Well, yeah, but it wasn't any good, man," he said and threw his little arms up in the air. "I ate it, but I didn't like it much."

"Oh, yeah?" Beanie said. "And, why not?"

"Well, all I had was a sandwich and some carrot sticks and my juice box. Plus, I didn't have a treat today. Annnd, you had me waiting all long after school for you again, and now I'm starvin' like Marvin out here in these streets!" He placed his small gloved hands on his stomach to help emphasize his point.

Beanie wanted to laugh at his baby brother. He was almost tempted to make a detour to the store, but he knew they didn't have time for that today. Scoop would get in there, not be able to choose what he wanted, and they would be in Mr. Sam's store all day. Then, they would be really late getting home. They wouldn't finish their chores and homework, their parents would find out what Beanie had been up to, and then it would be all over for him. There's no telling what their parents would do to him. He may not get off punishment until he turned 18 if he lived that long.

No way. He wasn't getting in trouble over his baby brother's sweet tooth. Beanie had plans to hang out this weekend, maybe even hop a bus downtown and see if he could sneak into a Hoyas game with the fellas.

"Look, buddy, I'm sorry I was late again, but we can't stop today, ok? Can't do it, man. Mom and Dad will get on our asses if we don't handle our business."

A look of disapproval flashed across Scoop's face, and the smaller boy shook his head at his older brother.

"What's up?" Beanie asked.

"You said a bad word, Beanie," Scoop said, his voice shrinking into a whisper. "Not supposed to curse."

Beanie thought about what he'd said, and he knelt in front of his kid brother. He zipped up the little guy's coat, adjusted his hat, and rubbed the top of his head.

"Sorry, buddy. You right, I shouldn't curse n' shit. I mean stuff. Damn, my bad, Scoop. Look, I shouldn't say those words, ok? But I don't want us to get in trouble. So, we gotta get home and we can't stop today, cool?"

His brother crossed his arms and opened his mouth to protest, but Beanie held up a hand to cut him off. "But...check it out, lil' man. If you work with me and help keep us out of trouble, I'll hook you up with a pack of cupcakes, and I'll even let you get down on my Nintendo for a whole hour this weekend. Any game you want."

Scoop's eyes lit up and he clapped his hands, but then his eyes reverted back to shrewd slits and he crossed his arms again. "Four packs of cupcakes, and four hours on your Nintendo, and ten dollars!" He held up the four fingers on his small right hand to illustrate his point.

"Four hours? Ten dollars?" Beanie said. "Man, you trippin'. No way. How about a pack of cupcakes and two hours on my Nintendo? You can even chill on my bed while you play, alright?"

Scoop considered this for a minute, even rubbing his chin and looking up at the sky for effect. "Ok, Beanie. Three packs of cupcakes, and three hours, and ten dollars."

"Two and two. Two packs of cupcakes and two hours on the video game. And five dollars. That's it. Take that or I drag you home right now kickin' and screamin'."

Scoop didn't hesitate at this offer. "Deal!" he said and stuck out his right hand. "Nice doing business with you, Big Bro!"

"Yeah, yeah, yeah," Beanie said and playfully slapped his little brother's hand. "Right. Now let's get home, you lil' hustla. You ain't supposed to scam ya big brother, ya know?"

They started walking again. Scoop was doing a much better job of keeping up now, riding high and feeling good about his new deal. Beanie was just happy to have avoided one of Scoop's temper-tantrums.

There was a little bit of daylight left in the sky, so they still had a chance to make it home before dark. Beanie would knock out the dishes, Scoop would vacuum, they would both get on their homework, and it would be all good. And all it cost him was a couple of packs of Hostess cupcakes, a couple of hours on his

Nintendo, and five dollars. Not bad. He could deal with that. Maybe he should start bribing Scoop more if it meant he could-

The loud chirp of a police siren interrupted Beanie's thoughts. He turned and saw a brown car creeping along behind them.

"Who's that, Beanie?" Scoop asked.

"I think it's the police, man. Dunno what they want though. Come on. We gotta get home," Beanie said and tugged at Scoop's sleeve to keep him moving.

The car pulled up beside the two boys and slowed enough to keep pace with them. Whoever was inside chirped the car's siren again, and Beanie and his little brother took another couple of steps. The cruiser's tinted passenger side window lowered and revealed two men Beanie didn't recognize. He glanced over at the men but then turned away. He placed his right hand on Scoop's back and nudged him along.

"Yo, homeboys!" the man in the passenger side seat said, showing them a toothy, predatory grin as he leaned out the window. He looked like a wolf eyeing a couple of stray lambs. "Didn't you fellas hear the siren? In case you didn't know, that means stop. S-T-O-P! You boys can hear and you can spell, right?"

Beanie stopped walking and placed himself between Scoop and the car. He turned and looked at the man again but didn't answer.

The car came to a stop when the boys did, and the man in the passenger seat looked them up and down. He was a clean-faced white dude with brown hair and blue, shifty eyes. Beanie could see that something was off about him. He couldn't see the driver as clearly, but from where Beanie stood, the man behind the wheel looked like a big black dude.

"Where you boys headed?" the man in the passenger side said. "Gettin' to be a little late, isn't it?"

"Home," Beanie said, placing a protective arm around his brother's shoulder. "We're goin' home."

"Home, huh?" the man said. "And where's that?"

"Right up the block," Beanie said and pointed up the street. "Our parents are waitin' on us."

Their home was just over the next hill and Beanie wished that he and Scoop had gone straight home today. If they had gone straight home, they wouldn't be out here now getting sweated by the police.

Beanie guessed that these two dudes were cops. Had to be. They looked and sounded like cops to him and their car had a siren. Besides, who else would stop two little kids around here and mess with them for no reason?

The man looked towards the direction that Beanie had pointed and then returned his hard stare to the boys. "And where are you two lil' bastards comin' from this late?"

"School," Beanie said.

"School?" the man said and looked over at his partner. "You hear that bullshit, Slick? That a joke or what?"

The two men shared a laugh, but Beanie was sure no one had told a joke.

"Son, don't try to play us. School's been out for a couple hours now. So, why don't you tell us the truth about where you two are comin' from?"

"Already told you, officer," Beanie said as he tried, but failed, to put a hard edge in his voice. "Comin' from school."

Beanie wasn't scared of the police, but he'd learned not to trust them and to avoid them whenever possible.

"It's detective, son. And my partner and I don't like your tone, and we don't believe that shit you talkin'. So how about you stop jerkin' us around and give it up. Let's do this easy like, ok?"

"Give what up?" Beanie said, stepping backward as the man exited the vehicle and stepped onto the curb in front of them. He was a big man with broad shoulders and large, muscular arms. "I already told you, we're goin' home."

"So, you ain't out here dealing on these corners?" the man said. He was wearing faded blue jeans and a tight black sweatshirt. A shiny gold badge dangled from a chain hanging around his thick neck.

Beanie looked up at the man and shook his head.

"Well, we think maybe you are. Think you and your runner here decided the block was too hot today, so you're headin' home early. Or maybe there wasn't enough action out here. Either way, I guess you thought you could cut out without having to pay the piper?"

The cop crossed his arms across his wide chest, and Beanie could see his pistol peeking from beneath the bottom of his shirt.

"We ain't dealin'," Beanie said, his voice cracking with fear. He was for sure scared now. All he wanted was to get him and Scoop home safely. "We just comin' from school and we gotta get home."

With surprising speed, the huge man stepped forward and grabbed Beanie by his coat, snatching him forward and lifting him off his feet. "You think this is a game, boy?"

He pulled Beanie close and got right in his face. So close that Beanie could smell the cop's hot, liquor-laced breath. "Well, I got news for you. Ain't no games out here. We know you know something about the traffic on this block. Now get your skinny ass up against the car."

The cop lowered Beanie to the ground and shoved him hard against the side of his vehicle. Beanie knew he was in for a shakedown and a beatdown at least. He hoped that was all. They would find his money and take it for themselves. They would also knock him around some and then hopefully when they got bored, they would let him go. All of this because these cops were itching for a fight and had no one else to victimize right now. He and Scoop were just in the wrong place at the wrong time.

He looked over his shoulder at his little brother. He was standing just a few feet away, unmoving, his eyes as big as saucers and filled with tears, his mouth hanging wide open.

"Go home, Scoop. Get outta here. Go next door to Ms. Alice and wait for me."

Scoop didn't hesitate and took off running up the street as fast as his small legs would carry him. The cop's partner jumped out of their vehicle and started to run after Scoop. He was almost as big as the first cop and wore the same blue jeans and black sweatshirt.

"Come on, man. Let my brother go," Beanie yelled as the first cop held him in place. "He ain't got nothin' to do with any of this."

The man continued after his brother, but his partner called him back. "Don't bother, Slick. Let that lil' shit go. This punk here will do just fine."

*To be continued in* **DONE IN THE DARK**
*(available in summer 2019)*

*WELCOME TO*
*SCRIPTED VISIONS PUBLISHING GROUP!*

*"PUBLISHING & PROMOTING THE NEXT GENERATION OF LITERARY LEGENDS!"*

**SCRIPTED VISIONS CORE VALUES**

Innovative Creativity - Excellence & Achievement - Artistic Integrity

SCRIPTED VISIONS PUBLISHING GROUP is an independent publishing house delivering the very finest in modern literary entertainment. At Scripted Visions, our authors are members of the Scripted Visions family and an integral component of our publishing process. You, the reader, are essential to the success of Scripted Visions and our products are created not with budgetary bottom-lines in mind, but based on the needs and wants of our readership.

## *"The Birth of Scripted Visions"*

Shortly after the 2011 New Year, Tyrone Eddins Jr. found himself putting the finishing touches on his debut novel, BAD INTENTIONS. He also found himself in the midst of an extensive search to find a suitable publishing home for his book.

After querying several literary agencies & publishing houses without finding a suitable match, Tyrone researched alternatives to traditional publishing & discovered that many of today's authors have found success self-publishing their work. For Tyrone, the way forward was obvious and he decided to self-publish his novel.

However, that was just the beginning. After learning of the difficulty many authors experience in their attempts to break into publishing via the traditional conglomerate publishing houses, he decided not to stop at simply self-publishing his own book. Tyrone decided to form his own publishing house to publish not only his books, but also the works of other up & coming authors. So, in June 2011, Tyrone formed SCRIPTED VISIONS PUBLISHING GROUP with the mission of providing a vehicle on which to transport the voices of today's authors and tomorrow's aspiring writers.

*"Changing the Game"*

The Vision Behind Scripted Visions...

For writers, many things have changed in the today's publishing world. The "E-Behemoth" known as Social Media has not only circumvented physical barriers and made the world a much smaller place, but more importantly, it has blown the doors off of traditional publishing by giving today's author a powerful and wide-reaching platform on which to operate. Today's author now has an independent voice that has been emboldened and empowered, a luxury that our predecessors did not enjoy. Die-hard traditionalists may eschew these modernizations, but it is in these changes that Scripted Visions sees opportunity. Scripted Visions promotes author independence and serves as a conduit between the author and their target audience. Previous generations of authors were forced to rely on the middlemen; conglomerate publishing houses and literary agents, to help bridge the gap between their work and their target audience. So, what makes Scripted Visions Publishing Group different? Scripted Visions is a publishing house built by an author for authors. This means our authors work directly with a published author who understands the time, effort, and sacrifice required to write, publish, and sell a book. Scripted Visions authors will be mentored during each step of the creative process and beyond. With Scripted Visions, authors will be treated not only as artists, but also as business professionals and will have a key voice in the publishing and promoting of their work.

The end result? A successful, author-driven book creation and publishing operation. And with both our authors and readers in mind, Scripted Visions publishes books in a manner that maintains and enhances the author's original creative vision and ensures the reader receives the books in their purest form.

### *"All About the Words"*

Today's many impressive technological advances allow readers to enjoy the book of their choice in a variety of formats that best suit their tastes. Books are more accessible today than ever, but even with all of today's advancements; books, at their core, remain all about the words. It's in the words where a book is made or broken. It's in the words where a book lives or dies. It's in the words where Scripted Visions found its humble beginnings and it's in the words where Scripted Visions will continue to grow and introduce readers to the very best in literary entertainment from talented and upcoming authors.

## About the Author

Tyrone Eddins Jr. is the author of Bad Intentions and Done in the Dark, co-host of That's Game! Sports, and the CEO & Founder of Scripted Visions Publishing Group. He is a proud veteran of the Air Force and a proud native of the Washington, DC/ Maryland/ Virginia area (a.k.a. "The DMV").
He currently resides in Maryland.

www.ingramcontent.com/pod-product-compliance
Lightning Source LLC
Chambersburg PA
CBHW030813310726
48980CB00006B/477/J

* 9 7 8 0 9 8 5 0 6 6 6 1 1 *